THE
STRANGE ACCOUNT
OF
CHARLIE WENDIGO

MATTHEW E. KLINE

Brick Cave Media
brickcavebooks.com

The Strange Account of Charlie Wendigo

Copyright © 2024 Matthew E. Kline

PAPERBACK ISBN: 978-1-938190-95-7

Printed in the United States of America.

The characters and events in this book are fictitious. Any similarity to real persons, living or dead, is coincidental and not intended by the authors.

Cover Illustration Artist: James E. Shields

Brick Cave Media
brickcavebooks.com
2025

THE
STRANGE ACCOUNT
OF
CHARLIE WENDIGO

MATTHEW E. KLINE

Brick Cave Media
brickcavebooks.com

CHAPTER ONE
The Vampire in the Elevator

There were two irrefutable truths about Charlie Wendigo. The first—he couldn't make a decent cup of coffee to save his life. The second—he was magic.

One would think this second truth could be brought to bear against the first; that, if he were in fact magic, he could simply conjure up an adequate cup of joe. This first truth, however, was the result of a curse, visited upon him as means of revenge, for slights both real and imagined, by an angry gypsy barista, and gypsy curses are notoriously difficult to dismiss.[1]

While it's likely most reading this have encountered at least one individual who produced subpar coffee, it's doubtful any of you have ever met anyone capable of working magic. *True* magic.

I'll attempt to bring those inexperienced with the phenomenon a bit more "up to speed" in the paragraphs that follow.

Charlie Wendigo's particular form of magic, while appearing limited in scope, was actually quite

---

[1] The gypsies referred to within this book each self-identify as gypsy and as such are capable of working traditional gypsy magics; fortune telling, palm reading, curses, making those little pictures in the coffee foam, etc.

powerful in scale. Mundane, yet miraculous. For instance, he had the ability to draw any card he wished from an ordinary deck of playing cards. A common parlor trick, you might say, a simple slight-of-hand, the first bit of craft picked up by any ol' stage magician worth their salt. Nothing astonishing here.

That is—until you realize he could draw *any* card he wished: The Three of Hearts, the Ace of Spades, the Seven of Stars, the Thirteen of Keys, a business card for the now long defunct Abner's Bicycle Repair Shop on 5th and Walnut.

Any. Card.

But that's not all. If it were, his prestidigitations could easily be dismissed as simple acts of misdirection, loaded decks, and forced shuffles (this being the way I rationalized away his little miracles after my first encounter with the man.) If his magic were limited only to card tricks, do you think we'd be here now? Experiencing this symbiotic relationship between writer and reader? I certainly wouldn't be here. And of course, this second truth *would* bear impact upon the first.

No. Charlie Wendigo could also do coin tricks.

Again, you may think *smoke* plus *mirrors* equals *meh*. But understand this: when he makes a coin disappear, it *disappears*. Poof. The coin is gone. Forever. Not even he knows where it goes. And again, while this trick appears simple on the surface, the true magnitude of the feat is only discovered by digging deeper, gaining additional information. Accumulating insight *in addendum*.

Let's say, by way of example, he vanishes an ordinary nickel.

Yawn.

But that yawn quickly levels-up into a full-blown gasp once you realize you can now trace the path of that one-time nickel, back through the annals of commerce, by way of ledgers, spreadsheets, account histories, till audits and profit margins, all suddenly thrown off balance to the tune of five cents. All suddenly shorted by the nickel that never was.

See? That's miraculous.

This is the story of how I came to know Charlie Wendigo. It begins with a chance meeting, followed closely by a one-in-a-million coincidence. In retrospect, it's hard not to see the Hand of Fate actively playing a part in things—or, more accurately, smacking *yours truly* square across the face.

It was the last week of September 2017. I was in Baltimore, attending the dreaded Corporate Business Trip to the Main Branch, an annual week-long praise/criticize session[2] which sucked the life right out of countless, well-meaning, white-collar worker-bees in the employ of Devonshire Financial.

On the start of day two of "festivities," I lingered a bit too long in my hotel room, reluctant to leave it's strange yet comfortable surroundings. Subsequently, I found myself standing on the twentieth floor of the

---

2   Praise/criticize is a technique employed by many managers when interacting with their charges. The concept being that people are less likely to get defensive of a critical critique if you give a positive comment prior to heaping on the negative ones. So, for instance, your boss might compliment you on your tie before stating the third quarter divested interest report on the Northeast Subsidiary Holdings was overdue, your work on the Fredrickson account was rife with errors, and it was your fault a spreadsheet the company had been working on for the last three months became corrupted along with its backups. To those on the receiving end, praise/criticize has all the placating effect of being handed a balloon before getting punched in the face. Twice.

Baltimore Inner Harbor Radisson, running late and waiting impatiently for the elevator to arrive while doing all the things one does while waiting impatiently for an elevator—pacing, repeatedly pushing the call button, and alternately cursing at/directing various words of encouragement to an unreceptive inanimate object. Eventually, the elevator door slid open, displaying Charlie Wendigo to me for the first time.

I considered taking the stairs.

My first impression of the man was that he was mostly coat. He wore one of the "long and black" variety, cloak-like in appearance. In fact, he had the look of someone who would have preferred a cloak, possibly only settling upon this close second due to the unwanted level of attention his first-place choice would have drawn. He had what I could only refer to as skunk hair, a ragged black mop with a wide white streak running down the middle. He peered out at me with eyes on loan from a Siberian Husky, blue-gray in color, which would have been his most startling feature if they were not half hidden under heavy lids. He had a weight of enormous weariness to him, leaning against the back rail of that otherwise empty elevator, looking every bit as though returning from a long weekend of playing at being a vampire, LARPing around Inner Harbor with a clutch of like-minded brethren, returning at last to his cardboard coffin, secreted somewhere within the hotel's subbasement. And I was to have the honor of accompanying him on that morning's elevator ride.

Our long trip down from floor twenty to ground was experienced mostly in silence.

Mostly.

"You dropped a quarter," the vampire eventually

croaked.

"No. I don't think so," I responded, not bothering to look down, dreading the prospect of having to continue any sort of social interaction with this particular anti-socialite. Aren't they supposed to just brood? Silently?

He then made a point of stepping forward, scooping up the coin, and holding it up to me, so as to provide empirical evidence of my said dropping.

"Not mine," I maintained.

"Suit yourself," he countered. Then, in a quick, fluid motion, waving hand over hand, he made the coin vanish.

"Magic," I scoffed through an amused breath.

"Yeah. Magic." He briefly displayed his empty palms to me, with all the showmanship of a burned-out sideshow magician, before returning to his rail leaning.

Seconds later, the doors slid open, and I quickly disembarked. I was grateful to have somewhere else I needed to be. Even if it was corporate Hell and my impending eight-and-a-half hours of torment at the hands of middle management minions—demons armed with PowerPoint presentations in lieu of pitchforks.

It wasn't until later that night, returning battered and bruised[3] to the strange comforts of my hotel room, that I began to realize the startling significance of the deceptively simple coin trick I witnessed that morning.

---

3   This was meant only figuratively, an amusing way to describe the numb and addle-minded state I found myself in upon my return to my hotel room. The fact that I find it necessary to make the distinction here between a figurative battered and bruised state, as opposed to a literal one, should serve as a bit of foreshadowing.

I had been meticulously recording my expenditures, as one does when one is on soul-sucking business trips (impeccably, I might add, since I was a corporate accountant). The ability to balance accounts, down to the last cent, was my bread and butter, how I rake in the bacon, so to speak. I had just finished entering the day's expenses into a spreadsheet on my laptop when, to my horror, I discovered the balance was off. By twenty-five cents.

On any other occasion, this discrepancy would have set off a flurry of investigation. In this case, however, it was as simple as reviewing my perfectly balanced total from the previous day. Unfortunately, in doing so I discovered that it was now off as well. By twenty-five cents.

One quarter.

Missing.

In my weakened, punch-drunk, PowerPoint-prodded state, in that strange room, miles away from the grounding familiarity of home, I found myself thinking strange thoughts.

I recalled the coin trick performed by the depressed vampire during that morning's excruciatingly long elevator ride. What if that quarter *was* mine? What if he somehow made it disappear—not simply from sight but in a way that was so complete, so thorough, that all traces of it vanished as well? It was as though the quarter had been plucked from existence and all recordings of it retroactively erased.

I then proceeded to track the imbalance in my expenditures back three days to Sunday, shortly after my arrival in Baltimore, when I assumed the now errant coin entered into the life of Harry Long,[4]

---

4   That's me.

by way of change from the purchase of a Snickers.

In my situation and current condition, it was easy to imagine finding the newsstand where I had acquired that candy bar, and after a short inquiry, discovering their finances had been thrown off by one quarter as well.

I found myself in desperate need of a drink.

Thrown as I was, I still had enough of my wits about me to realize the substantial charge that would be tacked on to my bill if I raided the room's mini bar to the degree I would require, and the ramifications of having to explain the charge to Devonshire Financial's HR department. Instead, it was off to the elevator, back down, twenty to ground, and out into the Baltimore night. Mind still reeling, I made a stumbling beeline (if bees were wont to stumble) to the first bar I could find.

It was there I truly met Charlie Wendigo for the first time, long of coat and skunk of hair, maker of bad coffee, practitioner of card and coin tricks—mundane, yet miraculous. That was Charlie Wendigo in a nutshell.

Mundane, yet miraculous.

CHAPTER TWO
Men in Black

It is here I begin in earnest, the tale of my first meeting with Charlie Wendigo, and subsequent first adventure (for lack of a better term), falling a bit too easily into the role of assistant-slash-chronicler.

Consider me Doctor Watson to his Sherlock Holmes, if Sherlock Holmes wasn't that smart, constantly strung-out, and perpetually paranoid.

To reiterate: my sudden need for a drink that night led me out of my hotel, across the street, and into a convenient bar. It was something Irish, with a big O apostrophe in its name. I know that doesn't exactly narrow it down on the extensive list of Baltimore bars, but please bear with me. I'm relatively new at this chronicler thing.

I slid onto a conveniently empty barstool in the otherwise crowded O'stablishment and ordered a whiskey.

"Neat," I added.

I wasn't exactly sure what neat meant when attached as a modifier to the noun *whiskey*, but I had heard it in a movie once and always wanted to give it a try.[5]

5   Be advised it means the whiskey is poured directly from bottle to glass and immediately served, without the delay

It wasn't until the drink was before me, and it and I were both half-drunk, that I heard a familiar voice.

"I'm being followed."

I looked up from my drink long enough to register that I had inadvertently seated myself next to Count Blackcoat Skunkhair.[6]

Instead of thinking, *What are the chances?* and calculating all the ways the Universe had to align to put us both there in the same place at the same time, there was instead a sort of resignation, a simple acceptance that this was the way things were going to be from now on, an acceptance I acknowledged by slumping my shoulders and returning to my drink.

"I'm not following you; you just got here before me. You're...pre-following me," I said.

"Not you. THEM." He pronounced the word in such a way that I could hear the caps lock engaged. "When I say run—run."

The words barely had time to register before he shouted, "Run!" then bolted away, making a mad dash through the crowded pub, the act accompanied by a high-pitched scream which may or may not have been his. Arms flailing and coat flapping, he disappeared down a short hallway adjacent to the restrooms. Then, evidently realizing it was a dead end, he shuffled his way back through the now silently staring crowd and slid back onto his perch beside me.

Sitting bolt upright, staring forward at the large

of adding mixers or flavors, or even adding ice for that matter. Which allowed me to start forgetting that missing quarter as quickly as possible.

6   At this point I didn't know his real name. My mind had offered this up as a temporary nametag to pin upon him, still blissfully unaware of ever requiring a more permanent one.

mirror-backed bar, he whispered, "Did they see?"

I was still slumped over my drink. "I'm pretty sure *everyone* saw."

"Yes, but did *they* see?"

"The *THEM?*"

"Yes. Over there." I looked up in time to see him nodding toward the mirror. "The MIBs."

"MIBs?" I caught sight of the *THEM* in question, reflected in the mirror. Two men in black suits and dark glasses were sitting in one of the booths along the wall behind us. They were, in fact, looking our way.

"You mean the men in black?" I asked through a whiskey-fueled snicker. "What? Are you an alien?"

"Forget about the movies," he hissed, then added something that sounded like, "*Government propaganda,*" now barely audible over the collective revelries of reengaged patrons.

"Okay." I decided to humor him, at least for the time being. "If I help you get away from them, are you willing to tell me how you did the coin trick?" After mulling it over for a bit, he gave a slight nod.

I explained to him that if the two men in black were after him, he was safer there at the moment than anywhere else, surrounded by a group of people who were now all painfully well aware of his presence. I reasoned that for sinister secret-y agent types the less eyes on their targets when they acted, the better. This seemed to put him a little more at ease.

"I doubt agents Jay and Kay will try anything here," I added.

"Yeah. Okay." He leaned and whispered, "What does *neat* mean?"

I ordered him a whiskey neat of his own so the two of us could plumb that mystery together. We sat there in silence, nursing our drinks and occasionally glancing at the reflection of the MIBs in the wide mirror behind the bar. The two of them sat there in the booth, trying very hard not to look like they were looking our way. In fact, aside from directly after Skunkhair's mad dash across the room, when everyone had turned their attention his way, they hadn't looked at us once. It was after the third time my associate looked nervously in my direction, presumably eager for me to share my plan with him, that I realized I needed to come up with one. This was the way my thoughts progressed that night in the bar:

My first thought was that I didn't really need a plan. I viewed the men in black more as extras from the T.V. show *Mad Men*. They were simply a pair of well-dressed patrons, enjoying a few drinks after putting in a hard day's work at an ad agency in the 1960s. Any moment now, they'd get up to leave, eager to get to bed early so they could arise tomorrow, properly refreshed, ready to put in another day's work doing 1960s ad things and smoking as many cigarettes as they could before it became an unhealthy thing to do. I'd then explain to my neighbor that the two agents must have received new orders, playing along with whatever paranoid scenario he had running through his head. After being assured he was safe, I assumed Skunkhair would make good on our deal. He'd tell me how he made that coin disappear, and, more importantly, how in the world he managed to modify my expense report.

Next—when it became apparent the MIBs weren't leaving anytime soon, I imagined they *were* federal agents, watching some ne'er-do-well who happened to be present here with the rest of us do-well-ers. I imagined them tailing their suspect out the door at any moment. The rest of this line of thought then progressed the same way as my first.

Then—well after last call, when the majority of patrons had filtered out into the cool Baltimore night, there came a growing paranoia, possibly passing by way of osmosis from my increasingly nervous drinking companion to me, that the still lingering suited individuals *were* there for him. And now I, due to my proximity and apparent familiarity with public enemy number something, just implicated myself in whatever it was they were after him for.

Hacking! My God, yes! Hacking! He was a hacker, probably wanted for cyber embezzlement! Stealing money from time-honored financial institutions, one quarter at a time, then erasing his tracks. Like Richard Pryor in *Superman III*, and those three guys from *Office Space*. So small an amount that no one would miss it. But *I* missed it. I—

"Alright, you two! Time to go!"

A chill shot up my spine, receding once I realized it was the bartender, addressing our two would-be apprehenders. I watched as they moved toward the door without so much as a glance in our direction. Maybe I was wrong. It would've been simple at that point for one of the men to flash a badge, identify themselves, and take down Blackcoat Bonnie and Wrong-Place-At-The-Wrong-Time Clyde. Instead, they simply left.

Then it was our turn.

"Those guys were here all night," grumbled the bartender. "Just the two drinks between 'em." When he scowled at the similar pair of empty glasses sitting before us, I deduced it was time to go. I dropped a few bills on the bar, and we headed for the door.

Once outside on the sidewalk, I opened my mouth, about to run through the elaborate "You're safe, now tell me about the coin trick" speech I'd been mentally preparing for the last hour, when the vampire-hacker spoke.

"They're here."

I spun around, half expecting to come face to face with two members of the FBI's Cybercrime Division, only to find the sidewalk behind us empty. I turned back to a view similar to what I had witnessed hours before: a collection of flailing arms and fluttering coat, running off down the street.

Something made me follow. It was easy enough to catch up to him, as I possessed a more traditional running style.

The vampire made a sudden turn, entering a multi-story parking garage. He came to an abrupt stop near an early 2000s dark Lincoln town car. The Lincoln's rear window was missing, replaced by a sheet of plastic and a substantial amount of duct tape. The car also boasted a very large dent on its passenger side door.

"This is me."

"*This* is you?"

"Get in," he called, gesturing toward the passenger seat while wrenching open the driver side door.

He must have seen the fact I was hesitant, and rightly so; he was still a stranger. (On top of that, I made it a policy never to ride in the passenger side of anything that bore a passenger side dent that size.) As his side window lowered, he shouted, "I'll tell you how I did the coin trick!"

I don't usually curse, so the expletive I let out surprised me as it echoed around the parking garage, its reverberations cut short by my slamming of the

Lincoln's passenger side door.

Tires squealed.

I was thrown back, then to the right as the Lincoln shot out into the Baltimore night. The street, lucky for us, was un-customarily empty. Of course, it *was* late. So late, in fact, that it threatened to be early.

It was only after we had put several blocks between us and our possibly nonexistent pursuers that I was given a name to assign to the one responsible for getting me into whatever this was. Perhaps he thought it would put me more at ease, serve to relax the death grip I held upon his dash and door, if he weren't such a stranger.

"Charlie Wendigo," he said, extending a hand and a smile my way before turning his attention back to the road and rearview mirror.

After a moment he glanced over at me again. "Aren't you gonna comment on my name?"

"I'm not one to talk." I took the still offered hand and shook it once. "Harry Long."

"A hairy long what?"

"See what I mean?"

His eyes shot back to the rearview, and he turned pale. "Glove compartment."

"What?" I turned to look behind me. A pair of headlights were visible through the plastic sheet.

"Glove compartment!" he snapped. The car lurched to one side as he reached across and popped open the console.

"Jesus!" I yelled.

Wendigo righted himself and the car, dropping something into my lap in the process. "Let's go! Let's go!"

I looked down. There was something roughly gun shaped lying in my lap, a seven-inch long, L-shaped piece of translucent white crystal. "What?"

"Shoot them! Shoot them!" Wendigo frantically urged. "I'm not going back again!"

Ah! *Back again*, as in, back to whatever funny farm let its barn doors open long enough for the crazy horse here to run off. Right.

I figured I'd just turn in my seat, point the crystal toward the back, make some *pew pew* noises, and then dive out at the next convenient red light.

"How am I supposed to fire it?" I asked, attempting to humor him, "It doesn't have a trigger."

"It'll know when to fire!"

The interior of the car suddenly erupted in a blinding flash as a bolt of lightning shot from the crystal, ripping through the rear window's plastic sheet and slamming into the car behind us, accompanied by the appropriate, bowel-voiding sounds.

My shouts, made up of equal parts astonishment and terror, were quickly drowned out as three more bolts fired in rapid succession, slamming me back against the dash and filling the car with a blinding strobe and the smell of burning ozone.

The Lincoln screeched to a halt and Wendigo jumped out. I was left sitting in shock, staring at a burnt and smoldering chunk ripped out of the corner of my seat's headrest. Through the drifting shreds of plastic that were once his rear windshield, I saw Wendigo approaching what was left of our tail.

I exited the car and staggered back toward the now wrecked vehicle in a daze. The crystal gun was still held tightly in my hand, even though it had become uncomfortably hot. I was only partially aware of the fact that Wendigo was busy going through the wallet of the dark-suited corpse that had fallen out the passenger side door.

He gave me an appreciative look as I approached. "Nice shooting," he commented, quickly retrieving the crystal from my hand. He pocketed it before heading over to the car's driver side, presumably to rifle through the belongings of the other corpse.

The sudden realization of the implications involved with A) shooting a car, and B) looting its occupants, shocked me back to reality. I glanced around, expecting to see several eyewitnesses—a bevy of bystanders, a gaggle of good Samaritans, a lodge of looky-loos, all in the midst of their panicked calls to 911—but there was no one.

My eyes played across the car. Several jagged slices ran across its hood, disappearing briefly at the shattered windshield before continuing across the roof.

I looked down at the corpse that had been discharged from the passenger side. In the half-light, the face looked smoother than before, paler. Its dark glasses had fallen away, and to my horror, I saw that it had no eyes! There were only smooth, concave patches of skin where its eyes should be.

The corpse began to smolder.

Wendigo was pulling me back toward the Lincoln. "Come on! We have to go!"

He ran back to the car, and I reluctantly followed, still dazed, still confused, still waiting to wake from whatever surreal dream I had found myself in, and not at all prepared to hear this:

"The World will catch up to us soon!"

* * *

We drove for several blocks before we saw another

car. Then another. And then we were stopped at a red light—the first we had seen that night.

Signs of life slowly returned to the deserted city streets. There was a smattering of vehicles, a scattering of late night/early morning pedestrians, the occasional blare of a horn, and the sounding of other assorted city noises.

The World had caught up with us.

Wendigo asked me to open the glove compartment again. "There should be something that feels like a mummified hand."

I reached in and pulled it out. "What is it?"

"A mummified hand."

I shrieked and tossed the thing onto the dash. Wendigo scooped it up, whispered something to it, then returned it to the same spot. To my horror, the thing rose up on its fingers and began scurrying, spider-like, back and forth across the front of the car.

I recoiled as far from the amputated appendage as the confines of the passenger seat would allow. "What's it—! What's it doing?"

"It answers questions." The hand suddenly stopped, pointing with one finger through the windshield and off to one side. "In this case, I asked it to find me the nearest Denny's."

Wendigo shot me a smile as he made his turn. "I don't know about you, but I could sure go for an omelet right about now."

CHAPTER THREE
Denny's

I jumped out of the car as soon as it came to a halt in the restaurant's parking lot, eager to get farther away from that bizarre hand. Wendigo, however, casually tossed it back into the glove compartment as though stowing away a pair of sunglasses. Then, out of the Lincoln's trunk, he pulled a brand-new sheet of plastic and a half-used roll of duct tape. We quickly patched up the rear windshield before heading inside.

The restaurant was bright, but the people were muted. Scattered at various tables, the dozen or so patrons were either worn down after a long day or dreading the start of another. The waitresses moved between dull conversations and tired mastication, shuffling toward the end of their long shifts.

We were shown to a booth a short distance from the entrance. Wendigo slid into the side facing the doors. I assumed he wanted to keep an eye out for any more MIBs.

Our waitress dropped two menus down in front of us, but we already knew what we wanted. I ordered a Moons Over My Hammy, a late-night favorite of mine during my college years. It had a strangely calming effect as a familiar eye in the storm of weirdness.

Wendigo ordered his omelet (diced ham, green peppers, American cheese), a side of hash browns (extra crispy), rye toast, "And *coffee*." He pronounced the word the same way an excessively devout person might pronounce the word "communion."

He stared expectantly in the direction of the kitchen for quite some time before realizing I was glaring at him.

"You still want to hear about the coin trick," he surmised.

I gave a curt nod, and he immediately deflated, lowering his head, and looking a bit sheepish.

"I guess I can tell you now." He fidgeted nervously in his seat before meeting my gaze again. "It's magic."

Despite seemingly self-aware crystal guns that shot lightning bolts for bullets, I reflexively scoffed at the word. Despite being pursued by eyeless MIBs, despite animated severed hands with built-in GPS, despite not hitting a red light for ten blocks in downtown Baltimore—despite it all, I scoffed.

"Really?" he asked. "Still?"

Wendigo pulled his wallet out of his back pocket and withdrew a single bill, which he then slid to me across the remarkably clean, well-maintained table. "Here."

It appeared to be an ordinary one-dollar bill, but there was something off about it, as though I was experiencing it in crystal-clear high-definition. It was *too* real. It felt weird to the touch as well, like running your hand across a static-charged balloon. My attention was drawn to its serial number. Instead of the normal string of digits one would expect to find, it bore the words "THIS IS REAL MONEY" printed in their place. I stared at the eye in the pyramid on its reverse side and the eye stared back. I did this for what felt like a very long time. Possibly hours.

"They don't usually carry much," Wendigo said, shocking me out of my trance. "They don't need to. It'll vanish in a few days, but until then, well, go try the crane machine." He pointed over my shoulder toward a large, plush-filled claw game standing near the restaurant's entrance.

By the time I returned to the table, arms loaded with three stuffed dogs, a pair of yellow Minions, and a vinyl football, our food had arrived. I slid into the booth, dropping my winnings beside me. In a hushed whisper, I stated what he already must have known—the machine registered the credits but kept spitting out the dollar.

Wendigo waved off my attempt to return it to him. "Magic?" I asked, giving the bill one last hard look before slipping it into my pocket.

"Only as far as tricking the bill reader. Your current haul's more a testament to your considerable, non-augmented crane machine prowess."

Wendigo took a tentative sip of his coffee. Immediately, his eyes bulged, and he spat back into his mug.

"Does yours taste like someone wrung out an infrequently washed dishrag into it?" he asked, making a face which conveyed that his did.

I raised my mug, cautiously sniffing at it before taking an experimental sip. No. It didn't. As a matter of fact, it tasted quite good,[7] and I told him as much.

---

[7]   This should come as no surprise. One of the many things I like about Denny's is the fact that their coffee is always good, unless adversely affected by a gypsy curse, which they, of course, would have no control over. Another thing I like about Denny's is the benevolence they exhibit while trying to decide whether or not to bring litigation against well-meaning yet still

"Damn." He sighed then folded his arms and slumped down in his seat. The look of immense weariness I first noticed during the previous day's elevator ride had returned.

"Do you want mine?"

His eyes brightened. He leaned forward, then fell heavily back into his seat. "No. I shouldn't. Besides, something will happen to it," he grumbled.

Puzzled, I suggested he simply ask for a replacement, yet when the waitress returned, he ordered a Coke instead. He then sat, silently staring at his mug as though it had just betrayed him in some Machiavellian way.

"So, the coin trick? How do you do it?" I asked, attempting to take his mind off the coffee. "I mean, how did you figure out you could do it?"

"It was just something I did." Wendigo shrugged. "I saw a stage magician do it, and I thought I'd give it a try. It wasn't until later that I found out the coin's supposed to go somewhere—down a sleeve, palmed into a pocket, wherever. My coin didn't go anywhere. It just wasn't *there* anymore."

"Do you know..." I paused looking for the right word, "Do you know the *extent* to which you remove it?"

He gave another shrug. "Yeah. I think so."

I took a bite of my Hammy and thought for a bit while I chewed. Then, after swallowing, asked if there was anything else he could do.

"Card tricks."

"Really?"

"Yeah. It's just one trick actually, but it's a *good*

very novice chroniclers who inadvertently infringe upon their intellectual property while seeking only to extoll the many virtues of a beloved American institution. Good people.

one. You wouldn't happen to have a deck of cards on you, would you?"

"No."

"Oh. Okay." He took a long sip of Coke through his straw, gazing wistfully at my coffee mug.

"What about the rest? What was all that? The crystal gun thing and the hand and the MIBs?" Whatever levee the whiskey had built up to insulate me against the events of the night had started to give way. The impossibility of everything it had held back now threatened to flood my quickly sobering mind.

"They're things I...acquired. The MIBs don't like the fact I acquired them."

"I shot them!" I blurted—then, realizing the error of loudly professing my guilt in the middle of a restaurant, lowered my voice and leaned forward to add, "I *shot* them."

"Really? Did you pull the trigger? There wasn't one to pull, was there?" Wendigo brought a forkful of shredded potatoes up to his mouth. "In this case, it truly was the gun that killed."

"But I *aimed*." I was determined to find something to feel guilty about.

"More like...pointed it in the general direction. The Crystal Gun does most of the work. But you know, you pointed it pretty good. It works off your conviction." *Conviction*. The word stuck with me. It had multiple meanings.

"Besides, the MIBs, well, they're not exactly *human*..." Wendigo muttered through a mouthful of hash browns.

"That's a little dismissive." I raised my mug to take a drink, then set it back down, only slightly aware of Wendigo's rising and falling expectations. Drinking coffee with him was weird.

"If they're not human, what are they?"

This was a surreal conversation to be having, especially after a day spent looking at scores of precisely calculated, mathematically sound charts, graphs, and spreadsheets. Of course, maybe this was just things balancing out for me, the metaphysical "yin" to the all too real "yang."[8]

"The theory is, they came through back in the late forties as sort of walking ovum, got fertilized by Cold War paranoia, and grew into...well...MIBs."

"That's not like the movie at all," I reflected.[9] "Wait, came through from where?"

Wendigo smiled weakly while sawing through his omelet. "Someplace else."

"Where they wanted to take you?" Wendigo just kept on sawing. "In the car you said you weren't going back again."

His cutlery fell to his plate with a clatter.

There was a long span of uneasy silence before Wendigo picked up his knife and fork and returned to sawing. "I'm sure I say a lot of things in the heat of—things." He shrugged.

I decided not to press. Instead, we just sat and ate, the way people sometimes do in restaurants. Until I noticed the time.

"Crap!" I shouted, narrowly avoiding a classic

---

8   This was life kicking me right in the yin-yang.

9   *Men in Black* is a 1997 American science fiction action-comedy film directed by Barry Sonnenfeld and produced by Walter F. Parkes and Laurie MacDonald. Loosely adapted from The Men in Black comic book series created by Lowell Cunningham and Sandy Carruthers, the film stars Tommy Lee Jones and Will Smith as two agents of a secret organization called the Men in Black, who supervise extraterrestrial lifeforms who live on Earth and hide their existence from ordinary humans. [Wikipedia contributors. "Men in Black (1997 film)." *Wikipedia, The Free Encyclopedia.* Wikipedia]

spit take. "It's four a.m.! I have to get up for work in two hours!"

The MIBs, the magic, the property damage, the mummified body parts, were all suddenly replaced by the very real, very adult fear, of not getting in a good night's sleep.

And across from me, the sullen looking, skunk-haired vampire stared at me through weary eyes.

"I'll run you back."

CHAPTER FOUR
The Sleeper Awakes

I awoke the next morning to a pounding on my door.

Lying in bed, still half asleep, I managed to croak an annoyed, yet curious, "Yes?" My first tentative movements of the day sending a trio of plush toys tumbling to the floor.

"Mr. Long, you didn't answer your wake-up call." The muffled accusation came through the door.

My eyes snapped open, mind racing. Zero to sixty in one-point-five seconds.

"Yes! Sorry! Thank you!" I called in acknowledgment. My eyes darted to the digital clock, its numbers blinking urgently at me from atop the nearby nightstand, confirming my fear:

I was running late.

A dash to the shower, a quick once-over. Throw on some clothes. Grab my cell. Wallet. Keys to the rental car. The threat of showing up late for work reduced my morning ritual to a blur of efficiency heretofore unknown.

Then I was out the door and into the elevator, and once the doors had closed there was nothing to do but wait. Stand and wait and think.

Unlike the previous morning's ride, the elevator lurched to a stop on several floors, allowing people seemingly in no hurry at all to shuffle aboard, making the descent take even longer. It provided me with even more time to think.

I had slept through both alarms; the bedside clock and the one on my phone. Even the emergency back-up alarm, in the form of a wake-up call, had failed to rouse me. What were the chances?

Thinking of chances triggered memories of the previous night and the chance encounter with the odd-looking vampiric fellow that started it all in that very same elevator.

The doors finally opened on the ground floor, and I shot off across the lobby, leaving the herd of plodding elevatorites in the dust behind me.

Emerging from the hotel, I was struck by the blaring sounds of Baltimore inner harbor during morning rush hour. Grateful to be within walking distance of Devonshire, I fell in with a small group of pedestrians moving at a brisk pace along the sidewalk. The bumper-to-bumper traffic stood in stark contrast to the empty streets experienced last night.

Last night? Did that really happen? The plush animals sent tumbling from my bed this morning say it was real. And why did that suddenly seem more real to me? Realer than anything I could ever hope to accomplish at Devonshire. My pace slowed as I approached the intersection.

I found myself standing at the crossroads, both literally and figuratively. On the other side of the street lay another predictable day of Corporate Hell, and in the opposite direction lay *what?*

Adventure?

At that moment, completely un-cued, the wind stirred my hair.

From inside its yellow metal housing, the crosswalk signal flashed its open red hand haltingly in my direction. I took it as a sign.

"Yeah okay," I said, smiling at the flashing hand, "let's do this."

* * *

A few minutes later, I was walking across the hotel's roof, two large coffees to-go in hand, calling out to Charlie Wendigo.

"Good morning!"

He was faced away from me, looking out over the city. He turned his head and gave me a slight smile, appearing only mildly surprised, then turned his attention back to Baltimore.

"I checked with the hotel. You weren't registered as a guest. So, I thought maybe you were just visiting someone when I ran into you yesterday morning. Then I thought, *Maybe he was coming down from the roof.* That seemed more likely to me for some reason. Coffee?"

He gave the offered cup the same sort of look I presume the people of Troy gave to gift horses after their unfortunate experience with the first. Eventually, he took it from me, exhibiting a level of care usually reserved for the handling of Fabergé eggs. Despite all his precaution, and the very good grip he seemed to have, the cup slipped from his hands and hit the rooftop. Spilled coffee joined the tar and bird-dropping littered surface.

Wendigo looked down at the widening pool the same way a child looked at a dropped ice cream cone.

"Here, take mine," I offered.

"No. I better not," he grumbled, then turned back toward the city.

I set my coffee on a nearby surface, well out of Wendigo's line of sight, thinking it unfair to drink it in front of him. Stepping forward, I joined him near the building's edge.

From our vantage point, the view of the city and harbor was breathtaking—though I doubted that as the sole reason Charlie Wendigo was there that morning.

"So, what are we doing?" I asked.

"*We*? Don't you have work?"

"I decided to take the day off," I admitted. "It's difficult to return to a world of spreadsheets and pie charts after one has fired lightning bolts at overgrown embryos from somewhere else."

We exchanged brief smiles, then turned back, looking out across an expanse of glass and steel and street and water. Out in the harbor, boats were doing what boats do, going nowhere fast or nowhere slow, depending upon the whims of their owners. I never realized before how appealing that was.

My silence prompted an explanation; Wendigo began to speak. "We're looking for empty spaces. Look for places where there aren't any people or cars. No movement. An absence of...things." He added an all-encompassing gesture. I started scanning the cityscape, the same way a tourist scanned the waves during a whale watching expedition. Only, in this case, I wasn't looking for whales; I was looking for nothing.

"It'll tell us where they're active."

"They? You mean the MIBs?" Wheels clicked. Gears turned. "You're *hunting* them! Or are *they* hunting *you?*"

"Little of both, I guess." He gave a nervous laugh, "The Crystal Gun, the Answering Hand—they're after things like those. So, I'm after those things, too."

"So, you're trying to get these...magically charged *things* before the MIBs get them?"

"Their intentions seem a lot more sinister than finding the nearest omelet."

"Right." I started looking harder, only slightly aware of my cell phone buzzing in my pocket.

"Sometimes, I luck out. I hear about one of these things before the MIBs are onto it. I can rush into wherever, scoop it up, and get myself gone before they even realize there was anything there to scoop." He frowned. "This isn't one of those times. This time, they were here first. And I don't even know what it is they're after.

"The nothing space means they're active," he continued. "It means they're clearing out an area to work in, free from interruptions or prying eyes. They're free to drop their human costumes and cut loose with their weirdness. They hold back the World so they can tap into powers not of it."

Powers. Not of it. *Otherworldly* powers. A sudden realization dawned on me and formed into words which tumbled out of my mouth before I could stop them. "We were lucky last night."

"Yeah." Wendigo looked at me with a large grin. "I don't think they realized you were in the car, that I had an accomplice. I usually don't have much luck running and gunning."

I recalled the plastic sheet and duct tape repair job I first saw on the Lincoln's rear window, no doubt the result of a previous attempt at gunning while running. I also recalled the bit of duct tape I saw a few minutes before, on the latch to the door leading to the roof.

"I don't think we're supposed to be up here."

"I don't think we're supposed to be doing a lot of things. And we're gonna do a lot more things we're not supposed to do. You sure you want in on this?"

I wondered what exactly the "this" was I was getting "in on." Preventing assumingly malevolent... *entities* from getting ahold of magical whatsits? Armed only with a crystal gun, a creepy hand, a couple of card and coin tricks, and a bachelor's degree in accounting? Trespassing on a hotel roof, looking for nothing? How would I even know if I found it? There had to be countless side-streets and alleyways scattered across Baltimore—not to mention large sections of harbor—with nothing happening in them right now.

I remembered the strangeness of the empty streets we encountered last night, looking back now with 20/20 hindsight and a sober mind. There was nothing, nothing but us and them, and it went on for blocks. Maybe a mile. The nothing would be a big area, and that's why Wendigo was looking for it up here.

Two unrelated things occurred simultaneously: My phone, nestled in my pocket, launched into another flurry of buzzes, and I realized we'd been staring at the empty space all along. My finger shot out. "There!"

Wendigo looked in the direction I was pointing, across the harbor, to what stood at its opposite side: a collection of red, blue, and gray walls topped by a series of towering glass angles.

The Baltimore National Aquarium.

There was no one there. No throng of people

waiting for admittance. No early morning comings and goings of delivery trucks or vans. No employees visibly scurrying from Point A to Point B. Nothing. It was so large, so glaring an absence, that it was easily overlooked in our search for a presumed subtleness, a clandestine *less*.

"My God!" shouted Wendigo. He turned and dashed back across the roof toward the access door.

It wasn't until we were in the elevator, on our way down to the hotel's lobby, that a thought occurred to me. "Why didn't you just use the hand? Couldn't it have found whatever it was the MIBs were looking for before they did?"

"It can't see magic. Besides"—he gave me a broad grin—"I knew you'd be here to help."

I checked my cell phone on the way down in the elevator. Three missed calls from Devonshire Financial. For some reason, the notices all seemed angry.

There was also a text from Jane (no last name given).

Jane was a co-worker from another branch with whom I had become recently acquainted, likewise in town for the annual week of Corporate Hell. I had formed a bond with Jane over the past two meeting-filled days, much in the same way survivors of traumatic experiences forge fast kinships with one another. We had developed a coping mechanism in the form of silently noting how many times buzzwords and phrases like *moving forward, outside the box, organic growth,* and *synergy* were used during a meeting, then comparing our tallies in the aftermath.

We had somehow gotten into a discussion on pie charts the day before, which led to a far more enjoyable conversation on pies, which led to both of us lamenting the fact that the meeting wasn't being held at our Boston branch, since at least then we could get some Boston cream pie, which led to us both realizing that we shared the same favorite pie, which led to me suavely offering to take her out for some sometime. Which led to us exchanging numbers.

I figured that would be as far as it went, because that's usually as far as those things go for me—but there was her name, sitting on my phone's text message panel. I had obviously made enough of an impression for her to be concerned about my absence. I tapped the text open.

It simply read: *Where are you?*

On an adventure, I typed in reply.

I dropped the phone back into my pocket and waited impatiently for the elevator doors to open.

CHAPTER FIVE
Seeing Baltimore on Three Packs a Day

We paused in our journey across the harbor long enough for Wendigo to purchase three decks of Baltimore Inner Harbor Souvenir Playing Cards from a cart loaded down with an assortment of trinkets standing just outside a long two-story shopping mall that ran parallel to the water.

He insisted we needed the cards, and who was I to argue? He was the one with all the experience here. If we were going over his finances, it would have been a different story.

(Though, presumably, a shorter one.)

As he rifled through his wallet, I took the opportunity to check my voicemail. I was right; those were some angry calls. *Very* angry.

At first, I felt a flash of annoyance—as far as they knew, something could have happened to me. I could be lying in a ditch somewhere (which, for some reason, was the go-to place one cited as people winding up lying in when *things* happened). Then I realized, in all fairness, that this was not the case. I wasn't lying in a ditch somewhere. I had just decided not to show up. I *ditched* them.

Maybe they had experienced this sort of thing

before. Maybe other employees bailed on them mid-week, and they just assumed that's what I did.

Which is what I had done.

I cleared my throat over the sound of seagulls, distant boats, and other harbor things.

"So, out of curiosity, what does this job pay?"

Wendigo paused mid-transaction. "All the crane game prizes and vending machine fare you can stand?" he offered. I didn't think it would be enough. I had, after all, grown accustomed to a certain lifestyle. One that required a dwelling.

Maybe the thing we were after would be a new source of income, in addition to the disappearing MIB dollars, since I apparently had just sacrificed my old source of income for whatever *this* was. I looked off toward the aquarium. The only scenario I could think of was magic oysters.

"Endless pearls," I whispered, finishing the thought out loud.

"Oooo! Endless pearls," echoed Wendigo, suddenly standing beside me, "That would be nice." He dropped the rolled-up plastic bag containing his purchases into one of his coat's deep pockets. "Ready?"

"You have the...the gun, right?" My voice lowered near the end of the sentence, asking a question best asked in hushed tones while traversing crowded tourist areas.

"Yeah, I have it." He patted a section of his coat in a reassuring way. We then resumed our trek across Inner Harbor.

"Oh!" Wendigo added, "Before I forget. It only works in there."

"It only works in there? The...crystal?"

He nodded. "It only works in places where they're

holding back the World."

The fact that a statement like that now made sense to me should come as some sort of warning, possibly one included on a list of reasons to stop taking a specific form of medication and consult your doctor immediately.

My stance became slightly less confident. "Okay. I don't see us needing it out here anyway, but that's good to know. What about the hand?"

"Left it in the car. The crystal's easier to explain to security. Though...not by much."

***

We fell into a quick and steady pace, our footfalls beating a synchronized rhythm against the red brick causeway that framed the harbor. The aquarium loomed before us in the distance, growing in loominess as we approached. It seemed...*dead*. That was the best word to describe it; a place that should be alive but wasn't. One could almost imagine all the attractions inside, floating belly-up.

I felt a sudden pang of anger and latched onto it. It was a better thing to be feeling at the time than dread or fear. If the universe was setting me up to go all "John Wick" on a few MIBs over a dead dogfish, so be it. I had a lightning gun and combat knowledge gleaned from an extensive library of action flicks on Blu-ray. I was ready.

To my shock, Wendigo had stopped to chat with a few parents along the way, asking them what their plans were for the day. To my even greater shock, they cheerfully obliged him with answers. The results were strangely similar.

We're just down to take in the sights, they would

say.

Oh, are you planning to visit the aquarium? Would be his response.

Yes, but probably later on in the day. Avoid the morning lines, they would answer.

Well, there doesn't seem to be anyone there at the moment. He'd then indicate the aquarium with a sweeping gesture.

At that point, whichever parent he was conversing with would give him an annoyed look and state, *Yes, but we're doing something else right now.*

Like what? He would ask innocently.

And after a strange pause accompanied by a puzzled look, he'd get, *Like walking over there.*

Then the parents would gather their children and walk off across the harbor in a daze, always in the opposite direction of the aquarium.

After the last exchange, Wendigo turned to me and said, "I'm still trying to figure out how that works. The whole subconscious, 'I don't want anything to do with whatever's going on over there.' Seems like it would be a good trick to know." And then we were at the aquarium.

We stood before a wide, dark blue, slanted structure containing a row of ticket windows beneath a steel canopy. The words NATIONAL AQUARIUM TICKETS ran above the windows in bold white letters. A quartet of bored looking attendants, posted behind their windows at the ticket counter, momentarily brightened at our approach before Wendigo pulled me aside, back out of their view.

"Okay. Some of the workers must have arrived before the MIBs got here and started doing their thing." He reached into his coat pocket and produced the plastic bag from the gift cart. He quickly removed the cellophane wrapper from a fresh deck of cards.

"Why isn't the whatever it is working on us? Keeping us away?" My eyes scanned the sky. Even the birds seemed to be avoiding the place.

"I don't know. Maybe because we know what it is? We're aware of it?" He dropped the cellophane and empty pack in a nearby waste can. "You feel an urge? Like something telling you that you should probably be someplace else?"

"Other than a mild sense of self-preservation? No."

"Good," he said, fanning the deck out before me. "Pick a card, any card."

"Now?" I asked, surprised by his timing. I complied anyway, pulling a card from the facedown arc splayed out before me. I hid the card's face from him; in my experience, that was what you did when asked to pick a card.

"What is it?" he asked.

"You want me to just tell you?" He nodded. "Ten of Diamonds," I said, showing the card to him. It wasn't much of a trick.

"Now my turn." He handed the cards to me. I fanned the deck out as he had done, then held them out to him. He drew a card, hiding its face from me as well.

"Okay. What is it?" I asked, playing along with him.

"A Baltimore National Aquarium VIP Membership Card," he announced, displaying it to me. He grabbed the rest of the deck from me, dropped it in the trash, then strode off toward the ticket windows like he owned the place, leaving me standing in stunned silence.

"Okay," I breathed. "That *is* a good trick."[10]

I caught up with Wendigo just in time for him to indicate to a silver-haired matronly looking woman at the ticket counter that I was the *one additional free admission* his aquarium VIP status entitled him to. She gazed out at him through the ticket window. Frozen across her face was the unwavering, permafrost smile of those who have endured years of customer service.

It made our interaction with her even more unsettling, given the circumstances.

"I'm sorry, but we're having trouble with our computers. I'm having a hard time verifying your membership," Margret [11] admitted after tapping a few buttons on her console, smile resolute. "It's been a strange morning."

"Yes," agreed Wendigo, looking around the area. "Certainly seems that way. Tell me, is it usually this empty?"

"Oh, heavens no!" she exclaimed; her sentiment

---

10   Later, Wendigo confided in me that he discovered this trick much the same way he discovered his coin trick. He wasn't familiar with the suits or numbering of a standard deck of cards, so the first time he attempted a card trick he produced the Queen of Ravens. Those present at the time just assumed the card was part of the trick, so he was never corrected. It wasn't until weeks later he realized that such a card shouldn't exist in a standard deck of playing cards, but by then it was too late. In the space between he had already produced, the Five of Squares, the Ace of Jacks, the Three of Beetles, and a "Buy Twelve Dozen, get the Thirteenth Free!" punch card for the Donut Beat All Bakery and Café, in Rapid City, South Dakota.

11   Possibly her real name. From where I was standing all I could make out were the first three letters of her nametag "Mar." I batted around Marcy, Maria, Marilyn, Margot, Mariah, Mary, Maris, Marissa, Marla, Martha, Marsha, and the even more unlikely, Marble, Marsupial, and Marzipan before settling on Margret.

echoed by the three other attendants still manning their posts behind the counter. "Although it *has*, on the odd occasion, happened before. Some sort of fluke."

For some reason, her statement caused a burst of laughter to issue from behind the windows.

Wendigo waited until everyone recovered before continuing. "Really? It's happened before?"

"Oh, yes." Margret wiped a tear from her eye. "Usually on days when there's some other big event going on in the city."

"And *is* there? Some other big event going on in the city?"

"No." Her mouth was still smiling, but the rest of her face had stopped. Her voice lowered to a whisper. "It's the strangest thing. You're the only guests I've had all morning," she confided while handing us two tickets for admittance. Either the computer had finally kicked back approval, she didn't want to offend an aquarium VIP member, or she made an executive decision based on the lack of visitors. At any rate, we were in (or about to be).

As we walked away, one of the other attendants piped up, "Enjoy your visit! It's rare you'll find the aquarium this empty, just you and one other group!"

Wendigo stopped and spun, moving back quickly to the source of the troubling statement, a young man wearing a button-down fish print shirt, stationed at one of the other windows.

"Other group?" he asked, using the same voice and expression as someone asking to check the bottom of their sneaker after jogging through a dog park.

"Yes. All in dark suits. Some sort of business outing I guess."

"All?" Wendigo parroted, looking as if informed he had, in fact, stepped in something. "How many is *all?*"

"Seven."

And now he smelled it. "Seven?"

"Yes," the young man chirped, "But I wouldn't worry about it. It'll be just the nine of you in there. You'll pretty much have the run of the place. And it's a *big* place."

As we made our way toward the entrance, somewhere behind us Fishboy[12] called out, "You might not even run into them!"

"*Seven*," Wendigo breathed in stunned amazement as we approached the aquarium's doors.

"That's a lot," I commented.

"I only ever encountered them two at a time," he admitted through a dazed whisper. "They usually work in pairs. That's three sets and an...unknown variable." His hand rested on the handle to one of the large glass doors. He gazed through it with a look of uncertainty, as though trying to weigh an unknown risk against an unknown gain.

"Is that why you recruited me?" I asked. "Because they work in pairs? Thought you were evening the odds?"

"Hey! You recruited yourself!" he blurted, as though trying to absolve himself of any liability, both potential and impending. "Mostly."

I thought about being trapped for a third consecutive day in Corporate Hell. Enduring yet another gauntlet of meetings, another endless succession of charts and graphs, each accompanied by a narration duller than a voice actor reading lines for a computer chess game.

---

12   His real name.

"Hey, it's better than the alternative." I grabbed ahold of another door's handle. "Besides, how do you know the World didn't recruit me to help you? Maybe it's getting tired of being pushed around."

I swung the door open and stepped inside, leaving Wendigo standing behind in stunned silence.

My entrance into the aquarium was met by the sound of falling water. I was standing in a tall three-story glass-fronted structure, the aptly named Glass Pavilion, its ceiling part of the silvery angles we had watched grow increasingly larger as we made our way across Inner Harbor. Someone had pulled a thirty-foot tall waterfall from somewhere upstate, along with all its surrounding environs, and dropped it here, fully intact.

The water fell from above into a small pond, Its contents visible through a low glass wall before me. A large group of striped bass lazily drifted by (I was relieved to note they were right-side up). Birds tweeted, frogs chirped, and other things made other pleasant noises.

I had planned on visiting the aquarium, if time permitted, later in the week, provided I wasn't too burned-out from forty hours' worth of meetings to bother. But now I was here, a few days early, and I was—what was the word I was looking for…happy?

Hah, I thought, *tricked them*. My mind registered a small victory, over bosses and assistant bosses and assistant-assistant bosses.

"Ever been here?" Wendigo was standing beside me, looking up toward the top of the falls.

"Once. Years ago." I gestured up and around. "I don't remember all this being here before."

"Yeah. Maybe we should find a map."

"Gift shop." I pointed to a sign bearing an arrow

indicating one existed somewhere on the floor above us.

"There'll be plenty of time for souvenirs la—oh! Right. Map." Wendigo bounded over to the nearby escalators.

"You'd think with your VIP status you would have been given one at the ticket window."

"Can't really hold her at fault for forgetting. It's been a strange morning."

We climbed the stairs as they carried us up, our eyes scanning the Glass Pavilion's second story for any sign of MIBs as we arrived. It didn't take us long to find a sign of their presence.

There was a wide glass cylinder standing outside the entrance to the gift shop. "Was" as in "used to be"—the majority of it now lay in shards, scattered across the floor. A two-foot-tall fake, jagged stone stood at the bottom of what was left of the cylinder. Wendigo moved cautiously toward it as I nervously gave our surrounding area another quick look-over.

"Huh," Wendigo grunted. "At least now we know what they were looking for." He was staring down at a small placard at the cylinder's base. "Neptune's Trident," he read out loud.

"I'm sorry? What?" I asked, jogging over to him. I read the words myself. "Neptune? Like the *actual* Neptune?"

"Poseidon, more likely."

I just stood there, mouth hanging open, mind attempting to process the existence of mythical gods and the myriad of implications their existence presented,[13] before Wendigo added, "Kidding. There's

---

13   One of the implications involving Rick Riordan and hypothetical accusations of plagiarism.

a relatively short list of names you can attach to a presumably magical looking trident."

"Aquaman?" I offered.

"Whatever it is, it's safe to assume it was what they were after," Wendigo said as he wandered into the gift shop. I followed after him, about to voice my annoyance at his momentarily convincing me the Greek and Roman pantheons existed, when we both became aware of an odd smell.

It only took us a moment to locate its source. Two neat little piles of ash lay within the gift shop, one just inside the entrance, the other behind the shop's checkout counter. A half-melted Baltimore National Aquarium name tag sat perched atop each.

"Oh God!" I exclaimed. "Did the MIBs do this?"

"I'd say there was a good chance of it, yes."

I was suddenly gripped by an overwhelming fear, brought on by the reality of once-human ash piles, the reality of the foul and lingering odor, the reality of being in the same place as things that could do *this*. It was all catching up to me, this new reality, and just how dangerous it really was. "We have to call the police!"

"And tell them what? You think I wouldn't have already gotten them involved if I could? They like things a little more black-and-white than this, a little more cut-and-dry. They like suspects they can question who are native to this world and modus operandi that don't involve disintegration." He gestured toward an ash pile, which I thought was a little rude for some reason. "Besides, how are they supposed to get here if we *were* to call them? There's no guarantee that they wouldn't just subconsciously find other things to do until the World caught up with this place again. And by then it'll be too late."

"No," Wendigo said as he snatched a free map from the display sitting atop the gift shop's checkout counter with more conviction than anyone's ever snatched a free map before. "First thing they'd do is pull us in, interrogate us for a few hours trying to figure out what drugs we were on. Maybe hold us for a full twenty-four before reluctantly setting us loose. And then we're a day behind the MIBs and whatever they plan to do with whatever it is they've got.

"No," he said again. "Here, we *are* the police. We're the only police this place is gonna have until the MIBs are gone."

"But they probably *are* gone, right? I mean, they've already got what they wanted," I reasoned, gesturing at the shattered case.

"The trident was here, close to the entrance. They could have grabbed it and been off by the time we made it across the harbor, but they're still here. The World's still being held back. Can't you feel it?"

I couldn't, but I didn't want to admit it.

I could see the wheels turning in Wendigo's head as he unfolded the map. "They're after more than one thing. That's the reason for such a big group; there's something else somewhere else here. But where?"

He held the map up so both of us could see. I stood slightly behind him, peering over his shoulder. I was looking for the most likely place we could find a magic oyster, still dreaming of the possibility of endless pearls, when a strange voice suddenly barked at us in a series of warbles and croaks.

Wendigo slowly lowered the map to reveal four MIBs standing before us.

None of them were holding a trident.

CHAPTER SIX
The Gang Wrecks a Gift Shop

The garbled speech came at us again, more insistent this time. The four MIBs had abandoned their human guises, much like the ones from the bar had abandoned theirs prior to the abrupt end of last night's car chase. They were each pale and smooth, gaunt and alien, and—I assumed—eyeless behind their dark glasses. One of them was pointing something at us which must have been a gun, since Wendigo's hands shot up into the air, map fluttering slowly to the ground. I followed my associate's example.

The warbles and croaks continued. I judged them to be some sort of orders by their tone, and the fact they were issued by the MIB holding the presumed gun. Wendigo slowly stepped toward him.

"Look, uh...Slim, I can't understand you." His hands dropped down a little, assuming a more imploring pose. "How about one of you put your human suit back on, huh? Believe me, this'll go much easier."

The four exchanged looks for a moment, then the one holding the gun-thing stepped forward, its features suddenly rippling into something a bit more human in appearance.

"I said—"

That was all Slim managed to get out before Wendigo slugged him square in the face. The momentum of his punch spun him around toward me.

"See?" he said. "Much easier." He then made a mad dash for cover back inside the gift shop, arms flailing, coat flapping. One MIB moved to help its fallen comrade. One moved to retrieve the gun-thing that went skittering away when Slim hit the floor. One looked menacingly in my direction, opening its mouth, about to yell something alien and presumably derogatory. I moved to join Wendigo in the gift shop as fast as my feet could carry me.[14]

I ducked behind a display of stuffed manatees just as a solid beam of force took a big chunk out of its top, sending a collection of stuffing, bits of gray fabric and big black button-eyes flying everywhere. The beam hammered into the shop's rear wall, where it dispersed in a loud splash of television static and a shower of plaster.

"What the hell!" I yelped, glaring at Wendigo through a flurry of ex-manatee parts.

"Warn me next time!"

"How?" He was crouched down behind the end of the checkout counter. We were almost evenly positioned, both facing the rear of the store, backs against counter and display.

"Here," he offered. "You're actually a better shot

---

14   You'll notice that my reaction time here was considerably slower than Wendigo's. It hadn't occurred to me that simply punching these interdimensional invaders was an option. As a result, I was just as shocked by Wendigo's sucker punch as Slim, though to my credit I wasn't now lying sprawled across the second floor of the Glass Pavilion.

than me!" The crystal gun skidded across the grey tiled floor in my direction.

"I thought you said you don't really shoot this thing!" I yelled, scooping it up. Two more solid beams ripped through the store in unison, distorting the air as they shot past. One tore through a nearby rack of sweatshirts; the other shattered a shelf full of expensive looking water globes and statuettes.

"It relies on your desire to shoot! Your conviction! You seem to have a stronger one than me!"

"It's pretty strong now!" I yelled back.

Each blast through the store had been proceeded thus far by a short, humming, *whoom* sound, which I wasn't hearing in that moment.

With the lull in firing, I took my chance, popping up and pointing the crystal. Lightning flung out before I could even aim. The bolt struck one of the MIBs in the chest, sending it flying back. I ducked behind the display and pressed to one side, peering out around its edge, keen on seeing what the MIBs would do next. A pair of stuffed manatees tumbled to the ground, their heads on fire—collateral damage.

There were three MIBs left. I couldn't tell if the one I took out was the same one Wendigo slugged or not. (Secretly, I hoped he had just finished being helped back to his feet when the lightning bolt struck him.)

Then there was the *whoom* sound again, slowly building up. To my surprise, it seemed to be coming from their mouths. There was a faint glow, a slight crouch, and *wham!*[15] Three more beams ripped

15   The sound used here to indicate a sudden occurrence, not the musical duo. George Michael and Andrew Ridgeley did not suddenly appear, singing about their desire to be notified prior to anyone leaving their presence. This must have happened quite often, people slipping away or sneaking off

through the shop, tearing through displays and smashing countless souvenirs.

"They're shooting at us!" I called over to Wendigo, appropriately annoyed at the omission of this crucial detail. "Why didn't you tell me they could do this?"

"They can do a lot of things! It's not always the same things! It's different every time! You want me to run down a list?"

"Not right now, no!" Three more beams shot by, two taking out a good portion of my cover, the other clipping a shelf behind the checkout counter. To my horror, their aim was improving.

I popped up in the wake of those beams. This time, two bolts shot out from the crystal in rapid succession, leaving only one of the MIBs remaining. I dropped down, expecting to see Wendigo suitably impressed, but he was busy pocketing decks of playing cards that had fallen out of a display behind the counter.

"I hope you plan on paying for those!"

He gave me a look like a kid caught with his hand in the cookie jar. "Yeah. Sure. I'll leave them some money. They'll just have to spend it fast."

I suddenly realized the last MIB might try to make a run for it. I leapt up and caught him with a bolt just before he could disappear around the corner and into the nearby Main Concourse.

It was then, no longer caught up in the heat of

---

without their knowledge, for them to decide they had to lodge a four-minute-long musical complaint. While others would have taken less drastic measures, such as changing their deodorant, the two managed to successfully turn their annoyance at being snubbed into a number one hit. And while the ability to make Wham! appear would have been an impressive one for the MIBs to exhibit, it would have been about as useful in the current firefight as say...a coin or card trick.

the moment, that I became aware of a different heat, along with the smell of singed flesh drifting up from my right hand. I yelped, dropping the crystal gun to the floor. "Damn, that thing gets hot!"

Wendigo stooped to retrieve it, using his coat sleeve as a glove. He stood up and looked out, admiring my handiwork as he dropped the crystal into his pocket. "Nice work."

Wendigo moved to the nearest MIB. He gave it a test kick before crouching down to relieve its wallet of any magic dollars it contained. I decided to do so as well, moving to the next closest body and patting it down.

"Hey, there's an ID here!" I called after officially looting a corpse for the first time in my life, coming away with a wallet identical to the one Wendigo held, save for a small card in a transparent flap contained within.

Wendigo shouted a warning not to look at it, but it was too late. A pain shot through my head, the mother of all migraines. I immediately dropped the wallet.

Wendigo scooped it back up and pulled three bills from it, handing them to me as my vision unblurred. "It's another trick. It's painful to look at their identification. They just sort of flash it at people, just for a second, so the pain doesn't really register, only subliminally. That way no one really gets to see their ID, and no one ever asks to see it again."

"Bloody hell!" I exclaimed, despite my not being British. I staggered on to the next corpse, still holding my head. "You have a real gift for warning me about dangers either during or after." My right foot struck something that wasn't shattered glass or MIB.

"I *told* you they had powers." Wendigo watched as

I retrieved the something from the ground. "What's that?"

I looked the item over. It was a short white rod, possibly ivory, carved with several odd symbols. A strange feeling overcame me—a sensation that it wanted to be pointed somewhere, and that things wouldn't be right until it was. Slowly, I brought the rod up and pointed it at Wendigo. It felt right. Like it was the only thing in the world I wanted to be doing at that moment.

"What are you doing?" muttered Wendigo, clearly a bit uneasy to have an unknown something pointed at him.

"I think this is the thing. The thing Slim was holding when you decked him."

"Well, can you not point it at me?" he asked, stepping to the left. The rod followed. Or rather, it wanted to follow, and I felt obliged to let it.

"I don't think so, no."

Wendigo dashed back to the right and the rod followed. It was certainly pointing at him, but not directly, just a little off center. Something suddenly clicked. "Where do you have the gun?"

Wendigo's eyes went wide. He reached into a pocket and pulled out the crystal gun. He held the gun out to one side, and the rod followed. True to my hunch, the crystal seemed to be what the rod wanted to point at.

"Oh my God!" he exclaimed, handing me the gun. I immediately lost all interest in pointing the rod anywhere, so I placed it and the gun together in the same pocket of my jacket.

"Do you know what this means?" he cried, grabbing ahold of my shoulders. "*Do you know what this means?*" He snatched the aquarium map up from the floor and began to scan it. "We need to find the food court!"

"Are you sure? Seems to me like it would mean something else."

"Downstairs!" he said, quickly stowing the map away in his coat as he shot back to the escalators.

"I know. We passed one on the way up," I said slowly, surprised he had missed it. "I'm beginning to see why you brought me onboard. You're not very good at this."

CHAPTER SEVEN
Fish Sticks

Back on the ground floor, Wendigo made a right and entered the aquarium's Harbor Market Kitchen, where he hopped a counter and disappeared into the food prep area.

There was a weird uneasiness to the café, as though it were waiting impatiently for guests to arrive or haunted by the ghosts of visitors past. I followed anyway, getting as far as the first available chair in the café's seating area before opting to sit and wait patiently for whatever mania had suddenly gripped my partner in crime to subside. It actually felt good to sit. I thought about my extensive library of action flicks; you never saw the hero just sort of sit and relax for a bit.

Of course, I was still keeping an eye on the food court's entrance, warily scanning for any signs of MIBs. Three was the remaining number, calculated by means of my well-honed accounting skills. We didn't need any of them sneaking up on us while Wendigo was indisposed.

"Ah ha!" Wendigo shouted, leaping up. He vaulted back over the counter, triumphantly holding up a box of aluminum wrap.

I raised an eyebrow. "Are we making hats now?"

"Funny." He pulled out the roll of foil and tossed the box aside. He asked me for the crystal gun, which he then quickly wrapped in a thick covering of aluminum foil.

"I carry a few rolls of it in my car," he explained.

"Of course, you do."

"Blocks magic." He gave me an odd grin. "The rod thing. Try using it now."

I pulled the ivory rod out of my pocket and held it loose in my hand, the way I had moments ago outside the gift shop. It didn't seem to want to point at Wendigo, nor the wad of aluminum he now held.

Wendigo gazed at the rod in awe. "I knew the MIBs had a way of finding this stuff, but I always thought it was one of their powers. Not a thing. Not something we could use!"

"You said their powers are different each time. Maybe this is some kind of backup? For when they don't have the ability themselves." I looked down at the rod. Then, I felt it urging me on again. It wasn't so much a pull as the thought of being pulled.

The fact must have registered on my face because Wendigo asked, "What is it?"

"It's, um...prompting me...again."

"Let me see!" Wendigo made a grab for it.

"I can point it!" I said, shielding it with my body. After all, I was the one who found it. Wendigo had the gun and the hand. This was mine—whatever it was. I wasn't about to start calling it "Precious" or anything, but it seemed like it wanted to stay with me. The rod didn't care for Wendigo very much. Again, just a feeling, a planted thought, but a strong one.

It wanted to be pointed off to the side—southeast,

by my calculations. So, I pointed it.

"It's picking up the trident," Wendigo surmised. "Or maybe it's the other thing the MIB's are after… Whatever that other thing may be."

"Wait! What if the other thing is this?" I asked, indicating the rod. "What if they were after the trident and this?"

"Then why not just leave?"

"Maybe it detected your gun? And they decided to see what it was pointing at?"

Wendigo seemed to consider this for a moment. "Well, the rod's still pointing at something, and I'm betting we'll find the rest of the MIBs wherever it leads."

I shrugged. His logic was sound. "So, what's over that way?"

Wendigo pulled out his map and started searching. "Pier 4 Pavilion," he said after a brief orientation. "There's a walkway across. We need to go back upstairs to get there." I couldn't recall a single action hero who did this much backtracking.

***

A minute later, we were standing in the aquarium's Main Concourse—a wide corridor which ran to the southeast and connected the Glass Pavilion and Blue Wonders (the two sections of the aquarium which sat at Pier 3) with a single large structure that sat on Pier 4, appropriately named…Pier 4.

The entryway to Blue Wonders sat directly to the south of us. Just past a deep blue expanse and a series of perpetually bubbling, water-filled columns lay five stories worth of assorted wildlife: rays, sharks, crabs, octopi, and other exotic sea creatures. The uppermost level contained a section of tropical rainforest, housed within another of those large silver angles of glass, visible from practically anywhere in the harbor.

I considered trying to convince Wendigo that we should search for the remaining MIBs along the glass-lined walls of the aquarium's Shark Alley and Atlantic Coral Reef exhibits, hoping to get the most out of our visit, but he was already well on his way.

We headed for the enclosed walkway which spanned the gap between Pier 3 and Pier 4, passing several more piles of ash along the way. We also came across two security guards with pieces missing from them, no doubt shouted at by our bazooka-mouthed friends.

I half gagged as I made my way past the guards, trying hard not to look at what remained of them. (I was thankful I had skipped breakfast that morning.) "How do they explain all this away? The damage and the...bodies."

"Gas main explosion," Wendigo called back from several paces ahead.

"Gas main explosion!?" I sidestepped a severed arm as I moved to catch up. "This?"

"Oh, yeah. I mean, they know it's not a gas main explosion, but like I said, authorities like things black and white, cut and dry. They just quietly clean stuff up, and if anybody asks what killed all those people or did all that damage? Gas main explosion. It's a lot easier than looking for truths they know they'll never find."

"Why not a terrorist attack?"

Wendigo stopped in his tracks, turning to face me. "No, you see—with a terrorist attack, people want someone's head, and they're not happy until they get one, because they won't feel safe until they do. If we're lucky, we're long gone before anyone shows up, and the MIB heads eventually disintegrate along with the rest of 'em after they bite it, so there's nobody's head left to give to the clamoring public. You hear about a gas main explosion, nine times outta ten it's to cover something like this up." He spun and continued his journey along the walkway.

I tried to recall any gas main explosions I had heard about over the past couple of years. I knew there had been a few. What if those had been other cases? Cases where MIBs just ran amok, with no one to stop them? "You think there are other people doing this? Fighting...weirdness that gets covered up like that?"

"Well, there's gotta be more than me. More than us. At least, I hope." Wendigo reached the end of the walkway and came to a halt, standing just inside Pier 4. He turned back toward me. "Where's the rod thing?"

Straight across from the end of the walkway lay the entrance to the aquarium's dolphin show. Reflexively, I wondered when the next show would start, forgetting for a moment that I had just engaged in a deadly shootout less than a hundred yards away.

I pulled the magic-sniffing ivory rod out of my jacket pocket and held it up. To my joy, and then immediate dismay, I found myself pointing it straight toward the entrance to the dolphin amphitheater.

We took up positions on either side of the amphitheater's double doors. Wendigo mouthed a silent three count at me, and in we went. Unfortunately, I completely misread the situation— he slowly nudged his door open, while I chose to charge through, bursting into the top of the stadium accompanied by the sound of my door slamming into the wall beside it, echoing through the amphitheater like a cannon shot.

The three remaining MIBs stood on the other side of the dolphin pool, looking my way.

For a moment, no one moved.

Here is a summary of what I observed during that millisecond:

Two of the MIBs were standing on either side of a low steel container resembling the sort of dumpster you see at construction sites, but on a smaller scale, around fourteen feet long and three feet high. It had a white lid that didn't quite cover it. This sat on a cement apron which ran around the dolphin pool, close to the water's edge.

The third MIB, dressed in something more like a black cloak than a suit, stood near them, holding Neptune's/Poseidon's/Aquaman's trident aloft in a very theatrical way.

Directly in front of the robed MIB there floated, in midair, a warbly section of roughly oval shaped water, about thirteen feet long. Inside this floated a bottle-nosed dolphin, also about thirteen feet long.

The cloaked MIB didn't wear glasses, and it had eyes! Eyes which, at the time, were boring a hole straight through me.

None of them looked happy. Except for the dolphin. Dolphins always look happy.

Then the water oval broke and fell, crashing down into the pool along with the dolphin, which gave a choppy laugh as it swam away.

Blackcloak shouted an alien-sounding curse and pointed in my direction. I took cover for the second time that day, this time behind one of the rows of low-backed bench seating. It didn't offer much protection, but it was all I had.

"What the hell are you doing?" came a voice from a few rows back.

"I thought we were going to rush them!" I admitted.

"*Rush them*?" Wendigo hissed, "Who do you think made those piles of ash!"

"These guys?"

"These guys!"

"We're really going to have to work on this communication thing."

I suddenly grew uncomfortably hot. I watched in amazement as the top edge of the bench back in front of me began to smolder, then burst into flames.

"Christ!" I shouted, scrambling farther along the row of benches, attempting to stay as low as possible.

"They have pyrokinesis! Stay out of their line of sight! *Yeow!*"

"Wendigo?"

No response. And it was getting hot again. It was some sort of spontaneous human combustion power. And I was the human the MIBs were about to combust. Spontaneously.

I scrambled farther along the row, but it was only a matter of time before I ran out of bench, and I was getting even farther away from Wendigo.

Then I had an idea. Wendigo had said the MIBs didn't like the fact he had the Crystal Gun and the Answering Hand—they probably wouldn't like the fact I had their magic-sniffing thing, either. I pulled the ivory rod out of my pocket.

"Hey!" I yelled, "I got your thing! Your magic-sniffing thing!" I held it up above the back of the bench and waved it tauntingly.

Relieved that my surroundings didn't immediately burst into flames, I craned my neck to peer over the bench. My plan had worked, sort of—the MIBs were hissing at one another and gesturing at me like they were arguing. I realized they didn't want to risk damaging their magic detector. It must've been valuable to them—valuable enough to attempt to close in on me and take it.

The two MIBs in suits were now working their way up the stairs, one on either side of the row of benches I was crouched behind.

Great.

Blackcloak was still standing on the cement apron near the bin, making small churning motions in the air with the trident. In the pool before him, the water was trying hard to match the trident's movements.

I crouched down and crawled farther along the row of benches. I thought maybe the MIB on the stairs closest to me might lose track of the row I was in. Maybe I could take him by surprise as he came into view. I could knock him down, then take cover somewhere else in the amphitheater, run and hide until they did whatever they wanted to do and wait for them to leave. Then, call into work with some made-up excuse and be back again early tomorrow morning, safe in Corporate Hell, where, sure, things were boring, but you didn't get burned alive. Like in actual Hell. Which was where I was.

Not much of a plan, but it was all I had.

Unfortunately, in the time it took to formulate it, the MIB had come into view at the end of the row, only a few feet in front of me.

The area behind me started to grow warm. Through the wavering air, I could see the MIB at the far end, gesturing at me with crooked fingers. Apparently, they didn't have to burn me, they could just heat things up to an unbearable level. For a start.

The one before me started gesturing as well. The air around me soon became too hot to breathe.

"Yeah. Okay," I gasped, slowly rising to my feet. I was done.[16]

There was a sudden high-pitched scream. I turned to see Wendigo tackling the MIB at the far end, sending the two tumbling down the concrete steps toward the dolphin pool.

Glancing back at the MIB closest to me, I saw its attention diverted toward Wendigo and its companion. Giving a yell of my own, I leapt at the MIB, sending us both falling onto the benches behind it. We tumbled down over several rows, bodies flailing, before landing on the concrete with a terrible cracking sound. Luckily, I somehow came out on top, though slightly worse for the wear.

The MIB, however, wasn't as lucky. It wasn't moving. Apparently, it broke something important.

Huffing and puffing, I dragged myself back out of the row to the steps, where I stood, looking across the amphitheater. After a moment, Wendigo rose up as well.

We exchanged a pair of weak thumbs-ups. We were battered and bruised,[17] but we were alive. Neither of us had managed to make an ash out of ourselves.

Suddenly, a spout of water slammed into Wendigo, sending him spinning up the steps toward the entrance. I turned to the stage just in time to see

---

16   As you are currently holding this book in your hands, you've likely guessed that I was *not* done, but pretend to be in suspense for just a bit, alright? I've worked hard on this.

17   See? Foreshadowing.

a second spout of water crashing into me, rolling me up the concrete, leaving me in a wet, sputtering heap at the top row. I barely had enough time to stagger to my feet before another spout threw me back against the wall. I tried desperately to fight against the current crashing into me, arms thrashing, but it felt like I was pinned beneath a waterfall.

Then, the pressure subsided, and I fell to the floor, heaving in lungfuls of air.

I began crawling away, only partially aware of water again rushing toward me. It slowly wrapped around me, trapping me in a sphere which rose to carry me down toward the stage.

I was desperate for air, but no matter how hard I struggled, I couldn't work my way clear to take a much-needed breath. The water moved with me, keeping me sealed inside as I launched into a full-blown panic.

Then, the sphere burst, dropping me hard at the feet of the last remaining MIB, the one with the cloak and the trident. I lay there in a fetal position, my arms wrapped around my chest, violently coughing up water, as Blackcloak's features slowly shifted into something more human.

"I think I'm getting the hang of this now." His voice oozed, and he gave the trident a little whirl in the air. Droplets of water orbited its tip like a tiny solar system.

"So...how about a little race? Let's see if you can hand me that Eldritch Dowser you've stolen before I fill your lungs with water to the point they burst." He took a few steps back, in what I assumed was a precaution. If true, I had never been so overestimated in my life. "Ready?"

There was a loud crack, and Blackcloak fell

forward onto the ground beside me. Wendigo was standing behind him, holding a thick metal pipe.

"Dibs on the cloak!" he shouted as he tossed the pipe over his shoulder, where it hit the ground with a horrible ringing clatter. Wendigo then offered a hand, pulling me to my feet.

"We've really got to move."

I limped over to where the trident had fallen and bent over to retrieve it, the action accompanied by a sharp pain in my side. "I think I might have cracked a rib." I had never cracked a rib before, but it sounded like the kind of thing that happened after being thrown around concrete by a waterspout.

Wendigo pulled the cloak off the MIB and tossed it to me, "Here," he said. "Wrap the trident."

I looked over at the metal pipe Wendigo had used on Blackcloak. "Why didn't you use the gun?"

He gave me a *Why do you think?* look and held up what I assumed was the gun, still encased in multiple layers of foil. "It looked as though time was of the essence. But, please, continue to critique my last-second rescue attempt. Which seemed to be successful, since that sounded a lot more like, 'Why didn't you use the gun,' than 'Glub, glub, glub.'"

"Yeah, yeah, okay," I muttered. "Thanks."

I sat down on the edge of the low dumpster and began wrapping the cloak around the trident. Suddenly, I was hit from behind by a spray of water. It was a smaller amount than the last few blasts I had suffered, but it was still enough to terrify me, and I reacted accordingly: with a loud yelp and a leap in the air.

The stadium filled with a long, choppy laugh.

It took a few seconds for me to realize the dumpster had an occupant. What I thought was a lid had actually been some sort of sling, in which was slung a snug looking bottle-nosed dolphin. The weight of the creature had caused the "lid" to sag, bringing horizontal poles on either end of the sling toward the bin's center, creating what looked like a dolphin-filled taco[18] hanging suspended in the water-filled container.

It laughed at me, blowing more water out of its spout.

"They got the dolphin into the bin," I muttered, stepping back out of its range. "He must have done it while we were taking care of the firestarters."

"Yeah. Nice work on the firestarters, by the way."

"You, too. And, you know, thanks for the save. Or saves." I smiled. Why did it hurt to smile? "I wonder why they wanted him in the tank so bad?"

"Oh!" shouted Wendigo, "Oh! Oh! Oh!"

"What?"

He was pulling something from Blackcloak's wallet. "Look at this!" He held up what looked like a black plastic card, but it wasn't all black. There was something on it, something either more or less darker than the rest of the black. It took a couple flicks in the light until I recognized it—it was the eye in the pyramid symbol.

Wendigo turned the card over. It bore a magnetic strip, similar to a credit card's, again either less black (or blacker) than the rest of it.

"I was wondering where they got their magic money from!" he exclaimed. "Magic ATM card!" He returned the card to the wallet then slipped the wallet into his right back pocket.

"What about the eyes?" I asked. "The MIB with the trident had eyes."

18 I realized at that point I was hungry.

"Yeah. They don't usually have eyes. Or really cool cloaks. You think he's the MIB equivalent of a boss monster?"

"He *did* seem smarter. Nastier."

"The guy was a real creep," came a third voice.

Wendigo spun around. "What?"

"I said, the guy was a real creep." The dolphin poked its snout up out of the tank. "Glad you guys came along when you did! Even though you do kinda suck at this." The dolphin then let out a long, choppy laugh that echoed through the room.

I decided to call him Fish Sticks.

CHAPTER EIGHT
Grand Theft Dolphin

It is important at this point in the tale to state that, when I came to Baltimore, *I did not come with the intent of stealing a dolphin.*

I assume, much like with murder, that there are varying degrees of dolphin theft, ranging from premeditated to a sort of spur-of-the-moment thing. The equivalent of a, *the keys were in the ignition, so we thought we'd take it for a joyride*, defense.[19]

In this case, *the dolphin was already in the box, so we thought we'd take it for a spin, Officer.*

Wendigo was chatting with Fish Sticks. I took the opportunity to pull the Eldritch Dowser out of my pocket and casually point it in the big mammal's[20] direction.

Yep. Magic.

The talking dolphin was magic.

Wendigo excused himself from Fish Sticks and took me aside for a moment. "We have to take him."

"Okay. Sure. Yeah." I was a bit rattled by recent events, yet to my credit, managed to respond with three whole words instead of just curling up on the

---

19   *Joyride.* Seems like such a harmless lark. Like *spree.*
20   Yes, I do know dolphins are mammals. I'm still calling him Fish Sticks.

ground in a fetal position.

"I mean, the MIBs were after him, so we can't... we can't let them get him," Wendigo said awkwardly. (At this point, I realized he was trying to convince himself more than me.)

"These guys aren't a threat to him any longer, but they could send others."

We both glanced over at Blackcloak, who was sans-cloak and slowly evaporating.

"They seem kind of fragile, don't they?" I remarked. Up until then, I could count the number of fights I'd been in on one finger—and Wendigo wasn't exactly the bruiser sort. Yet, the MIBs all seemed to crumble pretty quickly, in a fatal sort of way.

"Tell that to the bits of employees we passed back there. Or what's left of the gift shop," Wendigo snarked. "Besides, I think we're just getting lucky with sneak attacks and sucker-punches. Our technique seems to be working, though."

"Okay, so. How do we take him?" I asked, pointing at the bin. "The magic dolphin."

"Not sure."

"And where do we take him to?"

"Not sure."

Despite his answers (or lack thereof), Wendigo started to wheel the bin away. I moved to help him as best I could, setting the cloak-wrapped trident across the top of the container.

As it turned out, the bin was mounted on some sort of hydraulic jack, with a handle similar to a toy wagon. It still took both of us huffing, puffing, and straining to drag it across the aquarium.

We moved from the amphitheater through a backstage area, then to a service corridor beyond. We explained the situation to Fish Sticks as we went.

Freedom now lay before him, in whatever form he wished it to take, not enslavement at the hands of some shadowy organization for some nefarious dolphin-related purpose.[21] He was quick to pick up on the fact that the dynamic of things had changed, from kidnapping to prison break.

"There's a loading dock back here, right?"

I was about to ask Wendigo how in the world I was supposed to know, when I realized he was asking the dolphin.

"I think so," Fish Sticks chirped.

That was going to take some getting used to.

Wendigo pulled a set of keys out of his pocket. "Found these on the boss monster. Give me a second." He dashed down the hallway, returning a moment later to triumphantly inform me there was, in fact, a loading dock at the end of the corridor, and a short, flatbed truck parked at the end.

We moved the container down the corridor as fast as we could, which wasn't very fast. Then, Wendigo realized the bin was motorized. Even with the motor engaged, it moved just as slow, but we didn't have to work as hard.

The truck made a horrible creaking noise as we wheeled the dolphin's container onto it. There was a tarp to throw over the bin, with little elastic straps to secure it to the sides of the truck bed. We stood on either side of the bin, moving the tarp into position.

"Do we have a plan?" I asked.

Wendigo looked down at Fish Sticks. "Do we have a plan?"

"Well, you know, I'd like to go back into the big blue. The At-lan-tic. I got family there. It's where I went to school!" He gave another long, choppy laugh.

---

21   Too easy.

Wendigo and I rolled our eyes at each other. We covered the bin with the tarp, muffling the dolphin laughter until it subsided, then flipped it back off.

"But seriously," Fish Sticks continued, "If you get me to the water, I can get there. I'm pretty sure it's just a long swim to the south..."

"Just a long swim to the south," Wendigo repeated to me, reiterating just how incredibly easy this was all going to be.

Then his face went pale.

"We have to go. The World's caught up."

We threw the tarp over the bin and jumped down to the ground, working quickly to fasten the straps along the bed on either side, forming a low, tent-like canopy.

Seconds later, we climbed into the truck's cab. Wendigo took the driver's seat, and I took the passenger's side after tucking the cloak-wrapped trident behind the seat.

Something occurred to me as Wendigo started up the truck, causing laughter to spray out my mouth like water from a blowhole.

"What?" Wendigo snapped.

"It's just...I didn't realize your VIP membership entitled you to one free dolphin."

Then we slowly pulled out of the Pier 4 loading dock, the act accompanied by a bit more creaking, and a great deal of sloshing.

Somewhere, back in the aquarium, the first screams of alarm began to sound.

* * *

As the flatbed slowly made its way through the congested streets of Baltimore Inner Harbor, and the

World caught up with the aquarium, the day abruptly caught up with me.

My life, until that point, had primarily consisted of events happening very far away, in very abstract terms, to very different people. Accounting is mostly looking at those events, the activities of others, things that have nothing to do with you, and simply validating the numbers that result from them. Today's events however were happening directly to me, on very real terms. Dangerous terms.

And I loved every minute of it.

Sitting there in the passenger seat, carting around a stolen dolphin, after besting no less than seven MIBs, I felt like one of their magic dollars. I felt too real. All the demons of corporate hell had been exorcised out of me. I wasn't just a worker bee anymore. I was Harry Long—possibly more Harry Long than I had ever been.

It was in that moment I realized I had made the right choice that morning at the figurative/literal crossroads. To hell with Corporate Hell. I was on my way to becoming Harry Long, action hero, and I wasn't going to let anything stand in my way.

We made a quick stop back at the parking garage near the hotel to retrieve the Answering Hand from the Lincoln's glove compartment. Even with its help, it took a long time to locate what we needed.

A few hours later, I was making my way toward a specific boat docked at one of the Inner Harbor marinas. A boat with a winch and pully capable of unloading Fish Sticks, and someone onboard to drive it.

Captain McGruff[22] was busying himself untangling a collection of rope on the boat's deck as

---

22   Probably not his real name.

I approached.[23]

I was wearing a pair of dark glasses borrowed from Wendigo. The idea was to try to look and sound as official as possible. (Luckily, enough time had passed since our aquarium adventure that I had dried off a little.)

"Excuse me, sir?" I called from the pier. He looked up as I flashed him Blackcloak's ID, still in the wallet, also borrowed from Wendigo. "Agent Jones with the FBI. Can I talk to you for a moment?"

I got him to follow me back to a nearby parking lot where the flatbed was sitting. Wendigo was already working to uncover the bin as we approached. I climbed onto the back of the truck and gave McGruff a hand up.

"We just broke up a ring of dolphin smugglers operating out of Inner Harbor. It's imperative we get this guy back to his natural habitat as quickly as possible."

"*What?*" McGruff laughed. He started peering around, looking for the hidden cameras he likely presumed were recording footage for whatever prank show he was currently on. "Let me see that ID again."

I glanced over at Wendigo, who went wide-eyed as I pulled the wallet out and displayed the card for a second time.

McGruff quickly looked away from it. He glanced

23   Whenever someone first encounters a person on a boat, in movies or on television, that person always seems to be involved in manipulating rope in some way or another. This seems to be one of the main things people do on boats. Either having to deal with rope made up 80 percent of the nautical experience, or there were an awful lot of non-boat owning writers who for some reason felt having a minor character manipulating rope on or near a ship the quickest way to establish the character as an experienced seaman. The latter just seems like lazy writing.

down at Fish Sticks. "Now, what did you say this was about?"

"We want to get him back to the Atlantic."

"As fast as possible," Wendigo added.

"You two don't look like FBI," McGruff remarked gruffly.

"We were working undercover," I said.

"Undercover sting operation," Wendigo added.

"Undercover dolphin sting operation," I clarified with a nod.

McGruff looked at the two of us, then back down at the dolphin, no doubt trying to determine if it were real. "Okay, so what do you want me to do about it?"

"We want to commandeer your boat to take us down to the Atlantic, with you in it. Piloting it." Was that the right word? *Sailing* didn't seem right; the boat didn't have a sail.

"And how do you suppose we do that?" McGruff asked raising an eyebrow.

"You have that arm, winch, thing, on the side of your boat. We can hook the sling to it."

"And what? Hang him off the side? That's an oyster farming boat! That pully's for pulling in oyster cages! It's not designed for carrying dolphins!"

Wendigo and I exchanged sheepish looks, realizing we didn't know much about boats. Or the ways of the people who boat them.

McGruff sighed. "Why don't you check with the aquarium? They probably have some sort of launch you can use."

"We can't," I blurted.

"Why not?"

"The aquarium's on lockdown," I blurted again.

"Lockdown?"

"There was a terrorist attack," I blurted a third time. Across the bin, I saw Wendigo frantically shaking his head.

"Terrorist attack?"

"Or gas leak."

McGruff gave me a long, hard look. "Let me see that ID again."

Wendigo threw his hands in the air as I fished the wallet out and flashed the ID for the third time, causing McGruff to visibly wince.

"Look, I'd like to help you—"

"You would?" I failed to hide my surprise.

"But my boat's just not designed for it. And anyway, do you have any idea how *long* a trip that is?" McGruff hopped off the truck bed and started back toward his boat. "If you really want to get him back to the Atlantic as quickly as possible, just drive east."

"Thanks, Mr....Boat...Guy!" Wendigo called after him with a wave, before he leaned down and hissed, "Why'd you tell him you were with the FBI?"

"You said to sound official and convincing! Besides, I was wearing the glasses." I took them off. "They're magic...aren't they?"

Wendigo snatched the glasses from me "No! They're not magic! Don't automatically assume everything I have is magic!"

"Then why did you tell me to wear them?"

"Because I thought they'd make you look official and convincing!"

There was an awkward period of silence. Apparently, I had just impersonated a federal agent without the benefit of identity-masking or mind-wiping glasses. We *really* needed to work on our communication skills.

"Well, that went well," Fish Sticks remarked, then let out another long laugh.

I looked out at the harbor as we started covering the bin back up. "Why don't we just toss him in?"

"You know how to do that without hurting him? Or us?"

"Well, what about the trident?"

Wendigo frowned. "That seemed to involve a lot of trial and error to get the hang of. I assume that's why the MIBs were there as long as they were. Besides, there's a lot of nooks and crannies, inlets and waterways, for him to get lost in south of here—I guess dolphins have a nose for that sort of thing and he'd find his way out eventually, but the MIBs have a nose for him, too." Wendigo leaned in to murmur, "And there's always the chance of him being reacquired if he got stuck somewhere, rounded up and taken back to the aquarium, where he'd be a sitting duck if the MIBs tried to grab him again."

He shook his head as he snapped the last clasp closed. "No, his best chance Is out there, in the open ocean. So that's where we're going to take him."

"Hooray!" came a muffled cry from under the tarp.

CHAPTER NINE
Leaving Baltimore

I did some quick calculations and began to worry. It was around one o'clock in the afternoon. The trip from Inner Harbor to the Delaware Shore area would take around three and a half hours. Figure in an hour to dump the body, and we wouldn't be getting back until nine or later, well past five o'clock, and my first full day of *just not showing up for work.*

I thought it best if I checked out of the hotel and returned my rental car. Both were on the company's account, and once they discovered I was no longer working for them it would be understandable if they decided to cut me off. Of course, I could probably kiss any sort of reimbursement for my out-of-pocket expenses during this trip goodbye as well. Companies don't always play fair when you leave them on short notice, and especially when you give no notice at all.

That's okay, though. My expense report was off anyway.

* * *

Upon returning to the hotel, we noticed the police had cordoned off the aquarium. Several ambulances sat outside, along with a fire engine for some reason. A mob of news people and other assorted onlookers were gathered there as well.

The realization that we were tooling around town with evidence linking us directly to the aquarium, combined with my more recently committed felony of impersonating a federal officer, made us think it was best to leave Baltimore as quickly as possible and, ideally, in a way that allowed us to stay away for a very long time.

Wendigo told me he had everything he needed in his car. Whether that meant he had been living out of it or had the foresight of packing up and checking out of wherever he was staying prior to the events that morning, he didn't say.

What he *did* say was that he was eager to find an ATM, someplace out-of-the-way where he could try out Blackcloak's debit card, not knowing how long he had before it would disappear on him. He didn't seem concerned about the need for a PIN number, and I didn't want to burst his big green dollar-sign shaped bubble, so I didn't say anything about it.

We decided to split up. I would return to the hotel, pack up, and check out. Meanwhile, Wendigo would head out in search of an inconspicuous ATM. I'd then drop my car off at the nearest rental place, which was over near Camden Yards, where Wendigo would pick me up in the Lincoln in one hour.

During this time, Fish Sticks was going to hang out, literally, on the back of the truck in the parking garage near the hotel. He assured us he'd be fine for the short time left unattended and was looking forward to taking a quick nap.

Dolphins don't sleep in the same way we do. When they're tired, they rest one side of their brain, and then the other, never both at the same time.[24] Suspended in his harness, Fish Sticks had the rare opportunity to rest *all* of his brain at once, something he was really excited to try.

It was only after collecting my belongings from my room and boarding the hotel elevator for what I hoped would be the last time ever, that I realized I didn't have any way of contacting Charlie Wendigo.

I didn't have his number. I wasn't even sure he had a cell phone. I *did* have the Eldritch Dowser.[25] I could probably use it to find him if he didn't show up at the rental place for some reason.

Or maybe not. Maybe I'd go off on my own and just...do this. Just walk the earth like Jules Winnfield in *Pulp Fiction*, or Caine in *Kung Fu*, or David Banner in *The Incredible Hulk* TV show. I'd be another person responsible for one of those nine out of ten gas main explosions. Kicking MIB butt, securing magic hoodoos, consuming my fill of vending machine soda and corn chips. I did have my savings to tap into, to supplement my magic dollar supply, for when I wanted to live it up. I even had an apartment waiting for me just outside of Lancaster, PA, and a much nicer, more intact car there as well.

A base of operations and a means of transportation.

Yeah. I could do this.[26]

24   Apparently, anyone with half a brain could float.
25   I was determined to find some other name for the object. Every time I referenced it as the Eldritch Dowser, I recalled the way Drowny McSmoothface had said it to me as I lay in a soaking heap of useless at his feet. I would have preferred to remove that particular mnemonic trigger; however, the only thing that came to me at the time was Magic Pointer. So, for the moment, I endured.
26   In retrospect I realized this was just me trying to convince myself that I had still made the right decision, choosing

Then the doors opened up on the lobby and standing there was Jane.

No last name given.

"So, you just don't show up? No call, no notice, no nothing? They're all going mental at Devonshire. They're asking me about you because they saw us talking, so apparently, we're supposed to share some sort of *psychic bond* now. Like I'm supposed to be aware of you and your actions! Your whereabouts! And all I have is this!"

She showed me her phone. It bore the words of my last text to her, now appearing incredibly glib out of context.

"On an adventure!" she said out loud. "What the hell's that supposed to mean?"

During her tirade, I succeeded in navigating her away from the elevators and into a sitting area in the hotel lobby, right across from the front desk. Large, comfortable looking chairs beckoned to me, but I stood. I felt it best if I stood.

"We were supposed to go for pie!" she shouted, on the verge of crying. I'd seen this before. Meeting fatigue.

"Are we dating, now?" I asked, after an uneasy period of silence. "This feels like we're dating."

I consoled her as best I could, picked up my suitcase, and headed for the front desk to check out. Jane No-Last-Name-Given followed, standing behind me as an associate desk manager began the process of ending my stay. He informed me that the charge for my remaining days might be forfeit unless they

---

adventure over security, even if I failed to reconnect with Wendigo. In truth, I'd probably just find another accounting job, or the same one after making up a believable excuse. Possibly involving a gas main explosion.

could find someone else to fill the vacancy. I just shrugged. It was on the company card, and they were already mad at me.

"You're not checking out, are you?" Jane asked, baffled.

Both I and the manager turned to look at her.

"Are you just...done? Why didn't you tell me you were done?"

The manager gave me a stern look. I gave him a weak smile and motioned for him to continue the process as I took Jane off to one side.

"There was no one there to count their stupid little words!" she hissed angrily at me, then softened. "You left me there. You were the only one that made it fun. And then you left. And you *left* me there."

"I'm sorry. A lot happened since last night." The manager looked up and gave me another stern look. I motioned for him to continue.

"Adventure?" she asked.

"Yeah."

She looked at me like I had gone insane. "Have you gone insane? You leave all day, you don't tell a single supervisor, and now you're just walking out the door?"

I walked over, signed something for the manager, picked up my suitcase, and came back over to Jane, picking up where we left off.

"Yeah." I nodded.

"*Yes* to going insane or *yes* to walking out the door."

"Both," I replied, "I think it's both."

We stared at each other until a smile simultaneously broke across our faces and laughter bubbled up. Until then, I didn't realize how much I missed her laugh.

"Adventure," she circled back to the word, her curiosity piqued. "Like what sort of adventure?"

"Do you really want to know?" She said yes. So, I told her.

I told her about Charlie Wendigo, the skunk-haired 'vampire' I met in the elevator yesterday morning and the quarter he made vanish, from there and everyplace else it had ever been. I told her about running into him again at the bar last night and our run-in with the FBI agents who turned out to be Men in Black—not the fun, alien hunting, Will Smith/Tommy Lee Jones kind, but the walking personifications of Cold War Paranoia and Impending Atomic Doom Hysteria kind. I told her about the gun without a trigger that could shoot lightning and the hand without a body that could find a Denny's. I told her about Magic Dollars that were REAL MONEY and pulled one of the stuffed dogs out of my suitcase and handed it to her. I told her about waking up late that morning and, after realizing that numbers didn't really matter in this new world where they could just disappear, decided there was no real point in trying to keep track of them anymore. I told her I decided to do something else. I decided to trespass on the hotel's rooftop, go into the nothing space where the World was being held back, have a shootout with invaders from somewhere else, almost drown in midair, recover Neptune's Trident, and steal a dolphin.

At this point, we had walked out of the hotel, down the street to the parking garage, and climbed onto the back of the flatbed truck. I threw the tarp off the tank. "Say hello to Jane, Fish Sticks." He didn't say anything, so I threw the tarp back over him. "Probably asleep." I hopped back off the flatbed, and she followed.

I told her about trying to find a boat to get Fish Sticks back to sea, and the subsequent felony I committed while wearing magic glasses that turned out to not be magic. I told her I was now about to drive three and a half hours to the Atlantic, where we were going to attempt to release our stolen dolphin back into the wild. And then I was at my car.

"After that," I said, tossing my suitcase into the trunk, "I have no idea what I'm going to do. Probably break more laws and endanger more wildlife." I emphasized the period by slamming the car's trunk shut.

I looked at Jane, waiting for her to say something. She just stood there, staring off toward the center of the parking garage for a very long time. I thought maybe I broke her. Finally, she turned to me and said, "Take me with you."

* * *

A half hour later, the two of us were standing outside the rental place waiting for Wendigo to show. I wasn't sure why I had told Jane all the things I did. I guess maybe I was thinking it was the easiest way to get rid of her, scare her off. I should have known better. Jane had endured the trials of Corporate Hell. She was made of sterner stuff. Or at least stuff that wanted to get away from the endless meetings[27] just

---

27   Zeno of Elea (c. 450 BCE) famously described a paradox in which a tortoise and Achilles had a foot race. To simplify the concept; for a runner to win a race they must cross the distance between the start and finish line. But, before, they can do that they must first cross half that distance. And before they can do that, they must first cross half that distance. And before they can do that, they must first cross half that distance. And

as badly as I did.

She admitted she was currently AWOL from Devonshire.

I was still trying to figure out how I was going to explain the Jane situation to Wendigo when the Lincoln squealed into view and skidded to a stop in front of us. Wendigo leapt out and dashed around the car to me, shoving a bunch of bills into my hands, laughing like a madman.

"What's this?" I asked.

"Money!" he yelled, slamming his hand repeatedly against the side of the Lincoln. "Real, actual money! No THIS IS REAL MONEY fake disappearing stuff!"

I counted the bills. There was three hundred dollars, all in twenties.

Wendigo informed me that, after a bit of trial and error, he had discovered the most he could take out at once was six hundred dollars. He planned on trying again later, figuring there'd be a daily limit, or hopefully only an hourly one, restricting how much could be withdrawn. He assumed he had a couple of days to figure it out, having no reason to believe that the ATM card wouldn't last at least as long as the Magic Dollars did before evaporating. Maybe longer.

He was elated. "You know what this means? No more vending machine food! No more sleeping in my car, dreaming of one day scrounging together enough ones to pay for a Motel 6! No more hoping my money doesn't disappear before I can fill up my tank or pay

---

so on. The finish line is never reached because the distance can be broken down into infinite increments, each of which must be crossed first. Endless meetings work on a similar principle, only instead of distance to the finish line, it's time until lunch. Escape is only made possible due to a loophole in the fundamentally flawed logic—distance and time do not work this way. It only sometimes feels like they do.

a toll! This is...this is..."

Wendigo suddenly noticed Jane. "Who's this?"

"This is Jane. She wants to come along."

"You don't mind, do you?" she asked with a level of politeness honed from years of engaging in office politics.

"No. I...I hope I didn't make it sound too glamorous."

Wendigo looked down at the wad of bills clutched in his hand, over at the wad of bills in mine, then over at Jane. "This is...this is because we did some *stuff* today. I figured on three hundred each. I mean...we did some stuff."

"I heard," she said with a wry smile.

"You heard?" Wendigo looked at her, looked at me, then pulled me a few steps to one side. "What's the situation here?"

"I told her everything."

"Everything?"

I shrugged. "I owed her a pie."

* * *

Not wanting to leave Fish Sticks alone any longer, the three of us piled into the Lincoln and headed back to the parking garage. We checked on him as soon as we got back. This time the creature was quick to note our new member.

"Who's this?"

"I'm Jane," she said through a laugh, seemingly astonished to be talking to a dolphin.

"Jane?" the dolphin squeaked.

"Austen," she added.

"Your name's Jane Austen?" I asked.

"Like Steve," Wendigo commented.

"What? No!" I corrected him, "Like Jane Austen!"

"Steve Austin. *Six Million Dollar Man*," Wendigo said.

"No! Jane Austen. *Pride and Prejudice!*"

"I don't remember that show."

"I don't usually tell people my last name," Jane muttered, apparently feeling responsible for our confused exchange.

"Well, Jane," Wendigo said, shaking her hand over the dolphin bin. "Welcome aboard."

And then, with Charlie Wendigo hauling Fish Sticks in the truck, and me and Jane Austen following behind them in the Lincoln, we pulled out of the garage, made our way to I-95 North, and waved goodbye to Baltimore.

CHAPTER TEN
Joyride

"So, Neptune's Trident was right there? And they were using it to steal the dolphin?

Don't you think that's a little convenient?"

We were about an hour into our trip, driving along I-95 North toward Wilmington. I couldn't find anything good on the radio, and Jane was asking a bunch of questions I didn't have answers to.

"Yeah," I agreed. "But Charlie says he sometimes finds these things in public places. Sort of hiding in plain sight."

"So, who's hiding them?"

"He doesn't know."

"Okay..." She drew out the word to three times its length. "What if it's the Men in Black?"

"MIBs. We just call them MIBs."

"What if it's the MIBs that are hiding them? Storing them in places where they know they'll need them?"

"That would mean every time Charlie grabs something from someplace, he's taking it away from where it's needed," I commented absently, splitting my concentration evenly between the radio and the road.

I thought about it for a moment.

"You know, that actually makes sense. He did say the MIBs didn't like the fact he had the gun and the hand. If he was taking them away from where they were needed before they could be used, that could be why."

Jane looked at the glove compartment and scrunched up her face. "Is it in there now? The hand?"

"I think Wendigo might have it with him. He uses it as a GPS. But you can check if you'd like."

"That's okay."

After a few miles of silence, she asked, "So, how is the dolphin magic?"

I shot her a glance, "Well, he talks."

"Is that all?"

"Isn't that enough?"

"No." She leaned forward, deciding to take over the job of trying to find a decent radio station. "I mean, the trident has the power to manipulate water. It blasted you guys with, from what you said, incredible force. It almost *drowned* you. Why wasn't that enough of a prize? What made the dolphin worth more than that? Talking? I mean, other than making a really incredible late-night talk show host, what are you gonna do with that?"

"These are some really great questions. Maybe you should ride with Charlie for a while?"

"Would you mind?"

I was going to say no. I was also going to say yes. So, I didn't say anything.

Eventually, Jane found an oldies station. Turned out we were both big Van Morrison fans, and we wound up crossing over into Delaware singing *Domino* at the top of our lungs.

With some music to distract us, the next thirty miles went by quickly. We were just past Newark, about to pick up Route 1 South to Dover, when we saw the flatbed truck slow and pull off a ramp marked Cristiana Mall. A few minutes later, we too were drawing into its parking lot.

Wendigo drove to an empty section of the lot, as far away from the mall and other vehicles as he could get, then parked the truck and hopped out. He was waving the Magic ATM card at us as we stopped next to him.

"Thought we could stretch our legs and try this out again. Maybe grab something to eat?"

Wendigo briefly looked over his Lincoln, checking for any additional dents which may have been made in his absence. Jane and I climbed up onto the back of the truck to check on Fish Sticks.

We flipped open the tarp so I could ask our finned friend how he was doing. "You need your water changed or anything?" Changing his water would have been difficult. I wasn't sure why I asked.

Jane made a scooping motion with her hand. "Should we be ladling you?" She looked over at me, suddenly concerned. "Should we be ladling him?"

"No. I'm good," the dolphin chirped. "I *could* use a couple of fish, though."

I looked over at Wendigo standing in the parking lot near the Lincoln. He gave an uneasy shrug.

"We'll see what we can do," I said, and Jane and I covered the bin back up.

After re-securing the tarp, the three of us started our long walk across the parking lot to the mall.

"I have to admit," I said while we were still away from prying ears, "when I woke up this morning, I never in my wildest dreams thought I'd be releasing a dolphin into the wild today. That's, like, a bucket list kinda thing. A life milestone. It's something to tell our grandchildren. Not that we're going to have grandchildren. I mean, each of us will probably have kids. Independently. With other people. And then, you know, they'll have kids. And—"

"I know what you mean," said Jane, jabbing me in the ribs with her elbow.

Then she took hold of my hand.

Out of all the wonderous things that had happened so far, that struck me as the most wonderous.

* * *

We entered the mall near the crowded food court. The variety of smells drifting from a variety of restaurants were a painful reminder of the fact that I had yet to eat anything that day. I thought it best if we grabbed something to go and got back on the road as soon as possible. I started considering the different food options.

Wendigo pointed out a McDonald's as we passed by. "McDonald's," he said.

"Yeah." I nodded, acknowledging the McDonald's.

"Filet-O-Fish."

I stopped dead in my tracks. "We are not going to feed the dolphin Filet-O-Fish!"

"I don't know how many things we're going to find here with the word *fish* in it." He made one complete turn while gesturing around the food court. "Besides, beggars can't be choosers."

"I don't think that applies to dolphins!" I hissed at him. "Especially ones you're responsible for taking from an area of significantly greater fish availability to less!"

"Maybe there's a pet store?" Jane had taken the time to download the mall's app and was busy scrolling through a directory on her phone.

"I doubt they carry dolphin chow," I muttered, and Jane, to my delight, smirked at the joke. "But, you know, even if there's a place that sells fish food, we'd probably wind up having to clean them out. And there's no guarantee he'd even eat that stuff, whatever it is. What, *is* it, anyway?"

"It's settled then!" Wendigo announced, contrary to the fact that nothing had been settled. "Filet-O-Fish, it is!"

He shoved a twenty into my hand. "Get me one of whatever number it is you have to tell them to get the most nuggets possible, big Coke, and fries. I'm going to find an ATM. If you're not here when I get back, I'll assume you're out at the truck."

Jane tried to call after him with the location of the nearest ATM, but he was already gone.

She said, annoyed, "Does he always do this?"

"I just met the guy yesterday. I don't think I have enough data to determine the things he *always* does yet." We turned and headed back for the McDonald's. "Now, if you asked me if he's a pain-in-the-ass sometimes, I think I'd have enough information to be able to extrapolate."

* * *

The girl behind the register at the McDonald's didn't bat an eye when I ordered five Filet-O-Fish sandwiches, hold the cheese, hold the tartar sauce, and hold the buns. It probably wasn't the strangest order she ever took. I think she would've changed her mind if she knew their intended recipient.

A short time later, Jane and I were sitting on the back of the truck bed, working our way through our meals, and waiting for Wendigo to appear.

The tarp was completely off Fish Stick's bin, wadded up on the truck bed, close enough for us to toss back on if we suddenly needed to do so. We figured we'd let him get some sun for a bit. To our amazement, Fish Sticks had wolfed down the filets as quickly as they were offered.

We told him he had Wendigo to thank for his new culinary experience.

The last two Filet-O-Fish were still wrapped in the bag, set aside for Wendigo. It was, after all, his idea. It seemed only fair to let him feed the dolphin as well. How often did you get a chance to do something like that?

I was working my way through a Big Mac and large fries while Jane picked through a salad she purchased at a Saladworks on the other side of the food court. I looked off toward the mall while sipping my Coke, mildly concerned over the fact that there wasn't a streak of white hair headed in our direction.

Jane suddenly laughed. "You know, this is our first date."

"This?" I said with a grin. "No. This isn't a date. Please don't consider this our first date.

Food court takeout?"

"So, what do you consider a date?" she asked.

"Not this." I laughed, looking over at her. She was staring at me, wide-eyed, expectant. And beautiful. More beautiful than anyone who had ever stared at me wide-eyed and expectant before.

"I'd take you someplace fancy." I said.

"Fancier than the back of a truck in a mall parking lot?"

"Yeah," I smiled looking out across the car-filled expanse. "A nice seafood place back in Baltimore, with a view of the harbor. Just you and me, the evening lights, the moon. And all the ships. Sailing nowhere."

"That *does* sound nice," she purred.

"Of course, that's if we didn't steal the dolphin."

We both burst out laughing at the absurdity of this new reality, these events we were both experiencing.

"Hey," she eventually managed, "I didn't steal anything. At most I'm aiding and abetting."

And then we were just looking into each other's eyes, and I realized this was too easy.

No. Easy wasn't the word for it, and too dangerous a word to even be thinking next to her for fear of blurting it out. No. This felt...too right, too soon. It was like a safecracker who stands before the safe, sands down his nails, puts the stethoscope in his ears, places it against the door, moves to begin the delicate and arduous task of slowly working the combination dial, only to find the thing's already unlocked. There's supposed to be more of a... process to this. Isn't there? The whole thing made me nervous. This much of a reward should have required a greater effort.

But then, maybe I was making a lot of assumptions.

"So, are we, like...a *thing* now?" I suddenly felt like I was back in high school, not a thirtysomething professional with my own apartment.

"A thing? You mean like a boyfriend-girlfriend thing?"

"Yeah, I mean, that's something you establish right? We should establish that."

"This all sounds very official." Jane set her

plastic salad bowl down next to her, then turned to face me. "What do you think? Are we boyfriend and girlfriend?"

Earlier, I had fought a group of creatures that could punch holes in you with their voices, set fire to you with their minds, and drown you with a gesture. And yet, this was the first time today I said, "That's a little unfair!"

"Well, maybe I could give you a hint." She leaned toward me, then suddenly stopped. "Is there... something in your pocket?"

"Oh. Oh, yeah! Here!" I jumped to my feet and pulled the magic-sniffing rod out of my pocket. "This is really neat! I can't believe I didn't show this to you earlier."

Jane stood up next to me on the truck bed. I placed the Eldritch Dowser in her hand. She was unsure what to make of it, so I helped guide her.

"You just sort of hold it loose."

"Okay..." she said, once again drawing the word out. "Oh!"

"You feel it?"

"Yeah!" I watched as she slowly brought the rod around, pointing it at Fish Sticks. She looked at me with wide-eyed amazement. "There's something else!" she said, turning toward the truck's cab—I assumed she was picking up the trident or the hand. She spun a little too quick and stumbled over the wadded-up tarp. I got an arm behind her, catching her before she fell off the truck bed. We looked as though we had been dancing, and I had just dipped her. "And that's magic?" She looked up at me with a mixture of excitement and wonder.

"That's magic," I said, staring into her eyes. I hugged her hands to my chest and slowly moved in to kiss her.

"Hey!" Wendigo shouted through a crazed laugh, "You're not going to believe this!"

Jane and I separated from each other as Wendigo pulled himself up onto the truck bed, oblivious to the moment he had just destroyed.

He quickly started handing us money. "How much time passed? Between now and Baltimore?"

"I don't know, close to two hours?" I estimated, looking down at the bills in my hand.

"Okay!" he shouted. "Maybe a two-hour limit between transactions! Six-hundred-dollar limit per transaction! And a so far unknown daily limit! If there even is one!"

Jane held up her share, "There's two hundred dollars here."

"Yeah, I figured I'd be cutting you in from now on." He gave a quick look over at me, then looked back at her. "You're...sort of aiding and abetting now."

"Where's it come from?" She wondered, looking a little annoyed.

"It came from the ATM," Wendigo answered, confused as to how she could have missed that part.

"Yeah, but this isn't that THIS IS REAL MONEY stuff," I said, shaking my cut at him. "This is *real* money! Which means it's coming *from* somewhere!"

"Well, what if it's coming from everywhere? Money's mostly virtual now anyway. It's not like there'd be enough to go around if everyone suddenly wanted theirs. Right?"

Wendigo looked at me, then looked at Jane, unsure what to make of the angry looks he was receiving.

Wheels turned. "Did I interrupt something?"

Jane hopped down off the truck bed, grabbed

what was left of her Saladworks, and stalked off to find the nearest trashcan.

"Look," I said, gathering up my trash. "It's just, me and Jane both deal...*dealt*, in finance. I think we both have a problem with the idea of money not being...firmly...anchored."

"Yeah. Okay," Wendigo acknowledged, slipping his bills into his pocket. "I guess I am kind of behaving like a kid with a new toy. But this is how I figure these things out. It's not like they come with instruction manuals. It's just nice to have people to help figure this stuff out with for a change."

I pushed the bag containing the Filet-O-Fish into his hands. "Here," I said with a slight smile, "feed your magic dolphin."

I hopped down off the truck bed and started off in search of a trashcan, passing Jane on her way back. "You okay?"

"Yeah," she said. "I'm okay." Then she kept walking, back to the Lincoln, where she climbed into the passenger side and slowly shut the door.

I didn't think she was okay.

At the trashcan, I noticed there were ten twenty-dollar bills lying in the garbage.

CHAPTER ELEVEN
A Trip to the Beach

The trip south down Route 1 through Delaware was spent mostly in silence. Jane sat in the passenger seat, arms crossed, not exactly brooding, but circling over it in a holding pattern.

It wasn't until we were near Dover that she spoke again.

"You took it, didn't you?" she grumbled.

"What?" I asked, concerned she had picked the moment traffic started getting dangerously heavy to start talking again.

"You took it. The money I threw away."

"What! No! It was in the trash! Why would I dig through the trash?"

She went silent again, but at least her arms were unfolded. Thankfully, she let things drop until we made it out of the other side of Dover.

"Look," I continued several minutes later. "What you did was what you chose to do. That money was given to you and that was what you chose to do with it. As a form of protest or whatever. But if you didn't want it, you could have just as easily given it back. Or found someone who could've used it. I'm sure the next person to use that trashcan won't have the same consideration as me."

"I wasn't really thinking about it at the time. I just wanted to be rid of it. Money just doesn't appear! It shouldn't be that—"

"Easy?"

"Yeah."

There was another long period of silence. We watched as a couple of cars weaved in and out of traffic, trying hard to get wherever they wanted to be before everyone else, unaware they were speeding past a talking dolphin, an animated severed hand, and two people trying to figure out the trick of how to become something more to each other.

"You're not upset that I took the money? My share, I mean."

"What you did was what you chose to do," she said with a smile. "Besides, from what you told me of your day it sounded like you earned it. Hazard pay."

She rested her hand on my leg. Things were starting to be okay again.

"Well, maybe after you're shot at a few times, you won't have the urge to throw your money away again."

We both laughed, but I suddenly realized that Jane getting shot at was the last thing in the world I wanted to see.

This had just become the opposite of easy.

* * *

We spent the next hour engaged in casual conversation, during which I discovered Jane lived in Norristown, Pennsylvania, about an hour and a half from my apartment in Lancaster. She had had a friend drive her into Philly, where she took the train down to Baltimore.

She had as much luck with relationships as I did: a few false starts, nothing too serious, and if serious, not for very long. She blamed it on her job.

"I think it was killing me," she said casually. "I think it made me into a very boring person. I think it permeates you, tags you with a certain smell, gives you a certain aura that puts people off. Numbers are cold, hard, and unyielding. And that's what I dealt with every day. How do you not become that? I mean, how do you romanticize two plus two?"

"By refusing to let it equal four," I offered.

"I think that's what we're doing now." She stared over at me for a few seconds, then shifted her gaze past me, out the driver side window, and beyond. "I think that's why this feels...right." She paused. "You know, the Delaware Bay's about four miles that way. Fish Sticks would have a clear run right out to sea from there."

"It's up to Charlie now. I got no way to talk to him unless he pulls over again."

"He doesn't have a phone?"

I shook my head, "I guess I could pull in front of him and signal to turn off at the next exit."

Just then, we passed a large sign reading *Slaughter Beach, ¾ miles.*

We silently decided to continue on. We were, after all, in the home stretch.

* * *

A half hour later, we arrived at the Delaware Shore. Wendigo began to slow, likely realizing what Jane had pointed out to me a few miles back after consulting a map on her phone.

Following Route 1 South was going to bring us in right between two of Delaware's most popular beaches, Rehoboth and Dewy. Neither place presented many opportunities to stealthily dispose of a dolphin.

The fact that it was late September worked in our favor (not as many vacationers present). Unfortunately, we had pulled into the area right around five o'clock, which meant an increase in the locals.

If we headed south far enough along the coast, we'd eventually hit Ocean City, Maryland. Jane remembered there being long vacant stretches of beach along the road in that direction from a previous trip. However, it was a well-traveled road.

If we had some sort of crane, we might've chanced it. If anyone stopped us, we could flash the headache-inducing ID and claim to be dolphin experts, relocating a dolphin who wandered into one of the bays and got lost. That had to be a thing that was done sometimes.

Right?

Or, depending on who approached us, Wendigo could produce a convincing card from one of his decks, claiming membership to Greenpeace, PETA, SPCA, WWF, the Flipper Fan Club, or any one of the other dozens of dolphin-releasing groups we theorized existed. We hoped the legalities would only come into question if approached by someone in authority. In that case, the plan changed drastically, the same way water drastically changed to steam—it evaporated.

Jane figured our best bet would be to head north up along the coast and into Cape Henlopen State Park. She said it looked like there were places where you could drive the truck right out onto the beach. There, we could hopefully rig up the tarp in such a way as to hide our attempts at dolphin levitation from anyone who might be there until we became good enough at it, and then, when no one was looking, fling him out to sea.

We pulled ahead of the truck and motioned for Wendigo to follow. We had a plan.

* * *

"This is a stupid plan," remarked Wendigo. He was sitting in the driver's seat of the truck, which was perched at the edge of Cape Henlopen State Park's northernmost parking area, looking down a narrow, sandy, scrub-grass lined path which led to the beach.

"You got a better one?" I gestured out toward the sea. The beach started about a hundred feet away from us. The Atlantic lay two hundred feet after that. "It's right there. I don't think we're going to get closer anywhere else."

Jane had started down to the beach on foot, scouting ahead for possible dolphin-flinging sites.

Wendigo hopped down out of the truck and looked around. I noted the Answering Hand was scuttling back and forth across the dashboard, possibly searching for a better location (or maybe it was just nervous).

There were only a few cars here in addition to the Lincoln, and only a couple of vehicles visible down on the beach. It was cool with the evening approaching and a strong, salty breeze coming in off the water. I zipped up my jacket and followed Wendigo as he walked behind the truck, staring uneasily toward the parking area's access road.

"This is federal property. We're dumping a stolen dolphin on federal property."

"Technically *near* federal property," I reasoned.

"And what if the truck gets stuck in the sand?"

"It's a rental?" I shrugged. "Not in our name. We could pretty much just walk away from it. Couldn't we?"

He gave me an annoyed look then turned and climbed back into the truck. "Yeah, okay. Let's do this," he said, followed by the slam of the door.

I assumed that was what we had planned to do: dump the dolphin, leave the truck and bin, jump in the Lincoln and go. As a matter of fact, I had toyed with the idea of leaving the truck (along with the dolphin) on the doorstep of the Cape Henlopen State Park Ranger's office, hoping they'd take care of the rest. But they probably wouldn't just summon the equipment necessary to get Fish Sticks from the bin into the ocean, not without calling around to see if anyone was missing a dolphin first. And then we were back in one of those scenarios we just made a four-hour long trip to avoid.

Wendigo slowly drove the truck down the narrow path toward the beach. The tires sank into the sand. They were leaving deeper marks than any of the previously made tracks, but at least they weren't spinning out. I followed after on foot, bringing up the rear, glancing occasionally at the lot behind us. I was sure we were going to draw some attention—the flatbed wasn't the type of vehicle you usually saw on a beach, and we were clearly hauling something.

The trick would be to make sure we saw the attention heading our way first.

Jane met the truck on the beach, motioning for

Wendigo to make a left and head north. A couple of pick-up trucks were visible to the south of us, their tailgates opened and pointed toward the sea. People were visible sitting on the back of the one closest to us, drinking wine and watching the water. At the one farther down, a young man was tossing a ball to an eager golden retriever that was racing around the beach. We put as much distance between them and us as we could without driving into the Delaware Bay.

I plodded slowly after the truck. When I packed for my business trip to Baltimore, I hadn't figured in a trip to the beach. My shoes weren't affording me the best traction in the sand.

Although, in the time it took me to catch up, I had an idea.

"Cosplaying," I said as I reached the truck.

"What?" Wendigo had parked so that the bed was facing the sea. He was busy retrieving the cloak-wrapped trident from behind the passenger seat as I approached. Jane was already snapping the tarp straps off their hooks. She looked up at Wendigo.

"Dress up," she said. "People playing dress up. Adults."

"Is it like a sex thing?"

"No!" Jane and I both answered at once. Then Jane went back to removing the straps and I started helping Wendigo unwrap the trident.

"It's people dressing up like superheroes and fantasy characters. People from movies and video games. It's a big thing right now. Some people even do it professionally." I didn't understand why I was explaining this to someone who already looked like they were doing it all the time.

"Here, look," I told Wendigo. "You put on the

cloak, right? And while you're trying to figure out how to use the trident, me and Jane will act like we're filming you with our phones. Anyone who looks this way will just think you're a cosplayer shooting some sort of promotional video, not a madman standing on a beach waving a trident at a truck."

"Yeah, okay," Wendigo said, rubbing his chin. "That could work."

I think I had him at "cloak."

I looked down the beach toward the two nearest pick-ups, sitting a few hundred feet away, concerned about any attention we may be drawing. "Of course, we'll still have to time the...dolphin...flinging."

"The dolphin what now?" squeaked a voice behind me. Jane had thrown the tarp off just in time for Fish Sticks to hear that last bit.

"He meant *gently place*," Jane assured him. "The gentle placing...of the dolphin. In the Atlantic."

"Well, let's go!" shouted Wendigo the Water Wizard, now donning the cloak and striding toward the sea, trident in hand. "This dolphin isn't gonna fling itself!"

CHAPTER TWELVE
Magic 101

Up until that day, I hadn't had much experience with magic. The little I had gotten over the last several hours mostly involved dodging it or trying not to be killed by it, rather than actually wielding it. The exception to this was the Crystal Gun, which Wendigo pointed out wouldn't work outside areas where the MIBs weren't holding back the World, and the Eldritch Dowser. Neither of these seemed to be of any use in our current situation.

From what little I knew of magic, it seemed to be made up of equal parts conviction and the item's desire to do whatever it was you wanted it to do. There had to be a shared willingness.

I assumed Wendigo had a better understanding of it than I. It sounded as though he had been dealing with magic for a very long time, and in his dealings, had picked up considerably more knowledge than my three-fourths of a Wednesday afforded me.

Even so, after an hour of watching Wendigo twirl the trident around on that beach without so much stirring a drop of water in Fish Sticks' bin, I was about ready to take over.

"Are you filming? Keep filming!" he called to us.

"My battery's dead," I grumbled.

Jane plodded over to me. "Were we supposed to actually be filming him? I was just holding up my phone, but my arm got tired."

"The other guy was much better at this," Fish Sticks chirped. He then launched into one of his choppy laughs before all three of us quickly shushed him.

"I was afraid of this," grumbled Wendigo, dropping his arms and sulking back toward us. "It didn't even occur to me until we left the mall. We were in a dead zone when the trident was being used."

It took a second for his statement to register—then, I felt a chill run through me. It was just like the Crystal Gun, it needed to be...*outside* for it to work. All those rules that are usually in place to make water act like water had to be held back, along with the rest of the World, in order for it to work.

"No." I refused to let that be the case. A few minutes ago, I had watched as the couple in the closest pick-up closed the truck's tailgate, climbed in, and drove off. Now, our only potential witnesses were the boy and his dog farther down the beach.

Our chance of pulling this off without drawing any attention had slightly increased.

"No," I said again. "Look, the hand still works. The magic-sniffing thing works. There's stuff that works outside those places! Look at your card and coin tricks!"

Jane wasn't sure what to make of our argument. Her experience with magic had been with the ivory rod in the mall parking lot.

"Let me try!" said Jane, grabbing the trident from Wendigo. "You two can film a water witch for a while!"

She started pulling the cloak off Wendigo, almost

spinning him right around with her efforts. "Yeah. Okay," he said, quickly shedding it. "Here."

"She knows that's mine, right?" he groused, watching Jane slip on the cloak. "I'd say I had at least two days' worth of use yet."

I smiled at Wendigo. He did tend to act like a kid with this stuff. Of course, before today, he probably didn't have to share it with anyone.

I looked down the beach at the kid, who had just resumed playing with his dog again after taking a long break. He was more concerned about tossing the ball around than our act of swapping out actors.

Jane thrust the trident in the air, striking a pose similar to the way Blackcloak was standing when I first saw him earlier that day. I had mixed feelings about that.

"That's...that's not bad..." said Wendigo, a bit reluctant to admit it.

Jane began slowly stirring the trident's tip in the air above her. Wendigo hopped up onto the truck bed, scanning the water in the bin for any signs of movement.

A broad smile broke across Jane's face. Suddenly, she dropped her arms and began walking back to us. "That's all I got!" she said with a laugh.

"No!" Wendigo called down to her. "Keep going!"

Jane's smile disappeared. She slowly stepped back from us, gradually lifting the trident back into the air.

I looked back down the beach. The kid was still tossing the ball around. He had been facing in our direction, no doubt using the ball tosses as cover for keeping a curious eye on whatever it was we were doing up here. Maybe he'd soon lose interest and start throwing the ball in the opposite direction. Give us a chance to—

Wendigo interrupted my thoughts. "I see something. Keep going!"

I glanced down at Jane, who was gently stirring the air with the trident, then up at Wendigo near the bin. I thought I could see it now as well, small bursts of water, leaping maybe an inch above the side of the bin, like watching a jumping fountain that was just starting up. She was doing it.

I turned and looked back at the boy. He was playfully wagging a finger at his dog, scolding him for not retrieving the ball that was lying on the beach a few feet away from them.

"Oh my God!" I heard Jane gush behind me. "I'm doing it!"

I was about to turn back when I saw something strange. The boy had stopped just short of picking up the ball. He turned and started heading back toward his truck.

"Uh...Wendigo?"

"Come up here, Harry!" He called, motioning for me to join him. "You gotta check this out!"

I kept watching as the boy and his dog climbed into the truck and drove away, leaving the ball behind.

"Wendigo?"

I turned back in time to see Fish Sticks slowly rising from the bin, the container's water gathered around him.

Running to the truck, I leapt up onto the back. I looked up in the air. There were no birds.

There was nothing.

Lightning suddenly cracked past us, striking the trident. Jane let out an ear-piercing shriek and fell.

"Jane!" I yelled, making a move toward her.

Wendigo pulled me down. We were both crouched on the rear of the truck bed between the cab and the bin. Through the rear window and windshield, we could see two MIBs walking toward us. They were both holding crystal guns.

"Where's the gun?" I shouted. Wendigo could cover me while I went to check on Jane.

"It's in my coat!"

He wasn't wearing it. "Where's your coat?"

"In the truck!"

"Crap!" I watched through the glass as the MIBs moved closer.

"Oh no!" shrieked Wendigo. "Oh no, oh no! What if this was their plan all the long?

What if they wanted to put Fish Sticks in the ocean? What if we just drove him here for them?"

"Look! I need you to think! What do we have to work with here?"

Wendigo leapt to his feet, hands in the air. "We surrender!" he cried.

I ducked down and made my way back along the bin toward the rear of the truck, hoping Wendigo could at least keep them from shooting at us until I could reach Jane.

"Look! You guys win!" Wendigo conceded. "You get the dolphin, the trident, the gun, the hand, the rod thing. Hell, I'll even throw in a few decks of playing cards. I'll show you where it all is. Just don't shoot, okay?"

I got around the back end of the bin just as the MIBs came up alongside the cab. Both were pointing their guns at Wendigo. One had shifted to human form.

"Come down from there now!" he barked. "Where's the other one?!"

"Other one?"

"Don't push your luck, Wendigo!"

I crawled to the back end of the truck and peered down. Jane was gone, and so was the trident.

I leapt to my feet, arms up in the air. The two spun, training their guns on me. "So, you know who this is, then!" I said, nodding toward Wendigo. I jumped down from the truck bed and approached them. "I'm curious, how many of you guys do I have to kill before you know my name?"

"Harry Long," sneered the human one. The other one said something in their native tongue. I assumed something negative.

"Okay. That's—" They knew my name. I wasn't prepared for that.

Wendigo smirked. "I guess you killed enough." Hesitantly, I smirked back.

The two MIBs pointed their guns at us.

"Come on," chided Wendigo, "you know how unreliable those things are this close to water."

"*What?*" I yelped. "Are you *kidding me?* We just spent the better part of this morning *surrounded* by water, and you're telling me this *now?*"

Wendigo waved a hand dismissively, eyes still trained on the MIBs. "The crystals are useless out here. They only managed to hit Jane because she was basically holding a lightning rod. It's why they had to get so close to us—and now they're a little unsure, right?"

Wendigo slowly lowered his hands. I saw another sucker-punch coming; I just wasn't sure if it was going to be Wendigo hitting an MIB or me slugging him.

"I mean, those crystal guns know when to fire. I know that. He knows it." Wendigo nodded in my direction, not realizing how close I was to clocking him. "And I bet those guns aren't firing now because they're unsure. And if they're unsure, you're unsure."

I realized then what he was doing, he was messing with their minds, screwing up their conviction, counting on that shared willingness between wielder and item not being there, or trying to erode whatever there was of it.

Then, we both took a swing at the MIBs.

My blow landed, but there was a problem. This one was too solid. Like punching a bag of flour. I thought they were supposed to be fragile.

I looked over at Wendigo, who seemed to have the same realization. I turned back toward the MIB in front of me who suddenly lashed out, striking me with the force of a small car. I flew back several feet and hit the beach hard. A half second later Wendigo landed beside me, spraying sand everywhere.

"Ow," Wendigo moaned.

I started struggling to my feet, anger building. "We really have to go over that list of powers sometime." One of the MIBs yanked me to my feet and started dragging me back to the truck. The other shifted into its human form. "You're going to collect those items for us right now!" it snarled at Wendigo. "Or we're going to start pulling your friend's appendages off one by one!"

"Hey!" Jane suddenly popped up on the other side of the truck. "Catch!" She tossed the trident over to the human MIB. The moment he caught it, lightning struck the trident and knocked him to the ground.

Wendigo's hand shot out, snatching the trident as it fell. He spun, bringing it up around in one fluid motion, causing a spout of water to erupt from the sea and smash into the other MIB, sending him tumbling end over end across the sand.

I grabbed the trident from Wendigo—"*You!*"—stabbed it down through the chest of the human MIB lying before me—"*Don't!*"—I yanked it out and charged across the sand at the other MIB still struggling to his feet—"*Shoot!*"—I rammed the trident into him, pushing him back down into the sand—"*My!*"—Jane threw the crystal gun at me, and I caught it out of the air—"*Girlfriend!*" Lightning shrieked from the gun, raced down the trident, and blew the MIB apart in a spray of smooth chunky bits.

The three of us stood frozen on the beach for a very long time, trying to process what had happened. Everything just...came together. There was a shared willingness, a shared conviction between each of us and the items we wielded. We had just worked magic there on the beach, as though we had practiced for weeks. We did the disappearing MIB trick.

No; the exploding *MIB trick*, I corrected myself, absently kicking a chunk of something resembling whale blubber off my shoe.

I grabbed the trident and walked back to the truck where we slowly regrouped.

"That blast knocked me out, but not for long, I guess," confided Jane. "I crawled underneath the truck. I heard Wendigo say something about the gun being in his coat, so I snuck in and got it while you guys were distracting them by getting knocked all over the beach."

"I think we could have taken them," I joked as I handed the trident back to Wendigo. Wendigo just stared at me.

"You have some anger issues, you know that?"

Jane looked over at the fully intact MIB. (Well, save for the stab wounds across its chest.)

"I heard Wendigo say something about them using the trident as a lightning rod, and I figured I'd give it a shot—just, not on the receiving end this time. Those guns are really cool, by the way. We have three of them now, right?" Her eyes scanned the beach, searching for a glint of crystal among the sand.

"What about you, man?" I said putting a hand on Wendigo's shoulder. "That was some nice trident work. You shouldn't have any problem getting Fish Sticks into the water now!"

Wendigo's eyes suddenly went wide. "Oh no! No! No! No!" Jane and I traded a look.

"What?" we asked in unison.

Wendigo buried his head in his hands. "The World's already come back."

"What? No!" I looked around. A couple of gulls floated overhead looking for food, but that was it. "Are you sure?"

He just gave me a grim look.

"Why so fast this time?"

"I don't know," he huffed. "No building to focus on? No narrow city streets to help hold things back? It's a lot bigger here," he said, gesturing around.

"So, we're stuck again?" Jane asked.

Wendigo hopped up on the back of the truck bed and waved at the bin with the trident.

Nothing.

"Let me try," Jane volunteered, climbing up next to him.

I decided to let the two of them work at it while I retrieved the crystal guns. I pulled one of them off the still intact MIB, along with five Magic Dollars. The second gun would be a bit more difficult to locate. I looked at the splattered remains of the other MIB, now being experimentally picked at by a gull.

Realizing I was responsible for its current state, I suddenly grew sick to my stomach. I also realized that it was probably part of my new job description not to leave dangerous magic things lying around on the beach. Reluctantly, I poked around in that mess for several minutes, until eventually finding the other gun.

The two new guns had the same balloon static feel to them as the magic dollars for some reason. I returned triumphantly to the truck, the Eldritch Dowser and three crystal guns divided among my jacket pockets.

By that time, conversely, Jane and Wendigo had given up. They were sitting with their backs against the bin, looking out across the ocean, watching it slowly growing dark. Deflated, I took a seat next to them.

It was only a matter of time now before a park ranger would come down to check along the beach on what I assumed would be some sort of evening patrol. Hopefully the MIBs would disintegrate before they arrived; the gulls were already cleaning up the scattered remains.

"It's nice, isn't it?" Wendigo muttered, staring at the waves, listening to their subtle white-noise crashes.

Jane and I agreed.

"Thanks for this," he said. "I've been doing this for so long, by myself. It was nice to have some company finally. Even if it wasn't for very long." We both turned to look at him, unsure what to make of his statement. "Why don't you guys go? Take the Lincoln. Drive back to wherever."

"Lancaster," I muttered.

"Norristown," Jane murmured.

"Must be nice to have places waiting for you."

Jane looked sympathetic. "So, you really do live in your car."

"You saw the trunk when you put your suitcases into it."

"Yeah. There's not much there."[28]

"Yeah," he agreed. "You guys were gonna leave anyway. Once we dumped Fish Sticks into the drink."

"That's not...entirely...true," I attempted to counter. It sounded much stronger in my head.

"The dynamics change when you have someone you care about," Wendigo stated.

Jane nodded. "Yeah. You fight even harder. Like we did just now." We both looked over at her.

"There are three types of people in this world." She held up one hand, counting off the types on her fingers. "Those who believe might makes right and use their positions of strength to impose their will upon the weak. Those who believe money makes right and use their wealth to impose their will upon the less fortunate. And then there are those precious few who believe the only thing that should make right is *right*."

"I know what type of people I worked for. I know what type of people we just fought here on the beach. And I know what type of people I'm sitting with here now. I'm gonna figure out some way of getting this damn dolphin into the water," she said, slapping her hand against the bin. "And then I'm gonna keep on making two plus two equal *anything* but four with you guys for as long as I can!"

I looked over at Jane. "I love you," I blurted.

---

28   A duffle bag, a few sheets of plastic, two rolls of duct tape, and about a dozen rolls of aluminum foil. It looked like a psycho killer's starter kit.

"I know." She stated as a smile broke across her face, "I love you, too."

Wendigo sat processing things for a bit. It was unclear if he understood the reason behind Jane's apparently strong stance against basic math. (Of course, he seemed to accept far stranger notions with a practiced ease.)

Finally, he asked, "Should we all stack our hands in a pile in front of us now, or would that be unbelievably corny?"

"I'm sorry!" Fish Sticks suddenly chirped. "I must have fallen asleep again! That sling's pretty comfortable when the truck isn't moving."

The voice came from behind us, but a bit higher than it should have. We each slowly rose to our feet and turned, greeted by the sight of Fish Sticks floating in midair, three feet above the bin. "What'd I miss?" he chirped.

Wendigo, Jane, and I hopped down from the truck bed and watched in stunned silence as Fish Sticks slowly drifted past.

"Look, guys! I had a blast, but it's getting kinda late. I don't mean to be rude, but I'd really like to be off. That bin was getting a bit stuffy anyway."

We slowly approached the water, following in the dolphin's wake as it swam slow and effortlessly through the air. Once he was out far enough Fish Sticks spun to face us and gave a little wave with his flipper. "So long, and thanks for all the Fillet-O-Fish!" He then turned a little somersault and dove into the water.

We stood on the beach for a very long time before any of us spoke again.

"Magic. Dolphin," said Jane.

Wendigo threw his hands up in the air. "Son of a bitch!"

CHAPTER THIRTEEN
Night Moves

We abandoned the truck on the beach, trudging back up along the sandy path to the parking lot on foot, grumbling to ourselves and thinking about various acts of dolphin-related malice along the way.

Upon reaching the Lincoln, Wendigo tossed the trident into the trunk. Before I could offer Jane the passenger seat, she opened one of the back doors and crawled in, shutting the door behind her. As she curled up across the backseat, I could see her eyes drooping. Apparently, being struck with lightning had caught up with her.

I dropped heavily into the passenger seat, shutting the door with a bit more force than intended. Then Wendigo climbed in and started the car.

I opened my mouth to make a comment.

"Don't," he cautioned. Then we slowly and quietly drove out of Cape Henlopen State Park. We headed south along the coast. I think we were just driving. Giving us all time to cool off.

After several miles, Jane sat up in the backseat. "Where are we going?"

"South," Wendigo spat, then admitted he didn't know.

"Okay. We're done for the day, right?" asked Jane. "I want to be done."

I suggested we find someplace to stay for the night, adding that I meant no offense to the Lincoln, but felt we'd all be more comfortable in a nice hotel after putting in a long day of dolphin rustling and sand diving. Wendigo pulled the Answering Hand out of his coat pocket, but I took it from him and quickly tossed it in the glove compartment. I asked Jane to use her Answering Smartphone instead; we had enough magic for one day.

Wendigo pulled into a gas-and-go place. I filled up his tank while he ran inside to use his Magic ATM card. This time, Jane took her share of the money without a word.

I wasn't sure how I felt about that.

* * *

Jane figured we'd drive down to Ocean City since we seemed to be heading in that direction already. I wasn't too keen on the idea of going back into Maryland again so soon, but I was too tired to argue. She found a *Comfort Inn* on the boardwalk and fed directions to Wendigo as we went.

There we checked in, each getting our own room under our own name. It would've been nice to share a room with Jane, even if it was just to sleep, but it also would've been a presumptuous thing for me to assume, and, I thought, something rude to suggest so close to the beginning of whatever it was this was. Besides, I was sure Wendigo already felt enough like a third wheel without driving the concept home. Of there being an "us" and a "him."

The desk clerk had given us three rooms right in

a row on the fourth floor, facing the ocean.

We decided to clean up, change, and head out to find a place along the boardwalk to get some dinner. We were tired, hungry, and all still very annoyed at Fish Sticks.

We agreed to take out our anger on plates of seafood by proxy.

We hit the boardwalk around 9 p.m. It would be a late dinner at the end of a long day, but my quick shower had rejuvenated me. And now, the cool sea air and lights and sounds of the boardwalk at night stirred me even more.

The three of us wandered along the boardwalk, heading wherever it was we wanted. There was magic in that. There was magic in the immense freedom of it—knowing there was no clock to punch tomorrow morning, or ever again if I wanted it that way.

This was what adventure felt like.

I held Jane's hand as we walked. Wendigo kept himself a few paces ahead, keeping an eye out for a dining spot that was crowded but not too crowded— *crowded* because that would mean it was good, and *not too crowded* so we had a little privacy to talk.

Eventually, we stopped at a place with both "crab" and "shack" in its name. We spent the next half hour in said shack, taking out our aggressions on said crabs, pounding on the creatures with tiny wooden mallets and breaking their legs with silver nutcrackers.

Dolphin was not on the menu.

We were all wearing bibs. Magic artifact hunting, monster slaying adventurers should not wear bibs.

"You know, I guess it's really not his fault," Wendigo said at last, leaning back in his chair, tossing his bib aside.

"We did say we were going to take him to the Atlantic." I added, "Like he said, he just didn't want to be rude."

"It'd be like someone accepting an offer to drive them home and they suddenly jump out a block away from their house." Jane sighed. "Besides, neither of you bothered to ask him how he was magic."

"He talked!" We both defended at once.

The waiter, having steered clear of us during our therapeutic crustacean smashing session, sensed a break in hostilities. He crept in and began clearing away plates of broken shells.

"Can I get you anything else?" he hazarded.

Jane and I both asked for coffee. Wendigo requested one as well, then immediately seemed to regret it.

The coffee came out to us in little teacups on saucers. Wendigo managed to get his halfway to his mouth before the cup slipped away from him, hitting the table in a clatter of China.

"What the *hell* is it with you and coffee?" I snapped.

Wendigo stared at the dark pool on the tabletop. The droopy-eyed vampire had returned. He suddenly looked as though burdened by a terrible weight. Until then, I had assumed it was the responsibility of preventing MIBs from taking over the world with lightning guns, aquamancy, and talking dolphins, but now I suspected it was something more.

Jane grabbed some napkins and made an effort to mop up.

Wendigo just sat and stared. "I'm cursed."

Jane stopped in mid-dab. "What?"

"I can't have good coffee. Can't make it. Can't drink it."

"You're serious?" I asked.

He gave me a serious look. "I was involved with a gypsy for a bit. She worked at a coffee shop. It didn't end well. There was a lot of screaming and yelling and...cursing."

"What about espresso? Or cappuccino?" suggested Jane.

"It extends to all coffee-like and coffee-based beverages."

"Tea?" questioned Jane.

Wendigo bristled "No. Not tea! But then that's not coffee, is it?"

"So," I interjected, thinking it best to steer the conversation in a different direction. "About this new job Jane and I both find ourselves working, I don't suppose you have some sort of new employee orientation? A handbook maybe?"

"What? No. I'm not sure what I'm doing most of the time. How could I possibly orientate others?" Wendigo groused, "And no, no handbook."

"Well, there has to be something you can tell us. About this new job. I mean, I'm pretty sure it doesn't pay medical. You know, like our last one." Jane said it with a chuckle, but her words still sent a shiver down my spine.

The thought hadn't crossed my mind before, but we were facing an otherworldly threat, possibly without dental.

My look of concern prompted a response from Wendigo. "Okay, here's what I know."

He then proceeded to tell us everything (or at least the things he thought were safe enough to share.)

The MIBs were a side-effect of something he called the Babalon Working, some sort of occult ceremony, supposedly performed out in the Mojave

Desert by Jack Parsons and L. Ron Hubbard.[29] The desired effect of the Babalon Working was to basically summon up a woman they could have sex with.[30]

Parsons was a rocket scientist, but also a student of occult icon Aleister Crowley. He focused heavily on absorbing Crowley's teachings regarding the summoning of a conceptualized goddess.

Using an odd mix of ancient alchemy and modern chemistry, Parsons and Hubbard managed to open a door of some kind, and the MIBs snuck through, though not in finished form. They were only the *concept* of eggs, the *idea* of ovum. Fertilized at the point of contact with this new reality, they latched onto the uterine wall of our collective unconsciousness, growing large on fear and feeding on 1950's zeitgeist until being "born" into what we fought today.

The existentialism of it all made me feel uncomfortable, but at least it resulted in something I could punch.

Wendigo didn't know how many there were or if they were still being born—both of which, unfortunately, seemed like good things to know.

They seemed to be organized in some way, or maybe that was just something born out of our paranoid fear. With their dark suits and dark glasses, they appeared and acted like members of some unknown sinister agency, the subject of many conspiracy theories, and in their smooth-skin, alien-looking form, the subject of many more. But that morning's encounter with a "boss monster," a leader type, was evidence of a hierarchy, previously only suspected by Wendigo. And the Magic ATM card

---

29   Yes, that L. Ron Hubbard.
30   This predated the movie *Weird Science* by several decades.

reeked of organization. Of finances. Of *accounting.*

"What about the first time?" Jane inquired. "Your first encounter with the MIBs?"

Wendigo's brow furrowed as he pieced together parts of an old memory. "It was in one of those carnival sideshow type places, on the boardwalk at the Jersey Shore. You know; giant bugs, shrunken heads, cursed dolls, six-legged piglet pickled in a jar? Well, this place also had a severed hand that moved like a spider."

"The Answering Hand?" I presumed. He nodded.

"I couldn't tell you what I was doing in Jersey, or why I decided to visit the boardwalk. Something drew me there that night. Just me and nobody else. There wasn't another soul around for miles. At least, none that I could see. I thought it was incredibly strange for the boardwalk to be so empty, but by that time, I was already pulling the Three of Nails out of card decks and making coins cease to be. Strange was something I had come to accept as part of my life. I didn't realize it was the World being held back."

"So, I enter this place, this Sideshow of the Strange. And I see what I assume to be the owner being roughed up by a pair of dark-suited men."

"They were shouting, *where's the hand! We need the hand!* And suddenly the thing was scurrying across the floor, coming right at me. I screamed out, of course."

Recalling my own unsettling first encounter with the hand, I nodded in sympathy.

"So now all three of them are looking in my direction, and I just scoop up the hand and run. I guess I thought it would make the two men leave the owner alone and come after me. Which is what they did."

"I didn't realize they could turn into mist. I didn't get very far. They just sort of solidified in front of me, out on the boardwalk."

"Oh God," Jane scrunched up her face in a wince, "Then what happened?"

"They just took the hand from me. Took the hand and left, leaving me behind like I was nothing."

"It made me angry, being treated like nothing, angry enough to follow them. I spent the next two months getting the hand back from those jerks."

Jane and I laughed in appreciation of Wendigo's tenacity. He flashed a weak smile.

"During that time, I found out the authorities were looking for someone matching my description, in connection to the murder of the owner of the Jersey side-show. The MIBs had somehow framed me."

This revelation left me almost speechless. "My God." Was all I could manage.

"I decided I had to go on the run for a while."

"But you're not running," I countered, "not *away*."

"No." He said through a grin, "I'm running *at* them. I've been running at them the whole time."

"*Wow,*" Jane breathed over the rim of her teacup.

"So, you tailed a pair of MIBs for two months?" I asked.

"Yeah." He sounded quite proud of it.

"What were they doing?"

"Tooling around the rural Midwest, doing traditional MIB things."

"Traditional?"

"Knocking on doors. Questioning and or threatening people regarding reported alien sightings. There are books on the Men in Black phenomenon; some of it's true. I got one in the trunk if you want to brush up." Wendigo gestured vaguely in the direction of his car.

"Ah ha!" Jane exclaimed, "So there is a handbook!"

"Anyway," he continued, trying hard not to smile at Jane's outburst, "I had the feeling they were using the hand in some way. Maybe to find people to harass."

"Why aliens?" I asked, as if it were the one thing in all this that didn't make sense.

"I was wondering that too. There's a school of thought that believes that an advanced enough science would seem like magic to the lesser advanced. I think they were looking for people who reported encountering advanced science so they could track down magic."

"Huh," was my only response.

"So, how'd you wind up in Baltimore?" asked Jane.

"Got lucky. Spotted a pair and followed them. Unfortunately, I lost track of them in the city."

"And they caught up with you at the bar," I concluded.

"Right."

The waiter dropped the bill on the table and asked if we wanted any refills on our coffee.

We declined for Wendigo's sake.

"You want to see a card trick?" Wendigo asked Jane.

Jane looked over at me, uncertain what to make of the offer. When I nodded my head, she answered, "Sure?"

Wendigo pulled a sealed pack of cards from his pocket, unwrapped the cellophane, and handed the deck to Jane, asking her to shuffle. He had her spread the cards out, then he pulled one from the deck.

"Guess which one."

"*Queen of Hearts*?" she teased, fluttering her eyes.

Wendigo revealed the card. "Nope. A gift card for Carter's Crab Shack." Jane was stunned. I laughed and clapped my hands.

Wendigo got the waiter's attention and asked him to check the balance on the card.

"I don't use that one too often," he confided. "I never know how much credit will be on them."

It turned out there was only eighteen dollars and thirty-three cents on the card. We paid the rest of our bill with cash.

"On the plus side, if we ever need to wash the Lincoln, I got a Wizard Wash card with, like, two thousand dollars left on it. Pretty sure that's a lifetime supply of car washes."

I was going to explain to Wendigo that, again, the money had to be coming from *somewhere*. Gift cards were prepaid, so everything had to balance out in the end. Then I realized—maybe it didn't have to. Maybe things were a lot less...*solid* than I thought. Maybe the only reason things always seemed to balance out in the past was because I thought they should. Two plus two equaled four because that was what I was taught. So that was what I did—kept making all those twos plus twos equal fours, even when they didn't.

That was part of what you did as an accountant— you fixed discrepancies, searched for mistakes in the calculations, and corrected them. But what if some of those discrepancies weren't mistakes? What if we were fixing magic the whole time, unaware we were creating other mistakes somewhere else in the system to fix it? Forcing it all to equal out because that was what we were paid to do? What if we had been part of it the whole time? Part of the conspiracy? Part of how magic worked?

Jane suddenly hugged my arm. "You've been quiet."

She was right. We had made our way out of the restaurant and back up the boardwalk while I was lost in thought.

"It's been a long day," I said with a smile.

"You've got that right." She hung on my arm as we made our way back to the hotel.

* * *

Back in my room, I couldn't sleep. I kept going over the events of the day.

The world didn't end when Fish Sticks hit the Atlantic. The seas didn't turn red, or whatever. The MIB's plans obviously didn't involve getting the magic dolphin to the water. Or at least, nothing seemed to have happened as a direct result because of it. No, I decided, we'd done well.

Then I realized we hadn't discussed our next step.

What was our next move? Just head off and look for MIBs? Check the news for weird stuff, leap in the Wendi-Mobile, turbines to speed, and go? I guessed we'd save that discussion for tomorrow.

I decided to take a quick inventory, placing items on a small table flanked by two chairs near the window. The curtains were open; the view of the sea at night was reassuring.

I had three Crystal Guns, the Eldritch Dowser,

seventeen dollars' worth of THIS IS REAL MONEY, and almost eight hundred in real money—some of it was mine, but most of it was my share from the Magic ATM card. My first day on the job, and I had already accumulated a decent magic arsenal.

Wendigo had informed me the new guns were most likely cheap knockoffs, and lucky for Jane, not as powerful as the true Crystal Gun, which belonged to him. The fakes were meant only to threaten us. Chances were, they'd disappear in a few days, but we might get some use out of them until then. And, of course, the true Crystal Gun belonged to Wendigo. He'd probably ask for it back tomorrow. I also had no idea how long the Magic Dollars would last. Wendigo said they'd stick around for a couple of days, but that was a little vague. What was there to stop them from embarrassingly vanishing mid-transaction?

Maybe my arsenal wasn't so decent after all.

There was a sudden knock at the door.

I opened it to find Jane standing outside. She held up two large to-go cups of coffee.

"I thought maybe you'd like some more coffee. I would have had a second cup at the restaurant, but—"

"It's weird drinking it with him staring at you, right?" I finished, letting her in and shutting the door.

"Yeah."

I moved to take the coffee from her but somehow missed. Not because I was cursed. Quite the opposite. We were pulled to each other. Our lips met, and we kissed hungrily.

Moving back, unwilling to separate, we somehow managed to get the coffee cups onto the nightstand, despite our being oblivious to everything but each other, and an overwhelming need.

Clothes went away, removed with a speed and grace you only see in movies. Still kissing, hands reluctant to leave each other, we slipped back onto the bed.

"Easy," I breathed. I was reveling in how simple we fell into being in a relationship and now into being lovers. It made me feel like the star of one of those action films. I was James Bond about to bed some vixen wearing a double entendre for a nametag. And the word slipped out. And I realized, to my horror, that I was just Harry Long about to make love to someone I didn't feel I deserved. Someone who could wrongly mistake that word for a designation.

"What?" Her breath was hot on my cheek.

"I, uh...think I might have cracked a rib...earlier." In my defense, it was the truth.

She rose up, shadows and moonlight drifting in from the sea, playing across her body, catching her sly smile.

"I'll try to be gentle."

CHAPTER FOURTEEN
Breakfast Epiphanies

I awoke early the next morning without the assistance of an alarm clock, cell phone, or wake-up call.

Jane was snuggled up against me, still fast asleep. It was a strange sensation to wake to, but one I was sure I could get used to. I wanted it to be something I got used to. Something dependable.

The wrong word again. You'd be hard pressed to find a Hallmark card containing the word 'dependable.' A pick-up truck commercial? Sure. But Jane wasn't a pick-up truck. She was something wonderful. Dependable makes it sound like I'm taking her for granted.

I'm no good at this. I blurted *easy*, for crying out loud! Which was what I thought, but it wasn't that, either. What did Jane say? Too good, too soon?

I looked over at her, lying there in bed next to me. That's exactly what this was—too good, too soon.

But...maybe this was all just part of being an action hero.

I did my best to climb out of bed without disturbing her and shuffled off to the bathroom.

A few minutes into my shower, Jane slipped in

behind me, wrapping her arms around me, molding herself to my back.

After a bit, I turned around and opened my stupid mouth.

"That wasn't too soon, was it? I mean the sex, not the other thing...the actual sex. Not the...timing."

"No. I'd say the timing was just right," she purred. "I don't usually do this on the first date. The actual sex thing."

I laughed. "I told you not to consider eating food court takeout in the mall parking lot a date."

"I'm not. I'm considering battling killer aliens from another dimension while setting a magic dolphin free our first date. And as first dates go, it was a doozy."

"You *were* struck by lightning."

"And you kinda lost it there. Called me your girlfriend," she quipped.

I pulled her against me, suddenly getting serious. "You...getting hurt. Them hurting you. It..."

"That was what I was talking about. About fighting harder." She looked up at me. "I don't think this is going to be a weakness. I think this is going to be a strength." We stood there for a long time, holding each other as the water fell.

"It was a hell of a day," I muttered.

"The night wasn't that bad, either."

***

Later we were dressed, standing in the open doorway of my hotel room. Jane had thrown on her clothes from the previous night, just until she could make it back to her room. She was commenting on how she was happy that this particular walk of shame[31] ended a mere two doors down, when Wendigo threw open his door and stepped out into the hall, fully dressed and already wrapped in his black coat.

"Hey, I thought I heard you! You weren't planning on heading down to breakfast without me, were you?"

"No!" assured Jane. "I just wanted to check to see if Harry was awake first."

"This beats the hell out of sleeping in the Lincoln. A guy could get used to nights like that!"

"Yeah." I laughed. "Yeah, a guy could."

"I'm heading down to the lobby. Free continental breakfast!" he shouted, racing off to the elevator, finger pointed forward, like George Washington crossing the Delaware.

"He didn't notice I was wearing the same outfit from last night," marveled Jane.

"I think he's worn the same outfit for the last three days," I muttered, watching him dash off. Absently, I wondered what he did through the summer months. That long coat would make him stick out like a sore, sweaty thumb.

Jane gave me a peck on the cheek, then scurried to her room.

A few minutes later, we met back in the hallway and headed down to the lobby. When we arrived, we found Wendigo standing outside the hotel's breakfast area, sulking.

"What's going on?" I asked as we approached.

---

31   A term I first heard during my college years, used to denote the awkward morning trip after a night of revelry from whoever's place you wound up at (and possibly had sex with) back to your place of residence, performed while wearing the previous night's clothes, a hangover, and an aura of fresh regrets. Considering current efforts made by society to shame shamers who shame, it's possible the term may have fallen out of use.

He sniffed. "They kicked me out."

Jane frowned. "What happened?"

"I was just trying to get some coffee from one of the urns," lamented Wendigo.

A staff member happened to be walking by, large and clad in a great deal of powder blue material that was supposed to appear down-home diner waitress-y. "He tried sticking his mouth under the spout!" she scoffed as she wobbled past. "Could have gotten burned bad. Not to mention it's unsanitary!"

"I have money," Wendigo whined, "and possibly some sort of hotel VIP card!"

"Come on," I said. "Let's go find someplace you're not banned from yet."

***

It only took us a few minutes walking along the boardwalk to find a place that matched the same criteria as the previous night, crowded but not *too* crowded. Instead of "crab," this one had "pancake" in its name. I came to appreciate the naming structures of the area's restaurants.

Perhaps later, if time permitted, we would find one with the word "alcohol."

I ordered a seafood omelet, just because I never had one before, along with a glass of orange juice. Wendigo was working through a stack of pancakes tall enough to require warning lights to alert low flying aircraft, accompanied by a tall glass of milk. Jane went with a waffle topped with blueberries, light on the whipped cream. She opted for milk as well but couldn't help continuing to quiz Wendigo on the coffee-curse thing.

"Okay," she challenged, "what if we got, like, an

iced coffee with two straws? Would your curse foul it up for me too? Or would the fact that it was my coffee as well prevent it?"

"I don't know," muttered Wendigo, "but *iced* coffee?" He made a face. "It's already ruined."

It was then I had a striking realization: Wendigo was a coffee purist (or snob, I guess, depending on how you looked at it). That was why this curse hurt him so terribly. He *loved* coffee—possibly more than he loved a certain jilted barista. And when they parted ways, she made sure he would never enjoy his true love's company again.

"Can we do anything about it?" Jane looked at me, then back at Wendigo. "Can we make it our next mission or something?"

Wendigo sighed. "I don't think that would be a good idea."

"Okay, so what *is* our next mission?" Jane asked.

Wendigo shifted uncomfortably "I have no idea," he admitted.

"Okay..." Jane drew out the word.

"It's not like I get a tape that self-destructs or anything," Wendigo explained. "This is another reason why I thought you two might not stick around, there's a lot of downtime between things. I just kind of luck out at times and stumble over the next Golden Fleece that requires...fleecing."

"You don't *have* a Golden Fleece...do you?" I sputtered.

He gave me a condescending look.

"I wish you wouldn't do that," I protested. "We just netted 'Neptune's' Trident yesterday. Give me a break." I knew it wasn't really Neptune's, but it seemed reasonable there'd be a magical scrap of ram's hide out there somewhere someone decided to tag with the Golden Fleece name.

Jane suddenly pulled out her phone. After an elaborate series of taps, she explained, "I just set up alerts on a couple of Weird News feeds. That's a good place to start looking, right?"

"Yeah," admitted Wendigo. "That's good."

"And there's bound to be Facebook and, what? Instagram? Tumblr groups? A subreddit?" I offered. "All worth checking out. Of course, there's probably going to be a lot of fake stuff to weed through."

Wendigo brightened. "Yeah. But it's good! Better than waiting to stumble over something again!" He attacked his stack of pancakes with renewed vigor.

"And what about the hand?" Jane scrunched up her face in feigned (or possibly real) disgust. "Couldn't it point us to the next thing?"

"It can't find magic," I answered.

"Yeah, *but*," Wendigo corrected, "I can use it to find the MIBs, provided they're outside the nothing spaces and they're not ones with magic-blocking powers. I used it to find them a couple of times in the past." A smug smile flickered across his face. "I think that's why they don't like me having it."

"We got the magic-sniffer, too," I offered. "The Eldritch Dowser. But that obviously has limited range."

Wendigo pulled out the Magic ATM card to verify it was still there "Okay, I'll take the hand and the magic-sniffer, if I can borrow it from you. Take a stroll along the boardwalk and see if either can pick up on anything worthwhile."

I imagined Wendigo was considering the possibility of finding another Sideshow of the Strange. Maybe with another bit of magic hiding in plain sight.

"You two head back to the hotel. See if you can look at Facebook and that other stuff," he added. "Maybe we'll luck out and something will pop up. Until then, we have a MIB Gold Card, or Black Card, and a little bit of free time. Maybe we should consider having some fun?" I felt Jane's foot trail its way up my leg and smiled into my orange juice.

"You know, this is nice," Wendigo commented, leaning back in his chair. "I don't usually get to brainstorm like this..."

"Uh, Wendigo? You have that mummified hand someplace safe right? Not just sitting out?" I recalled how I had laid out all my magic objects onto the table in my room last night. "Be a hell of a thing for housekeeping to find."

Wendigo had a sudden striking realization. "Housekeeping!" He leaped up and bolted for the exit, inadvertently leaving Jane and I to cover our bill.

* * *

Back at the hotel, we met Wendigo as he was coming out of his room, dropping the Answering Hand into his coat pocket. He gave me the trident for safekeeping, and I handed him the Eldritch Dowser. I felt an odd pang as I turned the rod over to him, as though I were boarding a dog at a kennel for the first time.

Jane scurried into my room as Wendigo stalked off, slapping the *Do Not Disturb* placard on the door's handle, then kissing me passionately.

She beamed. "I...was considering having some fun."

Jane and I spent most of the day making love.

Sometime later that afternoon, I had the sudden,

striking realization that while Wendigo was out prowling the boardwalk, searching for magic, Jane and I were up there in that hotel room making our own.

CHAPTER FIFTEEN
Nothing

Wendigo returned later that evening to find Jane and I lounging in my hotel room (fully dressed), checking various feeds and sources on our phones.

"Nothing?" he asked.

"Yeah, uh...nothing." I glanced over at Jane, seated at the table by the window. She gave me a sly smile.

Wendigo stalked over to the window and dropped himself into the empty chair across from her. "Nothing." he echoed. "I found out there's a place called Mr. Frodo's near here—some kind of hobbit-themed restaurant—and a Ripley's Believe It or Not! I figured if there was going to be magic hidden in plain sight here somewhere, it would be at one of those, but nothing.

"Oh, here!" he suddenly exclaimed, quickly counting out three even piles of twenty-dollar bills onto the table. "They have arcades! I don't know how you guys feel about them, but I love them! And games! Like the shooting-water-in-the-clown-mouth-to-pop-the-balloon game! I don't know what they call that."

"I think that *is* what they call it," noted Jane.

"Well," I said, scooping my money pile up from the table. "Maybe we should go see about having some fun instead of spending all day cooped up in this boring hotel room."

"About time!" Jane smirked, scooping up her share. "I'd much rather be playing *Dig Dug* and popping clown balloons! And I hope to God we're planning on eating at Mr. Frodo's tonight."

"Well, yeah," Wendigo and I said in unison.

The first arcade we passed was closed for the season, but Wendigo assured us there was another one open farther along the boardwalk.

A short time later, we entered a large building filled with loud beeping, tweeting, and chirping arcade classics crammed next to a variety of redemption games and prize cranes, banked on either side by a pinball machines and Skee-Ball lanes.

I fed a dollar into an antique change machine from the 1980s mounted on a post near the rear of the establishment. The four quarters hit its metal bin with a nostalgia-inducing *shunk*, ejected with enough force to suggest a coin-loaded shotgun may be hidden behind its front panel.

Wendigo sidled up next to me at the machine. "You didn't use a Magic Dollar, did you?" he asked in a whisper.

I beamed, slipping the bill back into my pocket and collecting my four quarters from the machine's bin. "Yeah."

"*No. No. No,*" he hissed.

"What?" He was fine with magically pulling hundreds out of ATMs every chance he got without a care, but a dollar's worth of change was suddenly a no-no?

"The attendants in these places watch their coin

machines like hawks." Wendigo made a clawing motion with his hands before pointing toward a sign that read, *'Change for arcade use only.'*

"They keep an eye on who takes their change and how many games they're playing.

"There's x number of coins in here," Wendigo continued, tapping a knuckle against the change machine. At the end of the day the dollars in and coins out have to balance."

A smile broke across my face. "Are you...are you explaining accounting to me?"

"Look," Wendigo huffed, "You can get away with using the dollars on crane games because that's gambling. More people lose than win on those things, but the owners figure the occasional lucky player's walking away with an armful of prizes. A few missing dollars from their take could easily go unnoticed. With vending machines, there's the occasional glitch, a soda machine spits out two cans, a snack machine drops two candy bars. And then there's the shakers."[32]

"Change out those Magic Dollars here and you throw their balance off," he whispered. "And if there are cameras here, which I'm sure there are, we'll get accused of something. Hopefully we're long gone by the time anyone discovers anything's off, but I don't think it's anything we should have to worry about. You know, in addition to everything else."

"So *now* you're worried about balances?" I jibed.

He gave me a withering look.

"Yeah, okay. Bad choice on my part," I

---

[32] As in, "people who intentionally shake vending machines for the purpose of knocking loose free sodas and snacks," not members of *The United Society of Believers in Christ's Second Appearing* otherwise (also) known as Shakers. Although, to be fair, some Shakers could also be shakers.

acknowledged. "No Magic Dollars in change machines. But this is the sort of stuff you have to *tell me about!*"

Wendigo stood there, staring at the machine, then shrugged. "Eh, I guess two missing dollars won't hurt." He pulled a Magic Dollar out and fed it into the machine. *Shunk!*

"Probably three," I confessed. "I gave one to Jane earlier." I gestured to my approaching girlfriend.

"This is amazing!" she gushed, displaying a big handful of coins.

We set about blowing through our quarters and getting out of there as quickly as possible. Jane spent most of her time riveted to a *Mr. Do* machine, a close runner-up to the unfortunately absent *Dig Dug*.

Wendigo spent most of the time playing Skee-Ball. As it turned out, he was pretty good at it. I showed off my crane machine skills to Jane after playing a few of the classics.

On the way out of the arcade, I handed a very happy little girl a trio of hard-won Disney princess dolls, while Wendigo handed her mother a bouquet of Skee-Ball tickets.

Returning to the boardwalk, I looked over one of the Magic Dollars. My discussion with Wendigo in the arcade concerning the bills played over again in my head.

"What about casinos?"

"Too dangerous." He answered a little too quickly, as though he'd been waiting for it. "Even more eyes and more problems if people get suspicious. Besides, I don't know where you'd find one with machines that take one-dollar bills. It's all fives or higher anymore."

I was trying to figure out an alternative source of income; there was an assumption the Magic ATM card would eventually vanish with no guarantee of us ever finding another one.

Conversely, every MIB we ran into seemed to have a few magic bills on them for some reason.

I felt carwashes were the key, the older ones that hadn't yet switched to tokens or automation. We'd cut a path across America, hitting every old carwash we could find. We'd empty their change machines of quarters using our Magic Dollars, then use one of those supermarket coin machines to change our change into cold, hard cash—or, rather, soft, warm fiber.

We'd make a trail west, then double back east. The authorities would realize they had a rash of carwash robberies on their hands and start looking for us out in California or wherever. Maybe check those supermarket coin changers for signs of people depositing huge amounts of quarters. But by then, we'd be back cooling our heels up in Maine or wherever.

No. There wasn't enough of a return there. The risk versus gain was too far skewed.

Jane noticed I had fallen silent again.

"What are you thinking about?" She asked, giving me another one of her sly smiles.

"Oh, you know, robbing carwashes."[33]

It *was* what I was thinking of, on the surface. But I realized there was a deeper thought which prompted it. What I was *really* thinking about was the future. A Harry-and-Jane future.

I knew the salaries of two white-collar

---

33   Disclaimer: I am by no means suggesting nor condoning the practice of robbing carwashes. If you ever find yourself in possession of Magic Dollars, please turn them in at the nearest authority. Or prize crane. Repeatedly.

professionals would've provided a much better quality of life for us than disappearing dollars and an unpredictable ATM allowance, possibly being drawn from the enemy's bank account.

Subconsciously, I was looking for alternative means. Security. A secure future for me and Jane.

If my conscious mind had realized it at the time, it would've resulted in an uttering of what was quickly becoming a mantra for me and Jane: *too soon.*

Wendigo suddenly dashed ahead of us, pointing excitedly at a shooting-water-in-the-clown-mouth-to-pop-the-balloon game—surprisingly still open, despite it being late in the season for such activities.

Jane watched our friend greedily eyeing the prizes as we slowly approached the bank of water guns. "It's sort of like having our own kid, isn't it?"

"Yeah," I muttered, throwing another hypothetical shrimp onto my subconscious barbie. How soon would supporting a couple become supporting a family? Of course it wouldn't just be me. We'd be co-supporting. The two of us.

Why did a life with her feel so...right? Real? Certainly, more real than being there playing shoot-water-in-the-clown-mouth-to-pop-the-balloon.

We took up positions along the game stall, facing a long row of identical, creepy-looking clown faces, all with mouths permanently agape, frozen in their eternal screams. A large sign read, "One dollar per play."

We each placed a dollar in front of us on spaces specifically designed for them, a single, horizontal slit across the center of each separate place to stand. After casually scanning the boardwalk for any additional players who may be making their way to the stand, the attendant came along, sliding a thin plexiglass plunger into the horizontal slit, banishing the dollars into holding bins beneath the counter with an ease born out of endless repetition.

Jane's eyes went wide. From her position near the stall's far end, she turned and faced me, looking like a ghost. I realized what she had done—Wendigo and I had placed actual dollars in front of us, realizing that there were no sensors to fool, no mechanism to return the magic dollars to us after racking up credits, only a plunger and bin. We obviously had more experience with the intricacies of the shooting-water-in-the-clown-mouth-to-pop-the-balloon game than she did.

The bell rang, and instincts took over. We grabbed for our water guns and started spraying.

I noted the clowns were now slowly shaking their heads "no" on top of endlessly screaming. Despite their protests, we continued to spray water into their mouths until one of their heads exploded.

In retrospect, shooting-water-in-the-clown-mouth-to-pop-the-balloon is a terrifying game.

In the aftermath, Jane scurried over to us with her prize (a tiny stuffed heart) in hand. The attendant eyed us suspiciously as we huddled together.

She whispered her concern. "I gave him one of those magic dollars."

Wendigo glanced over at the attendant, which caused him to become even more suspicious. "There's nothing to do for it now. Depending on its origin it may only have a day or two left. Mixed in with the rest it probably won't even be noticed until it's gone. Most people tend not to notice they're different unless it's pointed out to them."

"Or they use one in a machine," I said absently. I glanced over at the attendant. He was now looking at us uneasily, as though we were planning something, possibly conspiring to obtain a greater prize. Perhaps one of the giant stuffed Pokémon which adorned the back of the stall, luring potential players with the unrealistic prospect of winning one without spending a week's pay or plotting some sort of kingmaker scenario. The attendant breathed a visible sigh of relief when we decided to move on.

We took a quick run through Ripley's Believe It or Not! Halfway through, I realized my internal scales had shifted regarding the things I now chose to believe or not.

CHAPTER SIXTEEN
Something

We returned to the hotel, boarded the Lincoln, and drove to Mr. Frodo's, located on the western side of the Ocean City strip. It offered a beautiful view of Assawoman Bay.[34]

Wendigo had played chauffeur, suggesting Jane and I sit in the back on the way to the restaurant. He tried finding some nice music on the radio. Whether or not he was successful was unknown due to the constant rattling of the plastic sheet across the rear window. Perhaps for his next trick, he could produce a gift card for an automotive glass repair company.

Inside Mr. Frodo's, the hostess led us to a large room adorned with faux gold and a vaulted ceiling. The ambiance seemed comprised of equal shares Middle Earth, Middle Ages, and middle class. We were seated at a wooden table, on almost comfortable wooden chairs, and handed a trio of surprisingly short menus. I quickly scanned the prices and while they were not unreasonable, they skirted dangerously close to being so. It was clear they were counting on fans of the material to pay a little more for the experience of eating there, and

---

34   That was its name. Assawoman.

while we were fans, two of us had roots in finance and the other was living out of his car. In an effort to better understand the assets we had available to us I brought up Wendigo's magic gift cards again.

I considered us incredibly lucky at the previous night's dinner when Wendigo attempted to use his Carter's Crab Shack gift card. There are, after all, an infinite number of numbers. The chances of producing a gift card bearing an astronomical sum should be far greater than producing one bearing eighteen dollars and some odd cents. Infinitely greater.

"Maybe there's a limit?" suggested Jane. "Like, say the restaurant has a hundred-dollar max on their cards, then the one you...magic up can't go above that."

"So, it has to be able to exist for me to make it exist?" Wendigo thought about this for a moment. "But I've made cards appear that don't exist, like the Five of Sparrows."

"Yeah, but you *could* make that," I offered, "if you had access to design software, clip art, and a card printer. You could make one. Maybe someone somewhere out there has." We were still trying to get the hang of this magic thing.

Wendigo had more experience with it than either of us, but he'd never had the need to try to explain it to anyone before. It wasn't until the need existed that he began to realize how little he knew about it. He'd just accepted it and that had been enough for him. He became visibly concerned when discussing his card and coin tricks, as though the thought of trying to define them, dissect them, realize them, would scare the magic off.

The three of us lapsed into silence, studying our

menus. Wendigo made a disapproving sound, and I looked up to find him frowning at the laminated sheet he held before him.

"What's wrong?" I asked

"I was expecting puns," he groused, gesturing at the menu with a free hand. "In the names of the dishes—there's no Middle Earth related puns. Where are the puns?"

"Like what? Two Towers Onion Rings?" I suggested.

"Crusted Salmon-rillion over Rice?" offered Jane.

"Frodo Fingers with Fries?" muttered Wendigo.

"That's a bit morbid, isn't it?"

Wendigo shrugged at me and went back to frowning at his menu.

The waitress appeared. Jane and I ordered the crab cakes with two glasses of a relatively inexpensive sauvignon blanc. Wendigo opted for Guinness braised ribs and some additional Guinness on the side, in a bottle.

"Something's been bothering me," Jane piped up after the waitress took her leave. "You said the MIBs are after you, and they were after the dolphin and the trident and the other stuff. Yet, you left Fish Sticks sitting alone in the garage in Baltimore *and* in the parking lot at the mall. Even now, your collection of magic stuff is back at the hotel. Why aren't you more worried about leaving these things unattended? Aren't you afraid the MIBs are going to get them while you're away?"

Wendigo explained that the MIBs only give off the impression of being members of a far-reaching, sinister organization with unlimited resources, part of the aura of fear and paranoia they exude. He didn't believe this impression to be true—

"If it were, why not just overwhelm me with sheer numbers and be done? Instead, it seems to take them awhile to do anything. So, either their forces are small or slow to grow."

"Or dwindling," I added, happily accepting my wine from the waitress, who chose that moment to arrive with our drinks.

Wendigo continued, stating it had to take some time for the MIBs to organize the assault on the aquarium. Until then, he had only ever seen them in groups of two. In Baltimore, there had been seven.

"Nine," I added, recalling the two from our pre-Denny's car chase.

"Eleven," Jane said between bites of crab cake, adding the two who assumingly tailed us from Inner Harbor to the Delaware shore.

"Okay, yeah," Wendigo acknowledged. "That was a *really* large group."

The question was then posited: what was the reason for such a large group? Was it a show of strength? A sign of importance? Or an act of desperation?

Maybe they knew Wendigo was on to them? That seemed logical, since the two MIBs we encountered at the bar were sent specifically to deal with him, maybe to get him out of the way before moving in on the aquarium. It was possible they'd amassed their numbers in order to frighten him away.

Then, there was the statement made by Wendigo at the aquarium—the idea that it was a large group due to there being two items to retrieve, two decidedly *important* items, though their significance was still lost on us. The trident was assumingly necessary to wrangle the dolphin. The dolphin's necessity was still unknown.

Then, there was the third concept: the possibility this was some sort of last desperate act they went all-in on for some reason. A circling of their wagons.

Our food arrived. We spent the majority of our meal in silence, mulling over the machinations of MIBs while enjoying some remarkable crab cakes and ribs.

Wendigo picked up the conversation after finishing his beer. "I figured we'd be safe for a little while. I think they know better than to try coming at us without holding the World back first. They want to chase away as many witnesses as they can. And it messes with recording devices. Nothing but blurred pictures and static filled videos. It takes some time to do the World-holding-back thing. I can usually sense it when I'm in it, just kinda snuck up on me at the beach because I was distracted."

"What does that mean?" Jane asked, spearing the last remaining bite of crab with her fork. "Holding back the World?"

Wendigo explained that the MIBs created a place to work where the laws of physics no longer did.

"A nothing space," I added. "They hold back the World so they can access powers not of it." I made air quotes as I repeated Wendigo's words from earlier. He seemed happy to be referenced in that fashion.

Jane pulled out her phone and started tapping.

The waitress allowed us an opportunity to turn down dessert and coffee before dropping off the check.

"You think I should try the gift card thing?" asked Wendigo.

"I think we should save that for further investigation in a more easily escapable venue," I stated, reaching for my wallet. "Besides, most of them have a number you can call to check their balance before committing to their use."

Wendigo's reaction indicated he hadn't thought of that before, or perhaps, if he did, never had a phone so readily available to implement it.

Just then, Jane shouted, "Ah ha!"

She startled the waitress, who had returned to collect our check.

"It's going to be a bit yet," I explained to the frazzled woman. "She just found her tip calculator."

Left to calculate, we huddled together as close as the table would allow.

"The nothing space?" Jane continued in a hushed whisper. "I did a search on our news feeds for things like that—and I found one."

"One what?" asked Wendigo.

"A nothing," Jane responded. "One square mile of it."

She tried her best to display her phone's face to the three of us at the same time, then gave up, choosing to read it out loud instead.

Apparently, an avid fisherman/equally avid conspiracy theorist discovered a strange spot just off the coast of Virginia Beach. Dubbing it the "Roanoke Rhomboid," the fisherman cataloged a number of strange phenomena surrounding it, first and foremost being the avoidance of the area by fish and fowl. He added that other ships seemed to avoid it as well. His own attempts made to enter the area bore strange results, such as suddenly remembering a bill he had to pay, a call he had to make, or there being a much better fishing spot in the opposite direction, each warranting his immediate attention.

The waitress warily approached our table. Wendigo politely waved her off, stating we were going to need more time, as it was turning out to be a very complicated tip calculator.

"That's something," muttered Wendigo, turning back to Jane. "That sounds like something."

I raised an eyebrow. "Is it just me, or is there some sort of nautical theme going on here?"

Jane looked up at us as she rummaged in her purse for money to throw toward the bill.

"The trident, the dolphin—is it possible they were supposed to be part of this? This Roanoke Rhomboid?"

"Only one way to find out." Wendigo rose from his seat. "Onward to adventure!" he loudly proclaimed, pointing again like Washington in the vague direction of adventure (which happened to be in the opposite direction of Virginia). The restaurant was happy to see us leave.

On the way out the door, Jane started laughing.

"What?" I asked, laughing along with her.

"I was just thinking of Bilbo and Frodo." She smiled. "You think they would've been able to run off to the Misty Mountains or traipse across Mordor if they were working a nine-to-five?"

I smiled and pulled her close. "Nah, they probably had to quit their accounting jobs, too."

CHAPTER SEVENTEEN
A Trip to Another Beach

We decided to leave immediately, thinking the MIBs already had a head start on us, doing whatever it was they were doing in the dead space off the Virginia coast. Of course, it could all just be a hoax, one of those fake posts we thought we'd have to weed out. Either way, we agreed the sooner we checked it out, the better.

There wasn't much of a plan beyond packing up and going. After raiding the hotel vending machines for drinks and snacks and hitting up another ATM, we were on our way.

It was close to eight at night when we left Ocean City. The trip to Virginia Beach would take us around three and a half hours, driving south along the coast and through the Chesapeake Bay Bridge-Tunnel.

Wendigo curled up in the back seat to get some sleep while Jane and I respectively handled piloting and co-piloting responsibilities, fueled by coffee served in two very large, very secure, to-go cups.

We figured we'd be pulling into Virginia Beach around eleven-thirty. On the way, Jane made arrangements for a late check-in at Best Western Seaside Suites—two bedrooms with a foldaway bed in the main room. I didn't bother asking her what she thought the sleeping arrangements would be. There'd be time for that later.

Jane found an oldies station playing soft rock hits from the seventies, so we drove along, listening to Gerry Rafferty moving "Right Down the Line," Al Stewart recounting bittersweet memories of his "Year of the Cat," and the gentle rustling of the Lincoln's rear window.

I suddenly realized I had no idea what I was doing.

Sure, the basic concepts were there—drive south, stop MIBs—but the bigger picture was fuzzy. There was just this urge to put an end to whatever it was they were up to. Maybe it was as simple as knowing they were one of the types Jane spoke of on the beach, the ones using strength to get what they want. But what *did* they want?

A hand, a gun, a trident, a dolphin—and what else? Did Wendigo have anything else squirreled away someplace? Maybe in that duffle bag in the trunk? Or in some foil-lined storage shed somewhere?

The MIBs seemed sinister. I felt threatened in their presence, and not just when they were shouting force beams at me, trying to set me on fire or drown me, or knocking me around the beach.

They induced anxiety, paranoia, and fear. But was I after them now just because they were...weird? Different? If I would've gone to work yesterday instead of venturing up to the hotel's rooftop, would I care about the Roanoke Rhomboid? No. I wouldn't even know what it was. And how would not knowing about it affect me?

Wendigo believed the MIBs were up to something and had to be stopped, or after something and had to be thwarted. That had been good enough for me.

Of course, I had already been looking for an out. An escape from a life bogged down by the eternal certainty of numbers. And if I would have gone to work that day, instead of up onto the roof and into the nothing space, who's to say Jane and I ever would have become this? Maybe we would have amounted to nothing more than another few days of counting corporate buzzwords and the unfulfilled promise of a Boston cream pie.

It wouldn't have been this—driving up onto the start of the bay bridge on a crisp fall night, surrounded by dark blue sky and deep blue water scintillating with rippling flashes of silver under a bright full moon.

ELO's "Strange Magic" began to play on the radio, and everything suddenly felt right again. It wasn't until the song had ended that Jane made an observation.

"We're being followed."

"What?" I craned my neck to see through the rearview mirror, but all I saw was a near-opaque sheet of plastic. I looked to Jane. She was hunched down looking at her side mirror.

"There's a car—an SUV, actually," she said. "It zoomed around a car that pulled in behind us then came back over. It's behind us again. I think it may have been behind us for a while. It's hard to say." She glanced at Wendigo, fast asleep in the back seat. "You think we should wake him?"

"Hold on." I accelerated the Lincoln and moved over into the passing lane trying to keep an eye on the SUV in my side mirror.

Jane murmured, "It's still following."

Traffic was sparse this time of night, moving in

clumps, but still moving. Still *around*. If it were MIBs following us, they weren't creating their dead space. They weren't holding back the World.

I found a slow-moving car and pulled in front of it, decelerating to match its speed. The SUV stayed in the passing lane for quite some time, keeping even with the Lincoln's left rear bumper, waiting for space to pull over. Finally, it relented and pulled in one car behind us.

"I think it *is* following us," I whispered, "and I think it doesn't care if we know."

"It's following us." Jane looked over at me. "Why does that seem sexy?"

"You think that's sexy, watch this!" I timed it so that when a large semi came alongside the SUV in the passing lane, I stomped on the gas and the Lincoln took off.

Wendigo jerked upright in the backseat. "We're going very fast!" He shouted, "Why is my car going very fast?"

Jane turned. "We're being followed."

Wendigo leaned forward and looked about. "There are other cars here. That's good."

I nodded and checked the side mirror. As far as I could tell, the SUV was still pinned in by the slower-moving traffic. Luckily, there were no shoulders to pass us on the bridge, just two very narrow lanes. I was hoping to catch up to the vehicles up ahead, put some additional obstacles between us and the SUV before we hit the tunnel, then really fly. Maybe we could make it to one of the pier-like rest stops along the route and pull off without being seen.

"If it was the police, they would've thrown on their lights, right?" Jane reasoned.

"Yeah," I agreed, smiling. "We've done some things

over the past couple of days that could have put us on their radar, and I don't know how legal that rear window repair job is—but yeah, I don't think it's the police."

"In the future I'd like to be consulted prior to speeding away from what may or may not be police!" Wendigo interjected.

"You were sleeping." I countered as we shot toward the tunnel entrance. "Besides, if it *were* the police, you could just pull a Get Out of Jail Free card from one of your decks."

The two northbound lanes and two southbound lanes of U.S. 13 were merging into one and one just before the tunnel.

This was not the leisurely, romantic drive across the bay I had hoped for. I glanced at Jane as I swerved around a car just before the merge. Its horn blared at us. "After we're done here, with the thwarting or whatever, we're heading up to Boston for some pie!"

The road sloped down, walls rose up, and we shot under the bay. The tunnel streamed past us, a blur of lights and tile.

Wendigo peered ahead between the seats staring down the tunnel, "There aren't any cars coming the other way," he muttered. "Why aren't there any cars?"

"I see the SUV!" Jane shouted. "It's coming up fast!"

I spotted it in the side view mirror. She was right; it was flying, driving erratic, angry. There was no doubt in the world they were after us, and then—

Jane gasped. "They stopped!"

"What do you mean they stopped?" I glanced over at the side mirror again. It looked like they were sideways across the tunnel. Did they crash, or—

"Look out!" yelled Wendigo.

A large black SUV sat across the tunnel ahead of us. I slammed on the brakes and skidded to a stop.

"Where's the gun?!" I shouted, snapping my seatbelt off, but I already knew the answer.

The crystal guns were packed away with the rest of my belongings.

In my suitcase.

In the trunk.

Wendigo placed a hand on my shoulder.

I spun, staring at him. "Where's the gun!?" I repeated in vain.

"I'm afraid it wouldn't be very useful here anyway." He pointed forward.

Through the front windshield, I saw four people were now visible, each dressed in dark blue pants and light blue shirts. They wore dark glasses like MIBs, but they also wore dark bulletproof vests with the letters FBI written prominently across them. Guns were drawn. Real guns. Loaded with presumably real bullets. An agent was advancing toward us, ID held up and out.

"Mr. Wendigo?" he called. "Mr. Charles Wendigo? We'd like you to come with us, please."

Jane slowly reached down to undo her seatbelt. "You have enough of those Get Out of Jail Free cards for all of us, right?"

Wendigo cautiously stepped out of the vehicle, hands above his head. As he did so, a fifth person appeared, stepping out from behind the SUV. She, too, wore one of the dark FBI vests—but that's where the similarities in attire ended. Instead of blue, she wore a colorful dress comprised of multiple layers, a white blouse with billowy sleeves, and a wide scarlet scarf upon her head.

"Hello, Charlie," she said with a smirk. "Long time, no see." Wendigo sighed heavily and dropped his arms.

"Son of a bitch," he muttered.

CHAPTER EIGHTEEN
Gypsy Curses

We were loaded into the black SUV and taken farther south along US 13. If it wasn't for the fact we were in the custody of federal agents, I might've enjoyed the ride; it was roomy, the seats were comfortable (*heated* even), and the rear window didn't flap.

We emerged from the tunnel and, ironically, pulled off at the next rest stop, where I had planned to go after losing our tail.

A sign stood in the middle of the off ramp, stating the combination rest area/observation pier was closed for renovations. We swerved around it and pulled into a parking spot in the vacant lot. Another agent brought the Lincoln up, parking it alongside us. He gave us a serious look as he climbed out of the vehicle. Not serious like *grave*—more serious, like *funeral home*. I decided to call him Agent Somber. Then we were escorted into a restaurant, also closed and under renovation. I grew nervous. I'd seen my share of murder mysteries; this was exactly the sort of setting that inevitably involved dead bodies in walls, either being recovered from or sealed up in.

They stuck Jane and I at a table on one side of

the place and took Wendigo to the other.

There they sat and talked—four agents, Wendigo, and the woman.

"I don't understand," whispered Jane. "Is that her? The coffee-curser?"

"I think so." I was trying to piece things together myself, but she did look gypsy-ish.

There was a very animated conversation going on at the other side of the restaurant. Wendigo and the woman were now standing, exchanging verbal jabs. The agents had stepped back to give them room, looking slightly embarrassed—except for Agent Somber, he kept looking somber.

There was something in the way the two yelled at each other. They looked as though they might have been something at one point in time—something volatile and stormy. Twice during their mutual tirades, Wendigo had gestured over at us. I wasn't sure what that was about, but it didn't look good.

After what felt like hours, Wendigo finally shuffled back in our direction, accompanied by two of the agents. His eyes were heavy, shoulders slumped. He was every bit that depressed vampire I remembered from our first meeting. His blue-gray eyes met mine as he passed.

"I'm sorry," he said simply.

Another agent approached. "We're taking Wendigo with us." I opened my mouth to protest, but I was cut off. "And the trident."

"Y-you know about the trident?" I stammered.

"We know about a lot of things. Be thankful that's all we're taking with us, Agent Jones."

Ah, okay. Impersonating a federal officer. That's right. That was something I did.

Then it was Agent Gypsy's turn. She slowly

approached us, fiddling with what looked like an oversized playing card in her hand. Great. More card tricks.

She had a rugged beauty about her, tom-boyish looks with the grace of a large cat. She padded her way across the empty restaurant toward us, wearing a sympathetic smile.

"You're her, aren't you?" I hazarded, "The angry gypsy barista?"

"Is that my nametag?" She motioned to where a nametag would be. "In my defense, I wasn't angry before I met him."

"He didn't say anything about you working for the FBI," Jane said.

"I didn't. Not back then. They recruited me. For Charlie. This was always about Charlie. But then you had to show up." She was still wearing her smile, but she gave me a saddened look. "He promised you magic, didn't he? And you had nothing to lose. Nothing but another day of being lost. So, you went."

I looked across the restaurant. Only Agent Somber remained. He was staring out one of the windows along the back, looking out across the bay. "What are they doing with Wendigo?"

"What they do with all bad men—take him away. Put him someplace where he won't do any harm. He's lucky they didn't Koresh him."

"As in David Koresh? The cult leader?" Jane asked incredulously.

"They think this is a cult?" I stared at Jane in disbelief, then turned toward the agent. "You think this is a cult?"

Her sad look grew sadder. "Wendi's always been a cult. A cult of one. But that's not why they're after him, not entirely—they know about the MIBs. They've known about them since the early sixties. They know he's been fighting them, but they feel he's doing more harm than good—counterfeiting, forgery, hacking, multiple counts breaking and entering, millions in property damage, transporting stolen goods across state lines.[35]

"The guy leaves a trail a mile wide...except when he doesn't. That's when they need me. We have a...connection. We always have. But you two," she lamented, "you didn't deserve this."

"It hasn't been *all* bad," Jane muttered.

Agent Gypsy was standing beside our table, still fiddling with the oversized card in her hands. Some sort of nervous tick? She seemed very nervous for some reason.

"I'm sorry." She blurted out, then stared at me. "You showed up and you stayed. You stayed because you had nothing to lose except another day of being lost—and there are only two ways to deal with someone with nothing to lose. You either kill them"—I shot a nervous glance over at the agent by the window—"or you give them something to lose." She sighed. "Both are...messy."

She turned the card so that its face was visible. I recognized it as a tarot. *The Lovers.* She slowly tore it in half and dropped it onto our table.

"I'm sorry."

* * *

---

35   Not all of this was entirely true, and in his defense, he had some help with the property damage. I suppose they had to distill instances where magic came into play into charges they could make stick. Putting someone on trial for counterfeiting and forgery sounded a lot better than persecuting a man for card and coin tricks or possessing Magic Dollars.

Jane and I sat for several minutes in that half-gutted restaurant, staring at the two halves of the card lying on the table between us.

I felt as though I had lost something, something tangible yet intangible, and important, very important. It was like losing your car keys or forgetting a significant memory—only bigger, far bigger than that.

I felt...deflated. Something that was filling me seconds ago, something impossibly vast, no longer was, leaving behind an empty space of equal proportions.

I looked across at Jane and felt...nothing. That wasn't right. That hadn't been the case for *days*. So, what changed?

The gypsy had left. All that remained was me, Jane, and Agent Somber still by the windows. After some time, he finally approached us with the practiced look of a funeral director. He dropped the keys to the Lincoln on the table.

"You two are free to go," he droned. "The doors will lock behind you. Take as long as you want, but I wouldn't take too long." He looked back over toward the windows. "A storm's coming." Then he left.

We sat in silence, staring at the torn card. The lovers that were now in pieces.

"It was easy," I said at last.

"It was too good, too soon," Jane muttered.

It was magic.

CHAPTER NINETEEN
Fear (An Intermission)

I'd like to pause for a moment and take some time to discuss fear. Fear's a nasty weed with deep roots—sometimes so deep it can root you right to the spot.

Fear is a strange thing. Or, rather, what we sometimes *choose* to be afraid of is strange. Take numbers, for instance. The fact that the series of unfortunate occurrences detailed in the previous chapter occurred while traveling along US *13* could be attributed to the superstitious belief that the number was unlucky.

The strong irrational fear of the number thirteen is called triskaidekaphobia. It will score you thirty-three points in a game of Scrabble.[36]

The Stress Management Center and Phobia Institute believes millions of Americans suffer from this fear. Playing the law of averages, there's a chance an afflicted reader may very well have skipped chapter thirteen, something I failed to consider while chugging along from chapter twelve.

If the thought of fear causing someone to skip over part of a story seems strange to you, keep in

---

36   Sixty-six on a double word space.

mind that in the case of some buildings, it's the *whole* story that's skipped, the floor numbering sequence going from twelve straight to fourteen. Of course, they still have a thirteenth floor, it's just not labeled as such. Presumably, this is done with the thought that any bad luck heading their way will board the elevator, get confused, and leave.

And here I may be accused of doing something subversive, since even though this chapter isn't labeled thirteen, and therefore easily avoided by those suffering from fear of that number, I wound up talking a great deal about it.

Here in this chapter.

The number thirteen.

Stephen King has triskaidekaphobia, but then Stephen King is afraid of a lot of things. Cats, dogs, clowns, cars, hotels, proms, and fans, to name a few.

In a quote regarding his fear of the number, he stated, "I always take the last two steps up my back stairs as one, making thirteen into twelve."[37]

One would think, with his money, he would've had the offending stairs removed and replaced it with a slightly deeper twelve or a shallower fourteen. Or an elevator.

If, God forbid, in his routine effort to avoid taking thirteen steps, stretching across the last two to make one, he tripped and fell, I wonder where he'd lay the blame. Would he fault the thirteen steps and his effort to avoid the number? Or would he develop an aversion to twelves?

Anyway—

The origin of the fear of this particular number is unknown. Most fears are primal, and thirteen *is*

---

37   King, Stephen. (1984, April 12). A Bad Year if You Fear Friday the 13th. *The New York Times*, p. C1

a prime number, but perhaps that's barking up the wrong tree.

One school of thought is that thirteen is unlucky because Loki crashed a banquet in Valhalla, becoming the thirteenth guest. This caused one of the gods to die.

Somehow.

Of course, this suggests the number was already considered unlucky (or un-Loki), and that simply his presence, bringing the count of those attending the banquet to that total, was enough to kill an immortal.

Another school of thought is that it's unlucky because Judas was the thirteenth person to be seated at the table during the Last Supper, and we all know how that turned out.

However, the fear or superstition surrounding the number thirteen seems once again to have existed prior to this explanation. That an effect was molded posthumously as means of explaining the cause.

Thirteen isn't the only number to be afraid of; it just seems to be the most popular.

There's also fear of the number five (pentaphobia or quintaphobia), fear of the number four (quadraphobia or quadrophobia[38]), and, for those of you who thought triskaidekaphobia was a mouthful, there's the cumbersome hexakosioihexekontahexaphobia, which is fear of the number 666.

For you completists, there's the all-encompassing numerophobia, also known as arithmophobia, which are terms used to label the extreme fear of numbers.

A fear of numbers would be particularly debilitating for an accountant, and yet I felt as though I may have it—to an admittedly lesser degree

---

38   Not to be confused with *Quadrophenia*, the sixth studio album released by The Who.

than a full-blown phobia, but it certainly felt like I was developing a strong aversion.

For instance, I had recurring nightmares in which numbers weren't behaving the way they should. When I say this, I don't mean they were leaping from a client's spreadsheet and trying to eat me—no, it was a subtler sort of horror. The numbers simply didn't add up. It may not seem like much, but to an accountant, it was terrifying.

Oh, and the account I was working on may have belonged to the Devil.

In retrospect, Wendigo's disappearing coin trick had been the perfect bait with which to set the Harry Long hook. It played upon that fear of mine, of numbers not adding up, not behaving right. What once had been a solid, yet simple example of my accountability, was suddenly thrown off by a quarter. It was impossible. And in my search for an answer to an impossible thing, I had found even more impossible things.

Before I realized it, the hook was through my cheek. I was landed, gutted, filleted, deboned and tossed into a bin at Whole Foods, skewed with a stake bearing a placard reading: *Suckerfish—Eight Ninety-Nine a Pound.*

But maybe it hadn't been intentional. Maybe he hadn't preyed upon my fear the way politicians, salesmen, scam artists, ad-men, televangelists, and insurance agents do. Maybe he had simply stumbled across it by chance. And that chance stumbling just happened to cause me to quit my job, throw my lot in with him, steal a dolphin, impersonate a federal—

My God. What if he *was* a cult leader? Just starting out, maybe? What if it was all just hacking, smoke and mirrors, a robot hand, and drugs slipped to me through coffee? What if that was the *real* reason he had all those "accidents" when it came time to drink?

No. That was silly.

But then, that's fear. It makes you doubt yourself. It also makes people behave in unpredictable ways.

For instance, the angry gypsy barista thought I had nothing to lose, and that by giving me something to lose, in the form of Jane, I'd be too scared to continue doing all the crazy things I had started doing, for fear of her getting hurt. For fear of losing her.

I don't think Agent Gypsy was counting on Jane becoming part of things. She probably thought my involvement with her would cause me to leave the fight, out of concern for the safety of "us"—and it almost did.

It at least had me questioning things, until Jane's stirring speech on the beach, the sentiment that fear of losing someone you care about should cause you to fight even harder.

So, fear is a strange thing. Sometimes it's a weakness, sometimes it's a strength. Sometimes it's rational (like fear of clowns), and sometimes it's irrational (like a multimillionaire author's fear of his back stairs). Sometimes it's substantial, and sometimes it's existential. Sometimes it's fear of the unknown, and sometimes it's fear of something that was once known never being known again...

But no matter the form it decides to take, how we deal with it, how we conquer it, that always remains the same:

We take the next step.

CHAPTER TWENTY
The Next Step

I don't recall how much time passed, sitting in that torn-up restaurant, eyes glued to that torn-up card.

Eventually, we left. Jane was the first to stand, to move toward the door. I silently followed.

True to Agent Somber's word, the restaurant's door shut behind us with a secure sounding click, an unmistakable note of finality. Also true to Agent Somber's word, the wind was picking up, and dark gray clouds were rolling in from the west.

There was a storm coming.

We stood in the parking lot for a long time—Jane, several yards away, looking out across the darkened bay; me, near the Lincoln, staring down at Wendigo's keys in my hand. The sound of cars racing past on Route 13, each containing people with places to go, drifted to us as the first tentative droplets, harbingers of the impending downpour, began to fall.

Jane walked over and climbed silently into the passenger seat of the Lincoln. I climbed in, started the car, and we slowly pulled back out onto South 13.

We drove in silence, through the night and the

rain, accompanied by the sound of fluttering plastic, the sporadic slap of the windshield wipers, and the hiss of the tires on the wet road.

Jane stared out the passenger side window.

I stared through the tear-streaked windshield.

We drove south because we had nowhere else to go.

***

Eventually, we reached the Best Western Seaside Suites. We checked in with minimal interaction—driver's license, credit card, a few nods, a signature.

We returned to the car to get our luggage. Jane pulled a small overnight bag from among her belongings. I grabbed my suitcase. We both stood in silence, regarding the empty spot that once contained Wendigo's duffle bag, until I gently shut the trunk.

Then back inside the hotel, up the elevator to floor four, room 412. The door opened into a combination living room/kitchenette area. A door to the left and right led to separate bedrooms.

The curtains on a large glass sliding door on the east facing wall were open, displaying a small balcony, a rainy night, and a windswept sea. The moon took that moment to break through the clouds, bathing the room in a dim gray light.

Jane quietly walked off to the right and through the door, shutting it behind her with another note of finality.

"Great," I sighed, then headed to the other bedroom.

It's a weird feeling to have been manipulated. Compromised. I thought all along that it had been too quick, too easy to love her—and she felt it, too.

We had fallen into it together. Of course, now we realized we didn't fall. We were pushed.

Pushed by what? A magic tarot card? A gypsy curse? And when? Was it what caused Jane to take an extra-long lunch and seek me out? Was it what caused me to be so open to her about all the impossible things that had happened to me? And then her to just accept it all, just from my word?

And what happened now?

I decided to take inventory again, just to occupy my mind. There was a small desk with a table before it in the corner next to a heavily curtained window. I started placing items onto it one by one.

Two of the crystal guns had evaporated at some point during the day, leaving me with the one true Crystal Gun and the Eldritch Dowser. I was down to seven of the Magic Dollars. I think some of them had evaporated as well. I had close to a grand in real money (two-hundred in my wallet, the rest stashed in a sock in one of my suitcase's compartments). The additional wallet with the migraine-inducing fake ID was still present.

Then I thought about what *wasn't* there. The trident was gone. The Magic ATM card was gone. Wendigo was gone. And Jane was gone.

It was just the ghost of her that lingered.

I turned and threw open the curtains. The rain was falling harder now, drops pattering against the window, storm winds rippling the waves. Out there somewhere was the nothing space where the MIBs were doing MIB things. They still had to be stopped, but I didn't think I could do that anymore. Then there was a murmur, a murmur that grew into a melody. Familiar and haunting.

I opened the door to my room.

Jane's cell phone was propped up on the table in the kitchenette. It was playing "Strange Magic." Jane stood in the center of the room, holding a single hand out to me, wearing a sad smile.

I took her hand and pulled her close. We danced there, in the center of the room, to the song and the wind and the rain.

Step. Step. Step.

And then I opened my stupid mouth.

"I'm kind of new to this magic thing, but the way I see it, it needs your...conviction for it to work. You have to desire it." Desire was the wrong word. I shouldn't have said desire.

"Yes, but whose?" she asked, eyes filling with tears. "Was it something we wanted, or Wendigo's gypsy friend? Whose...desire was it?"

"I...I can't be sure," I stammered. "It was... *uncharacteristic.* Things usually don't work out so—" *Don't say easy. My God, don't say easy!* "Things usually don't work out this way for me."

"Yeah. Me too." She rested her head against my chest. "I fell, we fell, into this too quick."

"But that's the way love is sometimes. Isn't it?"

"I don't know."

"So, what now?"

"Now? For now, we have this dance."

The song ended. Jane moved away from me, collected her phone, and retreated into her room.

This time the sound of the shutting door didn't seem so final.

* * *

Now, you may think me not much of a chronicler, since I lost my chronicle-e in less than three days' time, but as I said at the beginning, I was kind of new at this. I could hardly be faulted for the FBI suddenly dragging Wendigo away, no more than Watson could be blamed if Holmes were suddenly hauled off by MI5. The show, as they say, must go on. But what exactly *was* the show now?

I felt like Kurt Russel in *Executive Decision*, forced to step up and save the day after a more skilled and more experienced Steven Seagal, in his 1990s prime, bites it in the first act. Of course, if the plane hadn't been loaded with people and there wasn't a bomb, only a hint of possible nefariousness going on, what would have stopped Kurt Russel from turning that 747 north and flying Halle Berry up to Boston for some pie? John Leguizamo? Please.

At this point, I realized something. Agent Gypsy, the angry barista from Wendigo's stormy past, had stated that her intent was to have our love, our involvement with each other, push us away from danger. Instead, we plunged right into it. I was meant to return with Jane to the safety and security of the white-collar nine-to-five work-a-day. She wasn't supposed to hop onboard the crazy train with me. It was where our love had led us. And if we continued in that direction, perhaps we could find it again, waiting for us further down the tracks.

In my room that night, I looked out through the window, through the storm, out into the sea. Somewhere out there were the Roanoke Rhomboid and bad people up to bad things. It deserved at least an attempt. A quick once over. A look-see.

Bond wouldn't fly all the way to the Bahamas and then not bother to check out the villain's secret island lair. Batman wouldn't drive out to the old, abandoned toy factory, on the outskirts of Gotham, and then just park there and sit for a spell. The situation called for at least a token effort.

Then it was off to Boston for some pie.

CHAPTER TWENTY-ONE
Rainy Days and Fridays Always Get Me Down

In order to understand the attraction of throwing myself into the line-of-fire, of otherworldly invaders who could literally set you on fire, and sacrificing the ordered structure of a relatively normal life for the day-to-day chaos that was Wendigo's, you had to understand this:

Fridays had lost their appeal.

When you're depressed on a Friday, because you know in just two short days it'll be Monday and you'll be right back at it again anyway, then *what's the point?* That's when you can tell you're burned out.

The longer holidays start to look good: Christmas, Thanksgiving, three-day weekends, and week-long vacations. And then, even they begin to lose their appeal. Because you know, inevitably, Monday will come (even if that Monday is a Tuesday, in the case of some three-day weekends).

Eventually, Tuesdays feel like Mondays. Second Mondays.

Then Wednesdays start to feel like Mondays.

And eventually, you wind up with just a week of Mondays.

That's what work had become to me: a week of

Mondays.

I thought magic was my ticket to endless Saturdays, and for a brief time it was, but it turned out to be just another long weekend. Without the Magic ATM card to sustain us in our carefree MIB-slaying, artifact-hunting lifestyle, returning to that week of Mondays started to sound appealing, or if not appealing, inevitable.

So that's where the day found me that Friday morning—starting my fifth Monday, thinking about my seemingly unavoidable return to Corporate Hell.

And it was raining.

I rose around six, shaved, showered, dressed (in Friday business casual out of habit, which sometimes included pullover shirts and even jeans!), then shuffled out of my room and into the kitchenette.

Four simple white mugs were stacked next to an in-room coffee maker and a basket containing four premeasured coffee packets, sweetener, powdered creamer, and plastic stirrers.

While the coffee brewed, I stared at the four chairs surrounding the kitchenette's table.

Everything here was a reminder of our ranks having been dwindled.

I ventured out with a couple of Magic Dollars and returned with a selection of breakfast-type foods from the floor's vending area; my primal hunter/gatherer urges sated.

I grabbed my jacket and breakfast then slid open the large glass door and stepped out onto the balcony. I stood for quite some time, watching the rain fall into the sea, coffee and sweet roll in hand. Eventually, Jane emerged from her room and joined me.

"Thanks." She held up her mug of coffee and the

trail mix breakfast bar I had put on the counter for her, giving me a sad smile.

I hated that sad smile.

We stood looking out into a sea that roiled beneath a gray, cloud-filled sky.

"Not much change since last night."

"No," Jane muttered.

I wasn't completely sure we were talking about the weather.

"I tried reaching out to our fisherman friend. The one who posted about the Roanoke Rhomboid." Jane glanced at me, like she was attempting to gauge my commitment to the whole thing. "Turns out people who post anonymously on conspiracy group pages aren't the easiest people to get ahold of."

I laughed and we smiled warmly at each other. Better.

"So, what do you think we should do?" I asked, looking out across the water.

"I don't know." She took a bite of her bar, then quietly munched away while staring at the sea. Eventually, she added, "It's not like Baltimore. I don't think we're going to see it from here. There's nothing but nothing out there."

I was going to tell her I didn't come out on the balcony to look for signs of MIBs holding back the World—it was more to think—but I couldn't be completely sure I wasn't subconsciously motivated to do so. That's what happens when you feel as though you can't trust your thoughts, or emotions anymore; you start to question everything.

"Yeah," I said simply.

Then I had a thought. I moved back inside the room, leaving the sliding door half-open. I was aware of Jane watching me through the glass as I quickly searched through the drawers and cabinets of the kitchenette. I found what I was looking for in a drawer beneath the coffee maker—a roll of aluminum foil.

I rushed to my room and quickly wrapped the Crystal Gun and Blackcloak's ID in foil. I also wrapped my remaining Magic Dollars, just as a precaution. I returned to the balcony moments later holding the Eldritch Dowser.

If the MIBs were after something out there, it was taking some time to get it. The weirdness surrounding the Roanoke Rhomboid had been documented continuously over the previous week. If the MIBs were sitting out there, waiting on, say, a trident and a magic dolphin to help them get whatever they were hunting for, they'd still be sitting there, along with whatever magic thing they were presumably after.

A magic thing the magic-sniffer could sniff out.

Jane and I stood there, waiting for a breathless moment, only to have the sniffer sniff nothing.

Our shoulders slumped at the same time. Then Jane suddenly brightened.

"Okay! But this is good," she exclaimed through a true smile, "Wendigo said the range isn't that great on that thing, because otherwise it'd be picking up the Arc of the Covenant in that big creepy warehouse in DC or wherever."

"You mean the one at the end of *Raiders of the Lost Arc?*" I raised an eyebrow. "You know that's just a movie, right?"

She playfully elbowed me in the ribs, "You know what I mean. It would be picking up all magic everywhere. Like the Holy Grail or whatever"

She fixed her gaze on the Atlantic, a sparkle in her eye, wind in her hair. "If the MIBs are MIB-ing around in the Rhomboid, after something magic, the rod might be able to find them. We just need to get closer. We need to get out there."

"You think we could find it? The Holy Grail I mean."

"I think we could do anything if we set our minds to it. It's all about conviction, right?"

***

A few minutes later, we were standing in front of a rack in the hotel lobby, skimming over dozens of 'things-to-do' pamphlets. A few advertised boats that could be chartered all year long, for fishing expeditions, through the bay, up rivers, or out to sea. It was the last bit that interested us the most.

The plan was to pose as fisher-people—maybe buy some gear at a local shop and hire a boat to take us out. We'd state the magic-sniffer was some sort of superstitious, folklore-y thing and claim we used the ivory rod to find the best place to fish in the same way a pair of bent sticks could be used to find water. We didn't know anything about fishing, but together we had close to eighteen hundred in cash and a pair of savings accounts we could tap into if need be. That should count for something.

We were a little concerned about the weather, but as it turned out, fishing in the rain was something that was done quite often. A helpful young man at a nearby outfitter informed us that rain brings fish to the surface and can mask the ripples of your line hitting the water (the latter an issue more when fishing in calmer waters).

After stating we planned on chartering a boat, the clerk told us that a lot of the charter places had equipment you could rent as well, for tourists down on the weekend who just wanted to give fishing a try. We apparently had the look of novices about us.

He happily sold us matching sets of rain gear then went on to recommend Old Salty's Fishing Charters and Sightseeing Tours.

Old Salty's. The name reeked of white-bearded men in yellow raincoats and matching hats, moving rope around on decks. How could we refuse?

We drove south down Pacific Avenue to Lake Rudee, a body of water which provided several aquatic related businesses easy access to the Atlantic. Old Salty's was one of them.

We were largely disappointed to find a man around our age manning the desk—thankfully bearded, though with one not as white as we'd hoped. His name was Pete Bell. In my mind, I had already resolved to call him Salty Jr.

"What are you looking to catch?" he asked, eyeing us over, attempting to appraise our fishing skills. "A little early in the year for rockfish."

"Yeah," I agreed, trying to sound like I knew what I was talking about. My eyes shifted casually to a "Fishes of Virginia" poster hanging behind the counter. "Striped bass," I said.

Salty Jr. narrowed his eyes at me. "Rockfish *is* striped bass."

"Sea bass," corrected Jane. "He meant sea bass."

"We figured now would be a good time, the rain will bring them to the surface," I added, attempting to recover.

He gave me a smile that might have been a few more degrees condescending if not for the fact we were potential customers. "I know a good place that's only a few miles out."

A bit of haggling got us a four-hour excursion

for five hundred dollars. He gave us the option of extending the time if we felt it was necessary. He made it sound as though he doubted we'd *find* it necessary.

I put it all on my non-magical, fully anchored to my finances, charge card. I had only brought two hundred in cash along with me, and I wasn't sure what Jane had on her. The charge card seemed the easiest way to go.

"What are you doing?" Jane protested as I handed Salty Jr. my card.

I gave her a confused look, "Paying for the charter."

"I thought we were going to split it."

"What?" I asked. "Why?"

Jane looked at me annoyed. "Because I can pay for myself?"

"Don't worry about it." I muttered.

Out of the corner of my eye, I could see Salty Jr. smirking to himself as he punched something into the register. He handed me the receipt, and I quickly shoved it into my pocket, eager to put this transaction behind us. "So, what's the deal?"

Salty Jr. explained we'd be going out on the *Off the Hook*, a fully rigged, forty-two-foot Jersey Sportfisherman. I nodded in feigned appreciation; as far as I knew, we were about to board a giant angler from New Jersey who was going to paddle us out to sea.

After setting us up with starter gear and lifejackets, and going over some basic safety rules, we headed out into the marina. The rain was falling harder, and the wind had picked up a bit.

Salty Jr. had spent a great deal of time and attention helping Jane secure her lifejacket in the shop, something I noted with no small annoyance, but now he was at the wheel up in the boat's tower, and Jane and I were seated on benches in the lower cabin.

After a slow run through Lake Rudee to the Atlantic, we suddenly shot out to sea at an impressive speed. There were all sorts of knots involved.

We let Salty Jr. take us out to his "good spot" for sea bass. He slowed the engines to a stop and came down from the tower. We emerged from the cabin, going out into the rain to join him. He was only mildly surprised to spot the Eldritch Dowser in my hand.

"What's that?" he asked casually.

"It's a sort of fish finder?" I hazarded. "Handed down from my great-grandfather. Supposed to be lucky."

"So, you come from a long line of fishermen?" He smiled and nodded. I smiled and nodded back. "And now you're handing me a line as well."

I regretted how much I appreciated his turn of a phrase—but then, I guess the sea brought out the poet in everyone.

"You're after the Roanoke Rhomboid," he said simply.

CHAPTER TWENTY-TWO
Doing the Rhomboid Rumba

"How—?" Jane started.

"You think yer the first batch of crazies who came looking for it?" Salty Jr. held up his hands to us. "No offense."

"Almost none taken," I muttered.

"Had three groups so far, each with their own sort of voodoo hoodoo or Radio Shack gadget they soldered together in their mom's basement. Personally, I don't care. Your money's just as good as the next guy's."

"Did they find anything?" asked Jane. "Did you find it?"

"No. They gave up after a few hours; suddenly remembered they had something better to do than hopelessly searching hundreds of miles of sea at a hundred and twenty-five bucks an hour." He looked up into the stormy skies. "And they all picked much better days for it."

"So, you gave them the crazy discount as well?" I realized. This shocked Salty Jr. more than the Eldritch Dowser.

"Yeah," he stated with a bit more appreciation. "But look, you didn't have to go through this whole game. I'll refund your rental on the gear. I'll even throw in an extra hour, but I don't think you'll need it. Like I said—most gave up after only a couple of hours."

But then, I thought, *that's exactly how the nothing space works.* You suddenly remember there's someplace else to be other than there, so they must have gotten close.

"How's this supposed to work then?" he asked, nodding at the rod. He held out his hand and I handed over the Eldritch Dowser for inspection.

"It...uh...finds magic," I offered. It was a lot easier discussing this stuff with Wendigo and Jane. I suddenly wished we had access to a crane machine.

"Magic?" he said with a laugh. "Is that what you people think is out there?"

You people. He lumped us in with the crazies. I didn't care for being lumped in with crazies.

"It's nice." He handed it back to me. "What is it? Whalebone?"

I shrugged and absently pointed it out to sea. If I could get a hit, a pull, I could hand it to Salty Jr. and prove we weren't crazy. Then again...maybe his mind was a little too closed to magic for him to pick up on it anyway.

He watched me for a bit with an amused look on his face. I felt my anger growing. Finally, Jane pulled him away, asking to be shown the tower.

The two disappeared up the ladder and soon laughter drifted down from above. Flirty laughter, flitting down like tiny embers and landing on my already highly flammable disposition. I tried hard to put it out of my mind, concentrating on the rod and where it wanted to be pointed, but it wasn't asking to be pointed anywhere.

Eventually, Jane called down from the tower,

telling me that Salty Jr. agreed to take us up along the coast to see if the rod could detect anything along the way. I wondered how much coaxing had been involved.

I wrapped my arm around the ladder to the tower to steady myself as the boat turned and headed north. We went at a slower pace than our trip out to sea, but the ocean was choppy enough to knock me around if I wasn't properly braced. My grip on the Eldritch Dowser was stronger than I would have liked it to be, but necessary.

After running north for a little over half an hour, the engines slowed to a stop.

"Anything?" Jane called down.

"Nothing!" I yelled back, then added, "Ask him where the others were when they gave up!" playing a hunch.

The boat turned, and we ran south at a much faster clip, causing the wind and rain to lash against me. A little warning would have been nice. I sought shelter back inside the cabin. After what felt like an hour, the engines slowed.

I thought I heard Jane titter, "Stop," in a laughing, flirty, fire inducing way, just before descending the ladder and sticking her head inside the cabin. "Pete said this is the place."

"Oh, so it's *Pete* now?" I snapped. She gave me an odd look, apparently not realizing I had mentally assigned him a different name. And now I had a few more for him.

"Am I the crazy friend you're humoring?" I hissed as we stepped out onto the small open deck.

"Don't be like that," she whispered, folding her arms in front of her. "I told him we're doing research on contemporary urban legends for a *Wunderkammer* article, and the rod was just for pictures, for show. Lend some authenticity to the story."

I asked Jane what *Wunderkammer* was, and she said it was German for what was basically a collection of weird things. She always thought it would have been a good name for a magazine dealing with the strange. "I made it up," she added with a smile.

"I can see why we'd need the rod to add some authenticity to the fake article you're writing for your made-up magazine," I sneered.

The smile disappeared. "Whose idea was it to pretend to be fishermen?" she snapped.

Salty Jr. descended from the tower to find Jane and me exchanging angry looks.

"Okay..." He drew out the word the same way Jane had done in the past. (Of course, hearing her do it never made me angry.) He motioned out toward the sea around us. "What do you think of this?"

I made a token gesture with the rod as Jane took a couple of pictures with her cell phone.

Nothing.

We stood in silence for a bit. Salty Jr. asked if we wanted anything from the cooler before disappearing inside the cabin to fetch us a cola and an iced tea.

"Nothing," I muttered, shaking the rod.

"Are you sure?" Jane asked.

"Yes, I'm sure. Do you want to try it?"

"No," Jane said quickly, apparently sensing my defensive tone. "If you're not getting anything, you're not getting anything."

"Maybe Salty Jr. should give it a try."

Jane burst out laughing at what I had mentally dubbed the skipper stated out loud. I couldn't help but crack a smile. Our captain emerged from the cabin, can of cola and two bottles of iced tea in hand.

"What's so funny?" he asked.

"We were just thinking of getting a picture of you with the rod, for the article," covered Jane.

"No, that's okay." He handed us our drinks. "I don't think I want to be associated with this."

"No further than running my credit card," I jabbed.

The rain had slowed a bit. I was hoping it might stop and maybe the sun would come out to warm things up a few degrees—it had become a little bitter out there. But then, maybe I was feeling more than just the effects of the weather.

Salty Jr. plopped himself down on one of the benches that ran along the small open deck. He took a drink of his iced tea while looking the two of us over.

"What is it you think you'll find out here? A poor man's Bermuda Triangle?"

"Is that what you think it is?" asked Jane.

"That's what people seem to think it is." He spread his hands out in front of him, suddenly appearing sympathetic. "It happens sometimes. Something to do with the Earth's magnetic fields or the cooling of ocean currents, if you believe the global warming stuff. Places pop up where the algae and the tiny stuff the little fish feed on die. And if the little fish stop going there, the big fish stop going there. And if the big fish stop going, there's no point for the birds to go there. Or fishermen. They just stop. That's all. But then, that doesn't make for much of an article, does it?" He shook his head. "This Roanoke Rhomboid is no more different than countless other places scattered across the seven seas, and no more magic either."

"Yeah? Then why's this one got a name?" I asked.

He didn't answer. Instead, he looked at his watch. "It's been almost three hours, what do you say we head in, and I'll knock a couple of hundred off your bill?" Turning toward Jane, he added, "That's if you've gotten enough pictures of him playing with his rod." Jane laughed.

I went into the cabin to fume while Jane and Salty Jr. climbed up to the tower.

***

A short time later, we were back on dry land—or, more accurately, rain-slicked land. We stood just inside the entrance to Old Salty's Fishing Charters and Sightseeing Tours, divesting ourselves of our gear and de-vesting ourselves of our life jackets, while Salty Jr. processed our refund.

Handing back my credit card, he turned to Jane and gave her a broad smile. "I hope you have enough for your article."

"I'm sure you do," I muttered.

Ignoring me, he continued, "If not, maybe you could do something on the Neptune statue instead?"

Jane and I exchanged looks.

I turned toward Salty Jr. "Neptune statue?"

"Yeah?" Salty Jr. looked a little thrown by our reaction. "The statue's been there for a while, but it's getting a new trident installed right now. Something fancy. Maybe gold? Whatever it is, it must be expensive, cuz there's security involved. And you know the second the government gets involved in anything local, it brings out the conspiracy nuts. No offense."

"Government?" Jane and I asked in unison as I turned back toward her, broad smiles forming on our faces.

The act did not put our host any more at ease. "FBI, I think. You can see for yourself. It's only a few miles north of here, off Laskin and Atlantic." He looked at us as though fearing he had just unwittingly unleashed something.

Jane headed for the door.

"Here!" I handed him a dollar, pointing at a machine that was visible sitting outside in the marina. "Buy yourself a soda, Salty Jr.! No offense!"

"But soda's a buck fifty." Figures he'd complain.

"That's okay, I'm sure you'll have enough!" I called over my shoulder as I slipped out the door.

CHAPTER TWENTY-THREE
Seeking the Sea King

We climbed into the Lincoln, pulled out of the Lake Rudee Marina, and headed back up Pacific Avenue.

With a little help from Jane's smartphone, we located the statue of King Neptune, sitting two and a half miles to the north of Old Salty's. As it turned out, the statue sat at a point along the boardwalk,[39] embarrassingly close to our hotel. The area near the statue was cordoned off. Several large construction barricades stood at least two blocks out from the beach, blocking access to both Laskin Road and Atlantic Avenue. The long, white, extended arm of a construction crane was visible above the surrounding rooftops.

Returning to the hotel, we parked the Lincoln, opting to see how close we could get to the statue on foot.

There was still a light rain falling. Our raingear

---

39   If you were to walk along the raised path that runs along the Virginia Beach shoreline you wouldn't be walking on wooden boards, you'd be walking on concrete slabs. However, no one refers to it as the slabwalk. Similarly, very few of us dials a phone or rolls up a car window. Accuracy, at times, comes in second to the familiar.

with the hoods drawn offered us some anonymity, but we were still a bit nervous. If the FBI were present, there remained the possibility of being noticed and identified.

The statue sat across from the aptly named Neptune Park, a small venue adorned with a sign proclaiming it was "closed for the season." A government SUV and a white pickup with a construction company's logo on its side sat on the park's grassy lot.

King Neptune, as the statue was referred to, was created by American sculptor Paul DiPasquale. It depicted the mythological god Neptune from the waist up, emerging from a tall rock base surrounded by various sea creatures. It was a twelve-ton, thirty-four-foot-tall bronze statue, standing on a concrete slab adjacent to the eastern side of the boardwalk.

In short, it's something that's hard to miss.

Neptune's left hand palmed a giant loggerhead turtle, the same way Shaquille O'Neal would palm a basketball. The right hand held a trident—or, rather, it *normally* held a trident. It also normally faced to the west.

We arrived at the site just as the crane was being hauled away. A small crowd of people, likely attracted by the prospect of seeing a twelve-ton, thirty-four-foot-tall statue being lifted and spun 180 degrees, were now slowly dispersing, realizing the event had now de-evolved into a trio of men in blue FBI jackets talking to another two men wearing flannel and hardhats.

Considerably less impressive.

We hung back, using what was left of the rapidly dwindling crowd as cover, trying to remain as inconspicuous as possible. The five men were discussing something near the statue's base. There was no sign of Wendigo or our trident, but either could be sitting in the SUV or stashed in a nearby hotel room.

Jane must have thought the same thing—I saw her look up, eyes scanning the multiple stories of the Hilton that stood just south of us.

I was about to pull out the Eldritch Dowser to see if I could get a hit on anything, when one of the agents looked our way. I remembered the threat made in the closed-for-renovations restaurant back on the Chesapeake Bay Bridge-Tunnel, involving me being hauled in for impersonating a federal agent. Other than the threat, I didn't recall much else about him. It could have very well have been him staring at me that moment.

I turned and started heading back to the hotel. Jane followed.

***

I suspected, given the proximity of the statue to our hotel, the staff may have had some information regarding what was being done to it.

We returned to our temporary dwelling and inquired at the front desk. The hotel clerk seemed thrilled to be able to inform us about the statue. Of course, he also seemed thrilled to inform Jane that the restrooms were down the hall, to the left.

Apparently, there was an anniversary of the statue's installation coming up, and in light of this, a decision was made to turn *King Neptune* to face out to sea, the way the artist had originally intended. The statue was also supposed to be getting a temporary trident upgrade. It was something expensive, on loan from a museum somewhere, which was the reason for all the security. An official unveiling was scheduled for the weekend, but now there were rumors circulating that it was being postponed due to the weather.

"Hard to imagine people turning out to honor King Neptune would be afraid of getting a little wet," the hotel clerk said through his permafrost smile. "But there you have it."

"There you have it," I echoed as Jane returned from the ladies' room.

***

We decided to grab lunch at the hotel's restaurant, called "The Sea King's Bounty." The serendipity was not lost on us.

"So?" I asked, waiting for my fish and chips while sipping on my beer. "Did you get our good captain's number?" The words came out a little more icily than intended.

"Oh my God! You're jealous!" She laughed, which didn't help. "Is that why I was getting the attitude out on the boat? I thought you were just annoyed at not finding the Rhomboid."

"Look, I saw he was getting on your nerves, so I got him away from you." She took a sip of her iced tea, this one with alcohol. "I didn't think either of us could afford a mutiny. I don't know how to drive one of those things. Do you?"

I shook my head once. "What kind of name is *Off the Hook* for a fishing boat anyway? Seems like the direct opposite of what you should name one."

"You should have asked Salty Jr.," she said, bursting out laughing.

I joined in as well, only I was laughing more at myself than her use of the name. I realized I had been acting foolishly these past few hours, after all, it wasn't our boat driving friend sitting here enjoying Jane's company.

"I'm sorry," I said through a weak smile. "Y'know, for behaving like a jerk." Jane simply nodded.

Our food arrived. My smile broadened as an enormous piece of breaded cod with a generous helping of thick cut fries was placed before me. Jane had some sort of salad with crab or lobster bits, and a bowl of thick looking clam chowder.

"So, what's next?" she asked.

"I thought we'd head up to Boston. Get some pie. We should spend some more time together. I think we—" I realized she was staring at me, mouth agape. "...That's not what you meant, was it?"

She gasped. "So, you want to just run away?"

"What? No!" I realized I was drawing the attention of the other patrons and waitstaff, so I lowered my voice. "No. It's just...look." I gestured off in the direction of the statue. "Whatever it is that's out there, they've got it taken care of."

"*What?*" Jane snapped.

"Yeah. The FBI's onto it, whatever it is. You saw them at the statue. They just needed the trident and Wendigo. Hell, maybe Wendigo clued them in on it. Maybe he's even calling the shots now. Either way, they clearly don't need us. I'll bet you a Magic Dollar that statue's pointing at *our* Roanoke Rhomboid," I added, claiming ownership to the phenomenon for some reason. "They needed to spin it and mount the trident, so they could put the whammy on whatever it is that's going on out there."

"So, they pick up Wendigo last night and have a

crane turning the statue around by this morning?" Jane asked incredulously.

"It's the government," I countered, "They can do stuff like that."

"You've been watching too many movies," she said dismissively. "It takes them weeks to decide what type of paper to put the memo on to suggest a meeting to form a committee. There were plans to move that statue. Probably made weeks ago! They knew they were going to have the trident."

"And you've been reading too many conspiracy sites," I fired back.

"Wow! Really? Two days ago, it was sitting in a tube at the National Aquarium in Baltimore! We took it from the MIBs! We had it! You tell me how they knew ahead of time they were going to have the trident!"

"They have a gypsy!" Jane yelled.

The waitress suddenly appeared. "Is everything okay?"

"Yes!" Jane and I responded in unison, causing the waitress to quickly retreat.[40]

We ate in silence for a bit. Then I started feeling bad about losing my temper. "I'm sorry," I said, looking up from my fish. "It's just—"

"You lost something," Jane muttered, spooning absently through her chowder. "And you don't know how to get it back. And it's frustrating." She suddenly tossed her spoon onto her napkin and sat looking at me, arms crossed. "It doesn't feel right if you try to force it and it doesn't feel right if you don't try at all, so you don't know what to do."

"Yeah," I breathed, dropping my fork on the table. "So, what do you think we should do?"

---

40   I made a mental note to leave a big tip.

"We should stick around for a bit, at least until we can verify that it *is* our trident, *our* FBI guys, and *our* Wendigo's here somewhere."

I realized Jane was assuming a lot more ownership than I was over things that technically weren't ever ours.

"We're just making assumptions here. It could just be some sort of wild coincidence," she added.

"We get our trident taken from us by the FBI—and there just happens to be a different group of FBI agents down here mounting a different trident to the Neptune statue?"

"I did say wild," she admitted with a smile. "We should at least see. Like I said, verify."

I nodded. "Yeah, okay. And if we do? If we do spot *our* trident and *our* Wendigo?"

"I say we steal them back and take care of whatever it is ourselves!" She held her glass of iced tea out toward me as though preparing to toast.

"Just to be clear, I'm agreeing to that first part, the verifying things," I said, clinking my beer bottle off her glass. "We'll talk about imploding that other bridge when we come to it..."

CHAPTER TWENTY-FOUR
Separate Vacations

I relayed to Jane the information I'd gathered from the hotel's desk clerk while she'd been busy in the restroom.

There were three problems with said information: One, after some quick research via her cell phone, Jane discovered the statue was installed in 2005, making this an odd year to be celebrating an anniversary.[41] Two, there was no mention anywhere of the sculptor originally wanting the piece to face out to sea. The act of turning it wasn't being done to appease his wishes. Three, sticking our trident in the statue's hand would make it look like Neptune was holding a salad fork. The scale was horribly off. Not much of an upgrade.

It was clear the anniversary celebration was a cover story to explain why the statue was being turned and the tridents swapped out, but the *why* was still unknown.

We made a plan—something a bit more involved than heading north to Baltimore for some pie.[42]

---

41   2017

42   There were probably Boston cream opportunities to be had right there in Virginia Beach, but part of the allure was going right to the source.

Our first step was to establish a definite connection between us and what was going on at the statue. So far, it was mostly speculation; it was possible the whole thing *was* just a huge coincidence. Doubtful, but we both felt an additional level of proof was needed before we took action, whatever that action might be. For this, we needed to spot either a familiar agent, a familiar trident, or a familiar skunk stripe.

We decided to split up. Jane would walk along the boardwalk, armed with the Eldritch Dowser. There were certain nuances in the rod's use we hadn't fully figured out, but we still thought it was worth a try. If Jane could get a hit on something with the Dowser, it would probably be worth checking out.

While she scanned the boardwalk, I ventured out in the Lincoln with the Answering Hand. Wendigo said the hand couldn't sense magic, but I decided to try asking it to show me where the nearest trident was. Maybe it could point me to Wendigo as well.

Sitting in the car in the hotel's parking lot, I popped the glove compartment open to find the hand wrapped in several layers of aluminum foil.

Spinning it free, I held it up and whispered, "Show me where the nearest full-sized trident is." Then I set it on the dash and started up the car.

I felt as though I had to give the hand some sort of modifier, or else it might just point to the closest dollar store or souvenir shop with a plastic Sea King children's playset. Or maybe even wherever it was King Neptune's twenty-foot-long trident was being temporarily stored.

Of course, now it just might point to every costume shop. Or the closest place to buy a pack of gum. I crossed my fingers and filled my head with visions of our trident. The hand rose up on its fingers, skittered around on the dash, then pointed south. I called Jane on my cell phone and told her I had a hit.

"Roger," she replied.

"Over and out," I responded through a laugh.

Fifteen minutes later, I was pulling into the parking lot of the Virginia Aquarium and Marine Science Center.

"Son of a bitch," I muttered, staring at my second aquarium entrance in as many days, wondering if I'd run into a second talking dolphin, too. "There's definitely some sort of nautical theme going on here."

I spotted two of the standard government-issue black SUV's sitting in the parking lot and thought it best not to linger there, just in case someone could recognize the Lincoln. I pulled across the street into an overflow parking area and found a place to slot the car. I was about to toss the hand back into the glove compartment when I decided to play a hunch.

"Find Wendigo," I whispered.

The thing danced back and forth across the dash a few times, then flipped over onto its back, a move I registered as failure. I guessed Wendigo being there as well was a little too much to ask for.

I rewrapped the hand in the foil and shoved it into the back of the glove compartment then retrieved the pair of dark, non-magical glasses before shutting the console.

A light rain was still falling, allowing me to keep the raincoat on without looking too suspicious. Of course, the same dark clouds that brought the rain made the glasses glaringly unnecessary—but if there was someone there to recognize me, it would be by my face. The glasses were my only option and considerably less suspicious than a balaclava.

Though, not by much—I now bore a striking resemblance to sketches of the Unabomber.

It was twenty-five dollars to get into the aquarium. Prior to paying, I was informed the facility would be closing in less than two hours, which was fine by me.

The site was smaller than the last aquarium. It only took me a few minutes to find what I was looking for.

The trident was standing in a glass tube, close to their sea turtle exhibit. It was our trident. Or a very good replica. I also noted that there was an FBI agent standing guard and quickly retreated.

I managed to find a chipper aquarium representative who cheerfully confirmed things for me. She was told the trident was on loan from a museum in Greece and was on display there until later tonight when it would be moved to Neptune Park for installation on the statue, in preparation for tomorrow's ceremonies.

"The scale's a bit off though," she admitted with a slightly muted smile. "It's going to look like he's holding a shrimp fork."

"Salad fork," I corrected.

"Shrimp fork. A shrimp fork has three tines."

"I'll have to take your word for it." I glanced back over across the exhibit toward where the trident was displayed. "You didn't happen to see a vampire-ish looking guy? About my age? My height? Black coat, blue-gray eyes, white stripe down the center of his hair?" The attendant shook her head no.

***

Twenty minutes later, Jane and I were back in our room comparing notes. She didn't pick up anything with the Dowser, but she did manage to get some pictures of the statue with her cell phone of a scaffold being erected around it, and a tarp being thrown over it. She also had shots of additional agents coming and going, but still no familiar faces. I told her about finding the trident at the aquarium, the single guard posted, with assumingly more present, as indicated by the two SUVs in the parking lot. I also told her about their plans to move the trident later that night.

"We hit them while they're moving it!" Jane blurted.

"Jane, I admire your enthusiasm, I really do, but that's just crazy. This isn't *Fast and Furious...* whatever number they're up to. This is the two of us. And the FBI! Hit them?"

"Yeah, okay, I guess I'm getting carried away," she admitted, plopping down on the living room sofa, looking a little crestfallen. "So, what do you think we should do?"

"I feel like we're missing something." *Like an enormous, irresistible pull toward each other,* I thought, then quickly buried it.

"Okay." She stretched the word out again, and I smiled. "Here's something: why aquariums?" She went on to explain there was a big Navy base not far from us, and Norfolk, Portsmouth, and Langley were all relatively close. They were much more secure areas for storing something important like a magical trident. For that matter, why not put it in the back of one of the SUVs? And what was it doing at the Baltimore National Aquarium in the first place?

"Charging, maybe?" I offered. "What if it needs to be near seawater to charge?"

"Then why not just stick it in the ocean? Or on a submarine?"

"Maybe it needs to be near sea creatures? Sea life? And aquariums are the way of guaranteeing it a captive audience? And maybe we're overestimating the government's knowledge of this stuff." I was on a roll. "I know not everything's how it is in movies, but they always stress that federal agencies aren't exactly forthcoming with information, things they're willing to share with each other. Stashing it at a Navy base would require some disclosure, some explanation. What if knowledge of magic is something the FBI isn't too keen on sharing?"

Jane's brows scrunched together as she spoke. "So, the FBI knows about magic and the MIBs, and they're keeping it to themselves?"

"Yeah. Why not?"

"Okay, so what should we do?"

I thought about it for a bit, then gave Jane a broad smile.

"How do you feel about a stakeout?"

CHAPTER TWENTY-FIVE
Stakeout with Takeout

It took almost an hour to find what we needed: an oversized umbrella with a clamp at its base and a Chinese takeout place with a decent Yelp rating.

The rain was still falling in a light drizzle when we took our seat on a bench along the boardwalk. To the back of us sat a small hotel parking lot. Before us was the wide cement boardwalk, followed by a metal guardrail, and after that, beach and ocean. Several yards to the south, stood the statue. While seated, if we turned our heads to the right, we had a decent view of it along with a portion of Neptune Park.

I clamped the umbrella to the bench, and we pulled our takeout containers out of the plastic bag. We pretended to be just another couple, out on the boardwalk, eating dinner, and enjoying each other's company. The truth wasn't far from it.

The lie wasn't far from it either.

I started viewing our love the same way Schrödinger viewed his cat. I think Jane and I were both too scared to peek inside the box, to realize the quantum status of our relationship.

But then Jane snuggled up to me as we picked through our takeout cartons with plastic forks and played spy. "Now, *this* is sexy," she whispered.

And maybe that's what this was *really* about. I had wanted to get more information and figured this was the best way of doing so, an old school sit and watch. But I also think I was hoping to recreate that feeling as when we were being followed on the Chesapeake Bay Bridge-Tunnel. The same excited, adrenaline rush of fear, of high-speed chases and eluding the bad guys. Or at least the guys with questionable intent.

Then there was a pang of guilt. Wasn't this just a manipulation of feelings again? Only this time instead of a magic Tarot card, it was me? Of course, that's what dating someone, courting someone, was—wasn't it? A manipulation of feelings? It all seemed a bit gray to me, as gray as the night which slowly closed around us.

Maybe I was hoping for something else here as well. A moment of opportunity when the trident showed up and all eyes were directed elsewhere. A moment to stroll in and casually rob the FBI, the same way Bill Murray robbed the armored car in *Groundhog Day.*

Of course, he had days to plan that.

Or rather, one day.

Repeatedly.

At the very least, I hoped to see some indication of how the trident was intended to be used. At the very most, I hoped to see Wendigo.

We snuck occasional peeks at the agents milling about the statue as we ate. I was looking past Jane, eager to catch sight of a trident shaped package or a skunk haired vampire, when my vision suddenly focused on her profile. She was looking into her takeout container, pouting as she probed about it with her fork, her eyes lit up as she speared the last elusive shrimp, extracted it from the container, popped it into her mouth, then happily munched away. I became aware I was staring at her the same time she did.

"What?" She smiled.

"Nothing." I started, returning her smile. "It's just—I'm glad you're sharing this with me."

"Me too. This is *really* good takeout." She joked.

"No. This." I made an all-encompassing gesture, plastic fork in one hand, half empty sesame chicken container in the other. "This—adventure." I felt silly saying the word just then, but I wasn't sure what else to call it.

"Well, it's not like I have much of a choice. We only have one car." Jane muttered, peering into her container.

"Oh God!" I lurched forward, almost spilling my chicken. "I'm sorry! I didn't even—I mean if you want me to drop you off somewhere, or you could just take the car. I didn't mean to—"

A smile broke across her face. "Kidding. Besides, where would I go? I gave up my job for you and your adventure."

There was a moment of silence as those words sank into us. "No. That isn't fair. It wasn't you. It was the Tarot. The Lovers." She huffed.

I looked out into the ocean, at no point in particular. "I keep thinking about the start."

"When you met Wendigo in the elevator?"

"No. The start of us. I invited you out for pie. We exchanged numbers. That was before Wendigo. Before the Tarot magic ramped up everything. That was just us. That would have been our first date."

"Is that why you keep talking about going out for

pie?"

"I think we owe it to each other. Don't you? To see how things would have progressed. Naturally." I said, stabbing a bit of chicken with my fork.

Jane curled up onto the bench, leaning against my shoulder as she picked through her shrimp lo mein. "Do you remember back in Baltimore, when you ran through all the crazy things you and Wendigo did that morning?"

"I think I was trying to scare you away. I'm not good at getting close to people, I always seem to screw it up, and if you left, I wouldn't have to try again. *Fail* again. Even today, out there on the boat, I think I was trying to push you away."

"And yet here I am." Jane gushed, holding her arms out wide. "And yes, I do think we owe it to each other. Otherwise, I would have called a cab.

"Agent Gypsy said I was supposed to steer you away from this, from adventure." She continued. "Instead, we plowed right into it. I think that was us too."

So, there it was, we were both convinced the answer to the quantum state of our relationship lie in different directions. Jane surmised it was a bit farther down the path we had set out on together. Me? I presumed it to lie in the vicinity of two slices of Boston cream pie. Maybe we were both right. Or maybe we were both wrong and magic had damaged us along with any potential re-relationship irrevocably. Whatever love we had inside of us had burned bright and hot as a road flare, to the point of expiration. No. There was still something there. An ember to be fanned.

"I liked where we were, *what* we were. And I'd like to get back there again, it's just—I'm not sure how."

"Time?" Jane offered with a weak smile.

"I'm just glad you're here." I sighed.

"Me too."

From the angle Jane was sitting I could see that her take-out container was empty, she was only pretending to pick through its contents with her fork while sneaking glances at the agents at the statue.

Right. We were supposed to be watching them. This was, after all a stakeout. And you can't have a stakeout without— "Coffee?" I offered.

"Yes, please!" sang Jane.

I gathered up our empty containers, dropped them in a nearby trashcan, then went off in search of coffee.

In a few minutes, I returned to Jane, handing her a cup of coffee the same time an agent was handing a cup to another agent standing in front of the covered statue. Our mirroring of the act drew their attention; they both glanced our way.

"That's not good," muttered Jane.

Getting up and leaving at that moment could have implied some sort of guilt, so we just huddled close together, drank our coffee, and did our best not to look in their direction (which was the exact opposite of what you were supposed to do on a stakeout).

The sudden glare of headlights drew our attention to the park. Another SUV pulled onto its grass.

Two agents emerged from the SUV and made their way to the statue. One carried what looked like an oversized rifle case.

Jane raised her phone and snapped a picture. Unfortunately, one of the agents saw her and started walking in our direction. I grabbed the umbrella and guided Jane away, walking and fake laughing our way up the boardwalk. We tried our best not to think about the hands we thought were going to grip our shoulders at any moment. Thankfully, we made it back to the hotel without incident.

"That didn't go the way I hoped it would," I said, retracting the umbrella.

"On the plus side," Jane added, wrapping her arms around me, "that was my first stakeout."

***

Back in the room, we discussed our options. Jane sat on the couch. I stood by the large glass sliding door. If I stepped out onto the balcony and looked out past the privacy wall, I could probably see the statue from there. Maybe we should have just bought ourselves a decent pair of binoculars.

That case the agent was carrying had been the right size. The trident was there, being mounted onto the statue.

I restated my theory from earlier, that the statue and trident were now both pointed toward our dead spot—the Roanoke Rhomboid. It seemed obvious. The trident and the space.

There had to be a connection.

"The FBI's apparently using the trident to put the whammy on whatever the MIBs have going on out there. Whatever it is, it isn't our problem anymore."

"How can you say that? What about Wendigo?"

"I'd love to help him, but you heard the agents. I impersonated a federal officer. And I'll bet you the reason they were on our tail so fast was because someone reported us passing 'counterfeit' money on the pier in Ocean City."

Jane's mouth went wide in realization. "Oh."

"And I'm sure they could find some other stuff to

charge us with if they wanted to."

Jane sat in silence for a bit, turning things over in her head. "Okay. So why didn't the rod sniff out the Rhomboid while we were out there on the boat? We had to have passed the area."

"I was distracted?" I shrugged.

"Or maybe you didn't *want* to find it." Jane gave me an annoyed smirk.

And at that moment all my anger and frustration came bubbling up.

"What! You think this is easy? I was betrayed—we were betrayed—by magic! You think I don't feel that every time I try using one of these damn things now?" I scooped the Eldritch Dowser up from the table where Jane had it sitting and flung it across the room. It struck the wall, narrowly missing the T.V.

"Harry!" she yelled, moving to retrieve the rod, fearful it may have broken.

"This isn't fighting MIBs, who disappear neatly when you're done with them! This is the FBI. There are real, lasting repercussions for messing with them! Wendigo never had to deal with this!"

"How do you know?" she snapped back, fishing the rod out from behind the TV stand.

"Oh? You think he could've done better? You think he would have just gone up to the statue with his coin and card tricks and come away with the trident?"

"No!" she countered, straightening up.

"Well, what then?!"

"I don't know!"

The sound of her voice, filled with frustration bordering on hysteria, caused us both to lapse into prolonged silence, her cry echoing in my head.

Then Jane slowly brought the rod up and turned, pointing it south and slightly down. She looked at me, mouth open, eyes wide.

"Okay," I acknowledged. "Yeah."

"It's there," she breathed. "And it's...on. That's where the adventure is." She nodded toward the rod. "So, what do we do?"

"I don't know." After an uneasy pause, I looked up and gave her a weak smile. "Drive north and get some pie?"

Jane walked over, stuck the Eldritch Dowser in my hand, then went into her room and closed the door behind her.

"Great," I muttered. Then I noticed I was pointing the rod toward the statue. I went into my room and shut the door as well.

***

Hours later, I was awakened by a series of thumps. Or at least, I *thought* I was awakened by a series of thumps. I wasn't sure if I'd dreamt the sound or if it had been real. I lay awake in bed for almost a minute before the sound came again.

I rose, absently noting I'd fallen asleep in my clothes. I went to the bedroom door and listened. The sound came again—not at my door, but beyond it. Jane in the process of leaving maybe? Someone at the door to the suite?

I opened my door to find Jane wearing a sheer blue nightgown, standing just outside her room. She was looking at me as though she had seen a ghost. "Harry," she whispered, eyes wide with shock.

The sound came again. I realized it wasn't coming from the suite's door. It was coming from the opposite side of the room.

I turned slowly.

Out there, in the rain-soaked night, smiling at us from our fourth-story balcony, floated a dolphin. I slid the glass door open.

"Hey, guys!" Fish Sticks chirped. "I was thinking... You wouldn't want to see Atlantis, would you?"

CHAPTER TWENTY-SIX
Magic Dolphin

We floated out over the ocean like something out of Peter Pan, if Peter Pan were a magic dolphin and John and Wendy Darling were thirty-something professionals dressed in day-old Friday business casual and a sheer blue nightgown.

If I wasn't stunned out of my mind, I would've been concerned that Jane might have been cold, but I didn't remember it being cold. I didn't even remember when the sky turned to sea and we were suddenly beneath the waves.

"This is—" I breathed. Then I realized I was breathing. "I'm breathing!" I blurted. "Why am I breathing?"

"You don't want to breathe?" squealed Fish Sticks.

"No, that's fine!" I stammered. "Breathing's good!"

We glided above coral, across fields of seaweed, past schools of fish. I'm sure some of them could've been sea bass. Eventually, we moved out past the storm clouds. Above us the night was clear, and the moon shown down, lighting our way. Or maybe it was something else—moonlight from another source, or dolphin sight. Who knows? All I knew was I was flying through the Atlantic on my way to see Atlantis.

A thousand shades of blue danced in front of us. Jane's hand found mine and together we flew, like Superman and Lois Lane if they had a magic dolphin for a chaperone.

"I missed you guys," Fish Sticks chirped.

"We missed you, too," bubbled Jane.

"You wouldn't happen to have any of those Fillet-o-Fish on you?"

I told him he should've said something before we left the coast—we could've flown through a drive-thru first. We dipped through an arch of coral and shot forward into the deep blue.

"So, Atlantis?" I ventured after a bit. "What's it like?"

"Just a big glass dome and some ruins," the dolphin squeaked. "Still pretty neat. I thought maybe you'd want to see it."

"This right here is enough!" Jane gasped in awe, taking in her surroundings.

"And you don't have any problem going near it?" I asked.

"No," Fish Sticks chirped. "The other fish seem to have a problem with it, but not me." Jane looked over at me, suddenly concerned. I just nodded.

We were heading into the Roanoke Rhomboid.

***

After what felt like an hour, a large glass dome slowly came into view, sitting on the sea floor like a giant bubble. It was decidedly modern with a honeycomb appearance to it, a collection of clear hexagonal glass panels in a curved metal frame. It looked like a giant hotel desk call bell designed by the Tiffany Lamp company. (Certainly the largest I'd ever seen on the floor of the Atlantic.) It stood around six stories tall with a base roughly the length of a high school sports stadium.

"Is this Atlantis?" I asked.

Fish Sticks nodded.

"I don't think this is Atlantis," I countered.

The dolphin's smile became slightly less pronounced. "What do you mean?"

I grew concerned. I was expecting to find a couple of MIBs in diving gear, or manifesting some sort of underwater breathing powers, poking around in the center of the Rhomboid, looking for Davey Jones' Mystic Locker, sifting through the seabed for Blackbeard's Enchanted Beard Trimmer, waiting for friends of theirs to show up with a magic trident and dolphin to help with the search.

This was different. This was—what? Some sort of scientific exploration post? An underwater biodome project? Did they have those, or was that just a movie thing? And then there was the possibility that the MIBs had built this, that the last few we encountered had missed the final boat out and the trident and Fish Sticks were their tickets here.

Maybe Wendigo had been wrong. Maybe the MIBs gave off the appearance of being members of a large and sinister organization because they *were* members of a large and sinister organization. After all, something like this would require a lot of funding and a ton of resources.

A scary thought entered my mind: we were looking at MIB Base One...and we were in danger.

Just then a whirling spout of water shot by us, knocking us around in its passing. Fish Sticks quickly recovered, pulling us back into a tight little group, a v-like formation with him in the lead.

On the seabed, near the base of the dome, stood a trio of divers, each dressed in thick diving suits and large brass helmets. One stabbed forward with an arm looking as though it were comprised of coral, tipped with the head of a trident instead of a hand.

"Okay," Fish Sticks chirped anxiously. "This is new!"

"Get us out of here!" I yelled. We were out of our element—literally. I dreaded what a direct hit on our dolphin friend would do to us.

Another spout whirled by, throwing us around. I reached out to Jane, only to see her tossed away, a look of horror on her face—*she was holding her breath.*

"Fish Sticks!" I yelled.

He shot off after her, dragging me in his wake. I could feel the weight of the ocean pressing on me, the water trying to get in, past the dolphin's magic. Then I heard Jane coughing and sputtering. Suddenly, three spouts converged on us, knocking Fish Sticks back.

That was when the ocean hit me.

***

I awoke, coughing so hard I thought my lungs would collapse. Every time I tried to take a breath, my throat would seize up as I hacked up bile and seawater. I felt like I was going to die.

Finally, I managed a long, painful gasp.

I lay on a cool, metal floor, gasping beneath blindingly bright lights. I was only slightly aware of being picked up and hauled off. I managed to moan Jane's name.

It came out as a question.

I didn't get a response.

Eventually, I was dropped again. There was a loud metal clang. Then silence. Then darkness.

***

I slowly regained consciousness to the sound of my name being called.

"Mr. Long? Mr. Harry Long?"

I was lying on the floor of a small cell. I managed to pull myself up to my feet, coming face to face with an older, white-haired gentleman sporting an impressive beard, standing outside my cell.

He wore a white suit, looking a bit military in design. Something about it, along with his bearing, suggested Navy. He looked like a cross between the captain of the Titanic and the owner of Jurassic Park.

Neither were good comparisons to evoke, given the current circumstances.

He leaned slightly to the right, resting his weight on a black cane topped with a brass seahorse. "I apologize for the rude welcoming, we don't get many visitors down here. And the ones we were expecting, well..." He grinned. "I'm happy to say, you ain't them."

"Jane!" I cried, lunging at the bars. "Where's Jane?"

The man took a step back and gestured to a guard. "She's safe. We can go to her now if you'd like."

The guard moved to unlock the cell door. I noticed he had a sidearm holstered on his belt. It looked like a standard, non-crystal, gun.

The old man held out his hand. "Welcome to *Vanishing Point.*" I took his hand and shook it cautiously. We walked down a corridor and into a large open area. The man's cane tapped on the ground in a brisk, lurching gait. The guard followed a few paces behind us, attempting to appear casual and non-threatening, despite being armed.

The glass dome rose high over our heads, its hexagonal pattern holding back the weight of the Atlantic. It was like being back in Baltimore, peering up through the Glass Pavilion, though at least twice as tall. Catwalks crisscrossed the center area, leading to decks which ran like rings at intervals along the inner wall of the dome. There were small, sectioned-off areas scattered throughout the structure; I assumed they contained things like opaque-walled sleeping quarters and bathrooms.

"I'm Captain Adams, head of this facility," the bearded man explained.

I eyed him suspiciously. "You're not an MIB, are you," I said, more statement than question.

He laughed. "No! In fact, I'm the opposite. I'm the…Captain Ahab to their Moby Dick. I've hunted them for years. But I'm happy to say, my long hunt is just about over. You've come at an auspicious time!" He grabbed my shoulder as though welcoming a long-lost friend.

To my left, through the glass, I caught sight of one of the divers peering through the dome at me. To my horror, a white skull was visible through the diver's face mask.

"Project Sea King," Captain Adams said proudly. "All ex-Navy men, but they've still found ways to serve. Our first line of defense! Aha!" he brought his cane up before him like a sword, wielding it briefly against imaginary assailants, wide-eyed and frantic, before returning it to the catwalk's surface with a resounding *crack!*

"Unfortunately, they tend to follow their orders unwaveringly, and their ability to recognize friend from foe still requires a bit of fine tuning."

"So, which one of those *are* we?" I asked. "Friend or foe?"

He chuckled, which wasn't very helpful. It had been a genuine question. I was still trying to make up my mind myself—I was hoping his answer would contribute to the process.

"You were very lucky," the captain continued. "We scrambled a recovery team as soon as we realized what was happening. How in the world did the two of you manage to make it all this way?"

"Magic," I muttered.

"There's a lot of that going around."

The Sea King turned and lumbered off back to guard duty, seeming to lose interest in us. I noted most of its arms and legs were either encased in, or comprised of, coral and masses of barnacles. This fact didn't seem to impede its movements at all. It's one arm was tipped with a trident, like the others. I assumed these tridents were pale imitations of the original, like the crystal gun copies I recovered from the MIBs on the beach the other day.

We moved on, coming upon one of the opaque-walled chambers sectioned off from the rest of the dome. The guard opened its door, and we stepped through into an exquisitely decorated dining room. Three of its walls were adorned with thick blue tapestries while the fourth was comprised of the curved hexagonal panels of the outer dome. A large table, covered in a mosaic of polished coral, sat at the room's center, surrounded by thick wooden chairs adorned with carvings of sea creatures.

A selection worthy of any high-end seafood restaurant lay spread out across the table, but most importantly there was Jane. Her nightgown had been replaced by some sort of worker's jumpsuit.

"Harry!"

She leapt up from her seat at the table and dashed over to me, throwing her arms around me. We kissed passionately, that small ember of love that still remained fanned into a flame as hot and bright as any magic Tarot could produce. I broke away, still holding her tight.

"I thought I lost you."

She rested her head against my chest. "And yet I'm still here."

We stood there for quite some time until Adams cleared his throat. Jane and I reluctantly released each other, turning our attention back to our host.

"Okay, we are not going to do this." I fumed.

Adams looked confused. "I'm sorry?"

"This whole James Bond villain, Captain Nemo thing," I said, gesturing at the table. "The fancy meal right before you hunt us down with spearguns on the lido deck for sport."

"I'm afraid you misread the situation. You're simply my guests here until some important matters are attended to."

"That's exactly what Blofeld would say," I countered.

"Blofeld would at least have a decent dress for me." Jane muttered, looking herself over. "This is completely unflattering."

Adams pinched the bridge of his nose. "I told you, it's the only thing we had available."

The captain turned, eyes running across the banquet table until coming to rest upon the large brass octopus candelabra at its center, one tall flickering candle held aloft in each twisted snake-like arm. "I guess it does look a little villainous," he conceded.

"Look," Adams sighed. "If it would make you feel more comfortable, we'll eat in the cafeteria."

***

The cafeteria was bright and loud. Twelve long tables filled the room—simple, non-polished coral, hard plastic rectangles, surrounded by plastic chairs. A scattering of people occupied them, their excited conversations pausing only for a moment when we entered. One table emptied out of respect for the captain—or maybe it was something else.

Jane and I were given only slightly curious glances. Of course, Jane was at least dressed in one of their jumpsuits. I, in contrast, was still in slightly damp Friday business casual.

"Better?" Captain Adams asked.

I looked around the room. It was an odd group, but I saw the old cliques: the jocks, the brains, the outcasts. Only here, they took on different roles, as guards, intellectuals—scientists, technicians, maybe a college professor or two—and a trio who seemed like they'd be more at home on a commune in the sixties than a secret underwater base.

"Yeah," I admitted, slowly taking a seat. Jane sat as well. She had yet to let go of my hand.

Adams slapped his hands together. "Now, what can I get you? Breakfast? Lunch?"

"How about answers," I growled.

He nodded slowly, his face losing all expression. "Yes. Okay. Answers."

CHAPTER TWENTY-SEVEN
Answers

"A lifetime ago, I worked for the government." Captain Adams reflected. "It was a special division of the FBI, dedicated to keeping tabs on some of our top scientists. I was assigned to Jack Parsons."

"The rocket scientist guy," I interjected.

"That's the one. I was there when he got all loopy with L. Ron in the desert. Well, not *right* there, but keeping an eye on them, at a safe distance. You know about this?"

"The Babalon Working? Yeah, a little," Jane murmured.

"I thought it was all a bunch of hooey. I didn't think it was anything worth reporting...until it was too late."

A shadow passed over his face. "*Something came through.*" He pronounced the words imploringly, as though begging us to believe him, trying to move us to accept something he couldn't properly put into words, simply by stressing his statement.

Something came through.

"The MIBs," I realized.

"Yes!" He reached across the table and grasped my forearm. "What would grow into the MIBs! You understand!"

"Somewhat," I admitted. "They came from a place where they were little more than ideas, and they needed our thoughts to become physical. Our thoughts at the time were mostly fears, so... that's what they became."

Adams let out a long sigh of relief. "You *do* understand!"

The cafeteria had slowly emptied over the last few minutes—I assumed breaktime was over, or possibly the workers recognized when the director was about to take another one of his dives off the deep end and decided to get while the getting was good. I thought I saw one covertly twirling his finger next to his temple while making his exit with a colleague, the universal gesture indicating something may be off with someone.

The worker bees filed out back into the glass hive, leaving us alone with the "mad" Captain Adams.

"Well, understand this! Once I started to realize what had happened, I felt responsible. It happened under my watch. Understand?"

I nodded. Jane nodded. It seemed very important to him that we understood.

"I got ahold of Parson's notes."

"Wait," I said, "I thought his notes were destroyed along with him when the lab in his garage blew up."

"I got ahold of his notes," Adams repeated. "And I understood them. His mentor, Aleister Crowley, had been working on manufacturing a god, creating his own set of ceremonies and rituals designed to manifest a vision. The concept was based on a belief that past religious visitations, experienced by saints and the particularly devout, were the products of their own strong faith."[43]

"Their conviction," I muttered.

"Exactly! There was an attempt made to conceptualize a goddess, a female entity known as Babalon, to the point where a vision manifested. Parsons applied alchemy and science to Crowley's teachings and opened up a doorway out there in the desert where reality was already weak. Then the MIBs came through."

"What about Babalon?" asked Jane.

Adams ignored her question. "We didn't realize it at first—then things started to go missing. Very special things, from very special places. And then someone noticed that some of those special things were acting weird—throwing lightning, canceling gravity, calling up the spirits of the dead and making them dance. Something was putting our laws of nature on notice. And then the World was held back for the first time, on November 22, 1963."

Jane whispered, "The day Kennedy was shot."

I reeled. "Seriously? The *MIBs* shot Kennedy?"

"It was early that morning. Air Force One arrived at Dallas Airport to find it a ghost town. No reporters or cheering crowd—just three men in black suits standing on the tarmac. The Secret Service thought they were fellow government men, that the area had been cleared due to a security threat, and there just hadn't been enough time to notify them. The fools should have taken off immediately, instead they

---

43   It's similar to the way images of the Virgin Mary appear in toast or on potato chips. A terrible oversimplification, but the same basic principle is at play, amplified to the point of true materialization. For example: imagine instead a hologram of a Ferrari Testarossa. Now imagine being able to amplify the hologram to the point that you could climb in and take it for a spin on the Autobahn. Now imagine it being red.

moved to question the men." Adam's lip curled in disgust. "Before they knew what was happening, the president had been shot by some kind of invisible bullet, and those hacks working for him were scrambling to get the plane back in the air. Confused. Panicked. Afraid."

"Moments after becoming airborne, they received a call from Dallas tower saying they were clear to land. Slowly, they realized a threat that they chose to ignore, a threat they laughed away as the babblings of a madman, had just shot the president! Hah!" Adams bellowed, slapping his cane down on the tabletop. It echoed off the cafeteria walls like a gunshot.

A guard peeked in from outside, rolled his eyes, then returned to his post.

"They couldn't let the public know that creatures from another world had killed the most powerful man in the United States. This was the stuff of countless sci-fi horror movies from the fifties and sixties. Alien invasion! No one is safe! You could be next! It would have been chaos! Mass chaos," Adams added absently, as though losing his train of thought.

Then he started chugging away again. "They had to move quickly. Kennedy had already been traveling with a body double. There had been threats made on his life, and Texas was a dangerous place for him to go at the time, so precautions had been taken."

"The Feds proceeded to do a very quick, very sloppy cover-up. Favors were called in, unlikely alliances were struck, pawns were sacrificed, and so was the unfortunate body double, who no one bothered to tell that there just wasn't enough time to *stage* an assassination. For the sake of the country, it had to look real, and there had to be someone to blame the president's death on—someone who wasn't an invader from another world."

"Okay, but why?" Jane sputtered. "Why kill the president?"

"We think the MIBs needed to boost our collective fear and paranoia to birth more of them—there seemed to be a lot more of them after that."

"And there would have been a great deal more if the public wasn't given somebody's head," I realized.

Adams stabbed at me with a finger. "Exactly!"

He rose up from his seat with the help of his cane. "After that, they all started listening to me!" He strode toward the cafeteria door, motioning for us to follow. "Come along. I have things to show you!"

We walked out of the cafeteria, down a hallway between two sectioned off areas, and toward an elevator which ran up the center of the dome in an enclosed circular shaft. Above us, at multiple layers, thin catwalks ran out from the shaft like the spokes of a wheel.

I thought it would make a great place for a swordfight.

"This is exciting," Adams gushed, pushing the elevator's call button. "We don't get many guests here. There's no-one to really *appreciate* the tour."

We entered the elevator. To my surprise, we headed down, despite the fact we were on the ground floor of the dome.

Moments later we stepped out into a large, undersea chamber. The drone of running pumps echoed off the slick cavern walls. The only lights were too-bright industrial, construction site towers, which either spotlighted the stone or cast dramatic shadows on the walls. It all looked like a half-done movie set.

Jane was suddenly clinging to my arm. "I don't

like caves," she murmured.

"You're okay with secret bases hidden beneath the Atlantic, but you don't like caves?"

She shot me an angry look.

"Okay, sorry. I'm not entirely happy here myself."

Jane suddenly released her grip on my arm and walked off toward a large, imposing machine standing near the chamber's center—apparently, her curiosity had overcome her fear.

The machine was ringed with several workstations, manned by concerned-looking technicians. The technicians grew even more concerned when they became aware of Jane's presence. They relaxed only slightly once they realized she was accompanied by Adams.

Jane pointed to a giant metal mushroom at the machine's top. It was emitting tiny arcs of lightning, which danced about in the air above it. "That's a giant Tesla coil!"

She then pointed to several arrays of plastic tubes, mounted just below the mushroom, angled up and out. "And those are cloudbusters!"

Adams nodded. "Developed by William Reich, yes. You're just as surprising as your companion here, Miss Austen. It's amazing how quickly the two of you embrace all this weirdness. I could have used people like you."

He gestured to the machine. "What you see here was years in the making. Fringe science mixed with their magic. Without it, Vanishing Point Station never would have been possible."

"After Kennedy was shot, I was given my own team, comprised mostly of scientists and agents whose beliefs had made them outcasts, up until that point. We started carrying out tests, trying to figure out the science behind why certain items were gaining what seemed to be magical properties, and trying to figure out how the MIBs created their dead areas. They, in turn, were questioning and harassing civilians, anyone who may have witnessed our activities—trying to figure out what we were doing."

"We came close to a breakthrough, up in Point Pleasant, and they came close to stopping us. It was a weird time. Eventually, we had this." He gestured behind him at the hulking machine. "An artificial way of mimicking their dead-zone-generating powers. A smaller one's been installed under the statue of Neptune to the west of us on the boardwalk, but then I guess you've already surmised as much."

"You see, we think we've figured out how magic works." Our host began, tapping the end of his cane against the side of the machine.

"Imagine, for a moment, magic as a naturally occurring power signal. At one time, this signal traveled everywhere in our world, but something happened that disrupted it, weakened it. Maybe it became drowned out by all the other signals we put into the air—maybe we fouled it up with all the science we were beaming out there. Whatever.

"Now, imagine there were things designed, either intentionally or unintentionally, to pick up that power signal's particular frequency. When there's no broadcast, those items are about as useful as a broken television. But when the signal's on…"

"And that's it?" I asked. "That's magic?"

I thought about it for a bit. I thought about the Magic Dollars and how they felt like balloon static, how when I first saw them, I thought they looked more like a high-definition image of a dollar than an actual dollar. They were just…transmissions?

Some sort of energy holograms? That was why they disappeared—they just turned themselves off after a few days or burned out. I thought about the sound of the MIBs' shouts in the aquarium gift shop, how they dispersed with the sound of television static. I thought about the tin foil and how it disrupted magic, blocking the signal.

And that was why they needed the dead zones, the nothing spaces, places where all signals were blocked out. All the signals...except one.

"My God! That's it!"

Adams smiled. "Once we understood the nature of magic, we could make our own and create dead zones to power up our devices or catch reforming MIBs. Expensive as hell, but they had shot the president, so we had a blank check for a little while. We ended up finding some of those magic objects. Most we stored away; some we used as bait."

"Is that why the trident was at the aquarium?" asked Jane.

"Yes," answered Adams. "But! It was also there to be charged. It needs to be around sea creatures to do so for some reason."

"Yes!" I shouted. "Totally nailed that one!"

There was an awkward pause during which no one seemed to appreciate how absolutely correct I was about the trident.

"Anyway," Jane said to Adams, "you said something about reforming MIBs?"

Adams nodded. "You see, the MIBs are basically thoughts, ideas, the physical manifestations of fear and paranoia. You could no sooner kill them then kill a concept."

"But we—I—" I stammered, recalling our MIB-slaying rampage over the past several days.

"Oh, you did your best, just like we did. But here's the secret; the disrupting thing they do?" He wiggled his fingers in front of him to suggest disrupting. "They disintegrate in one place and reform in another. We thought them fragile at first, but they're really quite durable.

Enduring, you might say. We weren't killing them—only delaying them.

"Their goal was to spread fear, sow paranoia, and reap terror from the masses, using items through which they could somehow focus that power signal, along with their own abilities to harness it. Their goal, we assumed, was to create an army, an invading force. So, our first step was to figure out a way to contain them.

"Once we could duplicate their dead zone producing power, we discovered it could function more or less like one of those sticky-tape flycatchers, if you'll pardon the horribly oversimplified comparison." We followed Adams to a large metal door set in the wall. "Once rendered incorporeal, they drifted to the nearest dead zone to reform. We made sure they came to one of ours." He hit a button on the wall. The room flashed red, klaxons sounded, and the metal door rose.

Adams gestured toward the room beyond, and we stepped through. A long walkway ran down its center. As we moved farther into the chamber, lights clicked on, illuminating it in sections. The walls of the room were lined with cylindrical glass chambers, stacked three high, each holding a very alien looking MIB. They all thrashed about within their confines, mouths agape in silent screams, fingers scraping against the glass.

Machines moved what looked like the last two

tubes into place at the end of the hall. The MIBs we fought on the Delaware beach maybe? Reformed in some manufactured, temporary dead zone, three hours to the north of us, then transported here for storage?

I breathed. "This is—"

"Impressive?" Adams finished.

"Cruel," corrected Jane. "Your fly tape analogy was more accurate than you thought. Your solution is life imprisonment?"

"Oh, no. You misunderstand the situation." Adams grinned. "I intend to send them back!"

CHAPTER TWENTY-EIGHT
Vanishing Point

We were back on the elevator, thankfully heading up this time.

"So, how is this 'sending them back' supposed to work?" Jane inquired.

"We found another place where reality was weak, like the place in the desert where the MIBs originally came through. It took us a while, but we found it!" Adams said proudly. The elevator doors opened, and we exited into a higher level within the dome. Adams escorted us across a catwalk to an observation deck looking out over the seafloor. Below us was what looked like an airport runway. Small marker lights ran along either side of it.

At its far end stood a small collection of ruins, recently excavated from the surrounding seabed. In the space above the ruins, a vertical whirlpool was forming, its mouth slowly growing larger. At its center a dim light was visible. It hurt to look directly at that opening. I thought I caught a glimpse of stars before I had to turn away. Or perhaps they were hundreds of tiny glowing eyes, staring back out at me.

"We couldn't use the Mojave point again. Couldn't risk a tear." Adams made a jagged slice through the air with his cane. "We needed the trident to coax the damn thing open and to help power our Sea Kings. Necromancy will only get you so far."

"So, the statue's a transmitter," I muttered in amazement.

"What about the dolphin?" Jane asked. There was still a piece of the puzzle missing.

Adams gave her a puzzled look in return.

"What dolphin?"

I noted there were several of the Sea Kings lumbering out near the ruins, as though standing guard.

"You said the Sea Kings were for defense. What are you defending yourself against?"

He ignored my question completely. "And then, of course, there was another matter to attend to. I said the MIBs were basically an idea, but after reading Parson's notes, I started thinking of them more like a series of ideas, a train of thought. And like any train of thought there's the initial spark that gives it life." Adams held up a finger on one hand. "And the last closing thought that ends it." He held up a finger on the other.

"The Alpha and the Omega," he continued. "These were two very important ideas. Two very necessary ideas. We needed to make sure we had the first and last thought of what the MIBs were. Otherwise, what was to stop the train of thought from just starting up again? Another polarizing event, another burst of fear and paranoia, and we were back to square one. No." He brought his fingers together. "We needed the engine and the caboose and all the cars in-between before we sent them all on to the end of the line." He pointed behind him with his cane to the vertical whirlpool. "Back through Vanishing Point. We got our Alpha. You helped us with that."

He had lost me.

And then I found me. "Blackcloak? The guy at the aquarium! The one with the eyes!"

"Yes." He started walking back toward the elevator, step, tap, step, tap, step, tap. "And you helped us out with the Omega as well."

I was lost again. Then the elevator doors opened.

Inside, two armed guards stood on either side of a depressed looking vampire with skunk-striped hair. He brightened suddenly, raised his shackled hands, and waved.

"Hey guys!"

One of his guards was wearing a colorful multi-layered dress. "You have got to be kidding me!" She huffed. "What does it take to get rid of you two?"

"I told you there was a storm coming," the other muttered in a deep voice.

***

They stuck the three of us in a small white chamber, similar to a police interrogation room you'd see on TV or movies, only this one was in a secret base under the Atlantic. Adams had a guard shackle Wendigo to the table for safekeeping, fastening a short length of chain attached to a ring bolted to the tabletop to Wendigo's cuffs, before the two of them left to go make final preparations, allowing us time to say our good-byes. When I noticed they still hadn't taken Wendigo's handcuffs off I laughed

"What?" he asked defensively.

"They have you in handcuffs in an *underwater base*. Just seems a bit excessive."

"Well, I am pretty dangerous when I'm cornered,"

231

Wendigo bragged.

"Yeah, you might spray them."

"Not funny." Wendigo attempted to cross his arms in annoyance only to be stopped mid-action by his restraints. He then fumbled a transition into a casual pose before turning his attention toward Jane.

"I don't understand," said Jane. "You're a MIB?"

"Imagine my surprise."

"What? No," I protested. "They're mistaken, right?"

Wendigo explained that he apparently came over late in the game, latching onto the universal conscious at a time of great change. The fear and paranoia felt by the masses while the cold war was in full swing gave way to a counter movement. Thoughts of making love, not war took precedent. People were turning on, tuning in, and dropping out. When Wendigo manifested, the idea of being a member of a sinister organization that exuded fear and paranoia just didn't sit well with him. So, he went rogue.

"At least, that's what I've been told," he admitted. "But it fits; I have no memory of my childhood, or my parents, no place to call home or memories of there ever being one. I have powers." He wiggled his fingers. "I mean, I can't set people on fire or anything, but they're still powers."

I sat and thought, allowing the information to process. "That first car chase. When the MIBs were after us. You said that you weren't going back again."

"Yeah. I wasn't sure what I meant by that either. But I think I was picking up on the fact that I came from someplace else. The paranoia they exude brought my fear of having to go back there to the surface. And according to Adams, I have to go back, if you guys are ever going to be MIB-free."

"This is crazy!" I shouted, jumping up from my chair. "You're different than them!"

"Different time," Wendigo offered.

"So, what are you? Another Boss Monster?"

"I'm the opposite." Wendigo smiled at me across the table, fishing in his pocket. "I'm a Badass Monster Hunter—we all are. And we're not done yet." Wendigo pulled a quarter out of his pocket and held it up. "I think there's one last monster out there we need to deal with."

"What?" I asked, mind still reeling, "You're gonna Skee-Ball your way out of here?"

"This morning, I got the guard to toss a coin to determine whether or not to cuff me. I lost, unfortunately. But cuffing me still depended upon the toss." Wendigo made a simple magician's pass, bringing his free hand up and over the displayed coin. It disappeared—along with his handcuffs.

He got up and moved to the door, leaving Jane and me speechless. He was out the door and down the hall before we recovered.

"Okay," I said, turning toward Jane. "That was a pretty good trick."

Then we both scrambled after him.

CHAPTER TWENTY-NINE
Under the Siege

"So, what's the plan?" Jane called as we got close to Wendigo.

"What? I'm gone for a day, and you guys start working off plans?" he admonished. "I'm supposed to be exuding an aura of rebelling against rules and authority. Aren't you picking up on that?" Just then, red lights flashed and alarms sounded throughout the structure. We all froze in our steps.

"I'm picking up on it now a little!" I shouted. "Is that for you?" The whole dome shook.

"Oh no," Wendigo gasped. "We're under attack!"

"I thought they had all the MIBs rounded up below!" shouted Jane. "Who's attacking?"

"That one last monster I was talking about!"

I was confused. I thought he'd been referring to Captain Adams.

We ran down a side hall and onto a metal catwalk toward the outer dome. A trio of submarines hung in the water. The three of us slid to a stop, staring up and out at them.

"I have never been fired upon by submarines before," Wendigo breathed.

"Yeah," said Jane. "I think it's safe to say it's a

new experience for all of us."

The Sea Kings started firing their water spouts up at the subs. They struck the one closest to us just as it fired a torpedo. The projectile headed out across the Atlantic, detonating somewhere far behind us.

As the sub listed to one side, I spotted a familiar symbol on its hull—the all-seeing eye above the unfinished pyramid. Only, the eye looked as though it were winking, like one of those images that change when the surface it's on was moved.

"It's her!" Wendigo blurted.

"Her? You mean Babalon?" Jane marveled.

"The Cult of Babalon!" yelled Wendigo. "Minions of a living goddess!"

"Is this what Adams was afraid of?" I exclaimed. "What the Sea Kings were protecting this place from?"

An explosion rocked the dome, and fractures in the structure began to appear. The flashing lights and alarms were shut off, replaced by shouts from panicked workers and the terrifying sound of cracking glass.

"We have to get below!" shouted Wendigo. "They'll seal the dome off if it's breached!" We found a set of stairs that curved along the inner wall of the dome and raced down.

"I figured she might try something like this! The same conviction used to form Babalon went into forming the MIBs as well. Sending them back might mess with her conceptualization!"

"And what would that do?" asked Jane.

"She might cease to be. Or diminish, I'm not sure. Thing is, I don't think she knows either, but she's not taking any chances!"

We all grabbed the rail as the stairway suddenly shifted away from the wall. Above us, and a good distance behind, one of the glass hexagons had shattered. The Atlantic Ocean was pouring in.

"Nice design," Wendigo admired, gesturing up at the breach. "A solid dome would have just gone all at once."

"Yeah, great design!" I snapped. "We're still in a giant underwater bubble! And now the water's coming in!" I grabbed his arm and pulled him along down the stairs until we came to the next landing.

We moved out onto one of the catwalks that ran to the central elevator and looked over the side. On the ground floor below, technicians were scurrying to holes and disappearing down ladder-lined shafts, closing large bulkhead doors behind them, sealing them tight. A good foot of water had already accumulated. Consoles sparked. Flames erupted.

The interior of the dome looked a lot like a set from a James Bond movie, the type of set you'd see near the end of act three.

"Elevator!" I yelled.

"No, not the elevator! You're not supposed to use an elevator in a flood!" shouted Wendigo, dashing back along the catwalk toward the outer dome.

"That's fire!" Jane yelled.

"There's some of that too!" Wendigo ran off, arms flailing, coat flapping.

"Don't worry," I said to Jane as we watched him go. "If he dies, he'll just reform somewhere, right?"

"Probably in one of the tubes down in the basement," muttered Jane.

"Yeah, but at least he'll be dry."

I grabbed her hand and ran for the elevator.

One of the things I always considered strange in movies is the fact that whenever someone flees, they tend to flee up.

This is a trick used by filmmakers to heighten the sense of drama. Having the protagonists trapped on a rooftop makes for a far tenser scene than having them flee down and out onto the street, where any number of escape options would be available to them.[44]

Apparently, I had watched one too many movies.

"I'm not going back to that cave again!" shouted Jane.

"No! We're going up! Get as high as we can!"

"Then what?" Jane didn't seem to like that idea either. At that moment, the explanation that it worked for ancient monkeys and veteran Jedi didn't seem very convincing.

"There's bound to be, I don't know, escape pods? They'd put them up there if anywhere!

At any rate, it's better than staying here!"

Jane looked over the side at the rising water level. She nodded at me. Another explosion shook the dome, and scenic Vanishing Point station now sported two waterfalls.

We dashed for the elevator, stopping suddenly as its doors slowly slid open.

Step, tap, step, tap, step, tap.

The mad Captain Adams emerged from it onto the catwalk, looking considerably madder than the last time we saw him. Several more forehead veins were visible.

---

44   As it turns out, there's a science behind this—the concept of fleeing up. Supposedly, when our fight or flight instincts take over, and we opt for the latter, we reflexively seek higher ground, remembering a time when our great-great-great-great-great-great-great-great-great ancestors fled prehistoric predators by taking to the trees. Seeking higher ground also worked out well for Obi-Wan McGregor in Revenge of the Sith. Probably part of Jedi training.

"Where's Wendigo!?" he bellowed.

"He ran off somewhere." I gestured in the opposite direction of where Wendigo had disappeared to.

"I need him!" Adams lurched forward. "I need him, or all this was for nothing!" he roared, swiping his arm through the air before him.

Jane moved forward, attempting to coax him back onto the elevator. "We have to go! The dome is flooding!"

Adams shoved her away. There was a horrible flurry of motion, a slip, and a terrible scream as she tumbled over the side.

"Jane!"

She hung dangling from the catwalk. I'd seen this play out before; it was a classic action movie trope. Since when did my life become a series of tropes?

Adams lurched toward me as I moved to help Jane.

He brought the cane up, and with a yank, unsheathed a narrow sword, tossing the black casing over the side of the catwalk.

"Seriously?" It was my own fault. I was the one who thought it would make a great place for a swordfight.

"You're not going to stop me from finding Wendigo!" He stepped toward me, wild-eyed, suddenly walking a lot better.

"I don't want to stop you!" I reasoned. "I just want to help her! Help me pull her up and we'll hunt him together! I'll even carry the speargun!"

"Harry!" Jane yelled, "Catch!"

The black cane sheath was flipping through the air toward me. Jane had somehow caught it as it was flung over the side.

My hand fumbled for it. It bounced off my fingers,

but I managed to grab it. Adams swatted it aside and it clattered to the ground, slipping off the opposite side of the catwalk.

"I don't know how to fight with a sword! Why would you think I knew how to fight with a sword?" This came out shriller than I intended.

Adams staggered toward me, slicing his blade through the air.

"This is crazy!" I protested. "The place is filling with water! We need to get out of here!" I tried stepping to the side to get to Jane, but he lunged at me. I twisted in time to avoid the full strike, but the edge of his blade still caught me, cutting into my side. It took a minute for the thin line of pain to register, accompanied by the warm trickle of blood.

My hand went to the pain, and I stepped back from Adams. Behind him, I noted that Jane was starting to pull herself up.

"Okay!" I said taking another step back. "Big man! You cut me with your Princess Seahorse cane! Happy?"

"Princess!?" roared Adams, hobbling forward.

"Yeah! What? Are you, like, accessorizing? You have a bedroom tucked away here somewhere all decked out in seahorses, right? Canopy bed with four seahorse posts? Fainting couch with little seahorse legs?"

"I happen to like seahorses!" Adams raged.

"I'm not hearing no," I sang.

He slashed at me with the sword again and I pivoted back away from him. His limp was becoming more pronounced. Behind him, Jane was at least back on the catwalk again. I tried my best not to show relief. Instead, I kept goading him on, leading him away.

"You know," I said, "the thing about seahorses is the males are the ones that give birth. It's a role reversal that's really not experienced anywhere else in nature." The sword whistled through the air, and I lurched back.

"See? Despite living in a very enlightened age, I still thought it was my role to save the girl, but as it turns out, we could all learn a lesson from seahorses."

Unfortunately, I had overestimated his frenzied state. Wheels turned, an eyebrow arched. Adams spun and sliced. Jane stepped back, narrowly avoiding the blade.

Adams now slashed madly back and forth between us as the Atlantic poured in, and the water rose.

"Why didn't you head for the elevator?" I yelled at Jane.

"I'm not leaving without you!" she yelled back.

"No one's going anywhere until you tell me where Wendigo is!" Adams yelled, slashing his weapon back and forth.

A large, comfortable looking chair suddenly fell from above, slamming into Adams, knocking him over the railing and sending him plunging over the edge. There was a terrifying scream which filled the dome, drowning out the roar of the twin waterfalls, cut short by a loud splash.

We looked up. Wendigo waved down at us from the catwalk above. "I decided to go up for some reason!"

Jane and I raced to the rail, looking down at the flooded base of the dome. There was no sign of the captain.

"You seem to know a lot about seahorses," Jane

said, still looking down.

"I happen to like seahorses."

A pair of odd sounding *thunks* accompanied by a vacuum *hiss* echoed through the dome.

The water stopped flowing in. Above us, two submarines hung in the Atlantic, wide tubes snaking from each to the two holes that were made in the dome. The third submarine was nowhere to be seen.

Wendigo looked up, then back down at us. "I think we're going to have some guests! How do you feel about cultists?"

"Maybe we should make up Captain Nemo's banquet room? You know, break out the fine China, polish the conch shells?" I grabbed Jane's hand, and we headed for the elevator. We stopped at the level above us to collect Wendigo.

"Any idea where your angry gypsy barista went?" I asked as he stepped onto the elevator.

Wendigo looked puzzled. "That wasn't her."

"What?"

"The angry gypsy barista, the one who cursed me? That wasn't her. This was a different...angry gypsy."

"How many gypsies do you know?" asked Jane.

Wendigo's brow creased. His eyes slowly squinted, as though he were attempting a difficult mental tally. There must have been a lot of them in his life. He obviously had a type. Or a type had him.

"Okay," I snapped. "Never mind."

"So, elevators, huh?" he smiled.

"Yeah," I muttered. "Going up?"

CHAPTER THIRTY
The Roar of Babalon

The doors opened up at the highest level of the dome. A collection of armored men holding assault rifles greeted us.

"Okay," I said raising my hands. "Now this *really* feels like a James Bond villain thing."

I looked over at Wendigo. "I have to admit when you said cultists I was expecting more robes and less...Cobra."

There was a series of muted blasts, deep under the structure. Everyone turned to see several small, torpedo-like ships speeding away from the base of the dome.

"What the hell were those?" I asked.

"Escape pods?" offered one of the men with guns, trying to be helpful.

I looked at him, then back down at the stream of bubbles trailing in the wake of the ships shooting away from us. The technicians, scientists, guards, and hippies weren't scurrying below to seal themselves up, or prepare for their last stand against the evil invaders or sacrifice themselves for the greater good to make Project: Vanishing Point succeed no matter the cost. Captain Adams at least had the decency to go down with his ship; everyone else went down because that's where the escape pods were.

I roared, "Who the hell puts the escape pods in the basement!?"

We were led to one of the tubes and made our way up through it, by way of harness, cable, and the occasional chance purchase the otherwise slippery curved walls allowed. It was a very unsightly and ungainly process. It felt like trying to climb up one of those twisty slides you see at children's playgrounds, only five times as long, and moving slightly. If it had been an action movie, they wouldn't show this part, unless it was something with Jackie Chan. Jackie Chan wouldn't have had a problem with this. We'd marvel at how easily he scaled the interior of the tube, as opposed to the efforts of, say, a vampire in a long coat, a girl in a jumpsuit, and a guy wearing slightly damp business casual.[45]

Once aboard the sub, we were escorted down a long hallway to what could best be described as a throne room. It was narrow, as everything tends to be on submarines, but there were elements at work here to make it appear larger. The walls were lined with mirrors. In them, lights from tall gothic candelabras danced, endlessly reflected upon their surface, creating the illusion of a vast space. (Of course, maybe there was more than just smoke and mirrors involved there.)

---

45   Keep in mind at the time I was also attempting to keep the cut on my side protected, feeling as though it may split at any moment and spill whatever guts were on that side. I didn't realize that the wound I had suffered turned out to be the equivalent of a long papercut. All I knew was that it had been caused by a sword wielded by a madman at the bottom of the Atlantic. Fear of the effect was mostly generated by the cause.

Large, scarlet banners hung at intervals on either side of us, each bearing a golden eye floating above an unfinished golden pyramid. The eye looked as though it were winking, which was a hard look to pull off with just one disembodied eye. I was about to ask Wendigo what the significance of the symbol was when he gasped. I didn't like it when Wendigo gasped. He was supposedly from another world; the idea of something being shocking to him scared me.

On the opposite side of the room, at the end of a narrow red carpet, perched upon a golden throne, was the most beautiful woman I had ever seen. The more I looked, the more I realized how unnecessary my eyes had become. After all, what use were they to me after this? Any vision beyond this would be excruciatingly dull, agonizingly pale, wholly incomparable. My mind turned to sharp thoughts. I would pay reverence to this beauty by having her be the last vision I ever experienced. My eyes would have to go. Then, I thought, maybe they could stay. My eyes could stay if I just stayed here and never looked at anything else but her. She would become my world.

I mean, Jane was beautiful. For the short time we were in love, I'd realized I was a little out of my league, or definitely on the upper end of the scale of what my league should be capable of catching and retaining.[46] But at the time, I thought it was the lure of adventure, the excitement of the unknown, that helped grow the initial seed of attraction into fully-bloomed love and not the result of a magic-laced Tarot, wielded by a gypsy with ulterior motives.

But this? The woman was *painfully* beautiful. It

---

46   There was definitely a Billy Bob Thornton/Angelina Jolie thing going on.

hurt to look at her. It was like staring into the sun or an atomic bomb blast. That's what she was, an atomic bomb of beauty, fifty megatons of loveliness, perched atop a throne of gold.

"Don't turn away," Wendigo muttered out of the side of his mouth. "She doesn't like it when you look away. Of course, she doesn't like it when you look either."

"Nnnnuuuggghhh—" came my response. My eyes were watering.

Wendigo stepped forward. "Better let me do the talking."

The woman rose from the throne with a grace that brought me to tears (or rather, to more tears). Bits of red that could have almost been a dress clung to her in pleasing ways. She moved like water. No, she moved the way water *wished* it could move.

"Wendigo." The woman's voice flowed like melted butter. "We always meet under the strangest of circumstances."

"Glorious, Babalon! I'm afraid you have me at even more of a disadvantage than usual."

Two armored men moved forward from either side of the room and into my line of sight. They were wearing gas masks and air tanks for some reason. One knocked Wendigo in the stomach with the butt of his rifle and he crumpled to the floor.

"Why do you speak? It's bad enough you've taken so many liberties in my presence already," she cooed as she gracefully walked to his now kneeling form. "The impudence of your legs to stand, the insolence of your lungs to breathe, the audacity of your eyes to gaze upon my beauty, all without my gracious permission! I mean, the very nerve! I have half a mind to separate you from each of these offending attributes."

She drifted back to her throne and alit upon it. "Instead, I shall ask you a simple question. And I shall graciously permit you to foul my air with your quick and politely worded response." She leaned forward, smirking a terrifyingly beautiful smirk. "Where are they keeping my children?"

"Well, Mom," Wendigo breathed, slowly climbing back to his feet. "If you want, I could show you."

"How *dare* you address me so!" Babalon rose. Jane and I fell to our knees as waves of golden force rushed through the chamber. She had somehow weaponized beauty.

"There's a school of thought that claims I'm one of your brood," Wendigo went on. "Runt of the litter, you might say." The men in the masks moved in again, but the Goddess waved them off. "As for the rest of the gang—they're down below, loaded into a special chamber. It's neat, really. See, the whole thing's on tank treads, and it's designed to rise up out of the ground and roll down the path there into that swirling whirlpool in the ruins, which should look familiar to you. It's basically the highway home. It's a different offramp, but it still leads back to the old neighborhood."

The goddess suddenly looked nervous. I hated that she looked nervous. I wanted to make her happy.

"And you're really going to like this next part," Wendigo continued. "Earlier today, I got the man who runs the facility down there to bet me a quarter that he wouldn't press the button that started the whole process up."

"And guess what?" Wendigo pulled up a quarter, waved a hand, and vanished it. "I lost." A low rumbling ran through the walls of the sub.

"Wendigo!" Babalon bellowed. "What have you done!?"

The men moved in, rifles drawn. Wendigo yanked off their masks and ran toward us. The guards seemed more concerned about retrieving their gear then shooting their guns in our direction. In their desperate stumbles, they knocked over a candelabra and set one of the banners ablaze.

Wendigo collected us and got us out of the chamber while the goddess raged. The room filled with golden light, flames, and smoke. I screamed as we stumbled along the corridor. The enormity of the feeling we had in her presence was finally allowed to be expressed in a wail of unbridled longing. Jane was screaming as well. We kept screaming, until our voices cracked and our mouths went dry.

We staggered. Wendigo did his best to hold us up. "Yeah. She has that effect on people."

"She was so beautiful!" I wailed.

Jane nodded, "She was! I mean, I don't go that way, but *damn!*"

"You wouldn't want to go that way, either. Trust me. I've seen her drive men insane with a wink." Wendigo patted himself down, as though checking to make sure he wasn't missing anything. "She dials it back to seven when she has an audience she doesn't want to melt into a useless pool of nothing."

"Seven?" snapped Jane. "That wasn't a seven! *I'm* a seven!"

"You're an eight," I commented.

Wendigo nodded. "Yeah, definitely an eight. But she's on a whole other dial."

The sub lurched, suddenly struck by something hard, ringing it like an enormous bell. Alarms sounded. People were screaming.

A few guards rushed by, more eager to give their goddess solace than stop us. That's the nice thing about fanatical cultists; they tend to have a one-track mind. Of course, once they realized that killing us would be the soothing balm for their goddess' ailment, that one-track mind would quickly backtrack to us.

We managed to find our way back to the tube leading down to the dome.

"You'll be safer down there!" Wendigo yelled.

I balked. "But the dome's cracked and flooded! There's sparking wires and fire and I assume a half-dead, all-crazy Captain Adams lurking somewhere, waiting for round two!"

"Trust me!" Wendigo barked. "You'll be safer than here. So, you know, that's saying something!"

Jane gave Wendigo a hug, then entered the tube and slid down toward the dome.

I paused at the entrance. "What the hell are you going to do?"

He started walking away down the corridor. "I'm going to take control of this sub and drive Miss Daisy home!"

"*What?* How the hell do you plan on doing that?"

He was walking backward, still talking to me. "I got three decks of playing cards and a pocket full of quarters! I'm good!" He paused in the corridor and gave me a weak smile. "It's been fun, Harry."

I smiled back. "Yeah. I—"

The sub was thrown to one side, and I tumbled back into the tube. Rolling down around its curves, I quickly caught up to Jane. She had been making a more cautious descent, bracing herself against the sides. There was a sudden wrenching movement. The tube was pulled straight, and then taut, then it snapped back. Water rushed in, and we were flushed out into the Atlantic.

The salt water burned my eyes, but I forced them open. The end of the tube was snaking up and away from me, along with the sub. Down below, the MIB containment chamber, large and brick-shaped, was crawling along the road on the bottom of the sea floor, slowly making its way toward the vertical whirlpool at the end of the runway. A quartet of Sea Kings, possibly held in reserve to serve as escorts for the MIB transport, were firing up at the sub.

I felt myself being pulled toward the dome and one of the two neat hexagonal holes in its side. I tried fighting the current, but my arms and legs just weren't up to it, and my lungs were already aching.

This was it then: a plunge down an undersea waterfall into an electrified pool at the bottom of a secret underwater base. I had to admit, it's not the way I thought I was going to go.

Suddenly, I was swept back and away.

"Jesus!" yelled Jane. I spun. She was behind me, and beyond her floated Fish Sticks.

"I'm sorry," he chirped. "I really thought Atlantis would've been more fun for you two. I mean, seriously, I give it two starfish." He let out a long, choppy laugh.

I took a deep breath.

CHAPTER THIRTY-ONE
The Revenge of Captain Adams

Assisted by our magic dolphin, we shot down through the dome and flew to a safe landing on an upper observation deck.

"What are we doing?" asked Jane. "We can go! Get out of here! Why'd you tell Fish Sticks to bring us here!"

I dashed to the rail and watched as the Sea Kings kept firing up at the sub. The deck ran like a thin ring around the inside of the dome. I moved along it, searching the sea floor.

Jane staggered after me, still waiting for her answer. "Harry!" she yelled in protest.

I spotted the other two subs lying on the floor of the Atlantic. I didn't see any additional active Sea Kings; the rest must have been taken out by the subs during the initial attack.

"We've got to help him!" I yelled. "If Wendigo *does* get control of the ship, those things could knock him out before he gets to the portal!"

"So we shoot back to the pier, knockout their fake dead zone generator, and disable the trident!" argued Jane. "It's transmitting here, right? We stop it from transmitting!"

"That might shut down the suits, but it could also close the whirlpool!" I countered.

"There has to be something we can do!"

"Don't you think you two have done enough already?" croaked a familiar voice.

Slowly, I turned. Captain Adams was standing nearby, leaning on the rail for support. He was an odd combination of burned and soaked, looking like the aftermath of a small house fire and smelling the same way. His head was tilted at an odd angle. One hand held a revolver, pointed at us.

This was my fault.

"What do you mean, *you two?*" Jane said indignantly.

"You led Babalon right here!" Adams bellowed; he coughed with the effort, hacking up tiny, bloody bits.

"Why do you think the MIBs wanted the trident and the dolphin?" Jane raged. "They wanted to get out here and stop you! Free the others! And if her kids knew about it, I'm sure she did as well!"

"What dolphin!?" Adams screamed.

Fish Sticks drifted up alongside him. "Hi."

Adams spun to find a dolphin floating in the air beside him. "My God!" He lurched back and away, tumbling to the ground. The gun hit the catwalk and bounced off the side.

Jane and I moved to help Adams to his feet.

"Listen you old fool! We're on your side!" I snapped. "We told you, Wendigo's different. He's been fighting these things for years. Even now he's out there on that sub, fighting to send it through the whirlpool. With him on it!"

"He's sacrificing himself to get rid of Babalon. She's as much a part of all of this as the MIBs!" Jane reasoned, "She's the start of it all! She's got to go as well! To make all of this work!"

Adams lurched to one side. His hands reached for the railing to steady himself. I would have felt sympathy for his current condition if not for the fact he had pointed a gun at us seconds ago.

"Now I don't care if you believe us or not, but how about you stop trying to kill us!" I implored. "At least until we find some way to help him get through that whirlpool. After that you can have at it.

"But I'm pretty sure we can take you." I said through a slight grin.

"We have a magic dolphin." Jane added.

"But she's so beautiful," Adams moaned, turning his gaze toward the sub.

"You saw her! You saw Babalon! And you couldn't bear the thought of sending her away!" Jane chided. "But you can't take out a hive without killing the queen! That's like monster hunting 101!"

My God! He saw her. Of course, he saw her! He had been there! He was out in the Mojave Desert when the doorway between here and somewhere else opened, and the goddess first set foot into our world. He claimed he was keeping an eye on Parsons, but maybe he had been part of it. Maybe all this was his way of setting things right. He was fine with sending the MIBs back, but he was clearly in denial when it came to Babalon. Jane was right—he couldn't bear the thought of sending her away.

"But she has to go. Doesn't she?" Adams gazed at us through glassy eyes. "For this whole thing to work?"

I looked over the side. The water level was rapidly rising. That's the thing about domes: it takes considerably less time to fill the upper half of one.

The trapped air might keep the dome from filling entirely, but then you're dealing with pressure and cracked glass. We couldn't stay there much longer.

"Your dolphin," breathed Adams. "Can he get me one of the disabled Sea Kings?"

Fish Sticks shot out of the dome. Within seconds, he returned with one of the Sea Kings that had been knocked out during the initial attack.

We dumped what appeared to be skeletal remains out of the suit and started helping Adams into it.

"Maybe we should have had Fish Sticks bring back two," I said as Jane and I hefted the heavy brass helmet into position above Adam's head. "I could have helped."

"Well, the thing is, you have to be dead." Adams tittered as he pulled down the helmet. "Or damn close to it!"

The dome filled with his crazed laughter. The faceplate on his helmet suddenly lit with a warm blue glow and his face slowly dissolved, leaving behind a bare white skull. We gasped, stumbling back from the horror.

"Well?" the skull croaked. "What are you waiting for? Get me out there!"

The four of us rose up. We fought briefly against the current of the water pouring into the dome before rocketing out into the ocean.

Above us, the remaining sub had righted itself and was making its way back toward the dome when it lurched to one side. Wendigo was making his run for the portal. The vessel was surrounded by a dim glowing aura.

Fish Sticks released Captain Adams, and he fell like a stone, firing spouts of water at the Sea Kings as he plummeted, his hysterical laughter drifting up from below.

"I'm going to have nightmares about this day," I muttered.

We watched as the MIB transport breached the whirlpool. A blinding flash filled the water, and a flurry of bubbles sped toward the surface. A wave of force flew out from the vortex, disrupting the sea in all directions. Fish Sticks pulled us close together, and we plunged through the shockwave.

The transport was gone.

The whirlpool had been disrupted, diminishing greatly in size. It slowly spun up again, gradually growing larger. Below us, Captain Adams had knocked out two of the Sea Kings and was drawing a bead on the third. The sub plunged toward the whirlpool, its glow growing brighter.

Fish Sticks' smile was less pronounced. "That doesn't look good," he squeaked, then started to pull us away.

"No, wait!" I protested, but the dolphin didn't listen.

Spinning onto my back, I watched behind us as the sub dove for the whirlpool. Waterspouts shot up from below, buffeting the vessel, but it stayed on course. The intensity of the aura surrounding the sub increased, growing into a bright golden glare. Stress fractures began appearing along the ship's hull, allowing even more light to escape.

The sub's nose breached the whirlpool. There was another blinding flash as the sea around the sub imploded, wavered, and shot outward. The submarine was gone. Then the dome of Vanishing Point station flexed and burst. The ocean distorted as an enormous wall of force rushed toward us.

"Hang on!" yelled Fish Sticks. I rolled over on my

stomach, facing forward again. I managed to grab ahold of Jane, hugging her close to me, and then we shot forward with blinding speed, riding the edge of the shockwave.

"Yee-haw!" the dolphin squealed.

We flew like a bullet toward the Virginia coast.

CHAPTER THIRTY-TWO
Virginia is for Likers

Fish Sticks brought us in as close to shore as he could without breaking the surface of the water. We bid him a sad farewell, softened by the knowledge that we thought we had seen the last of him before, only to have him turn up outside our fourth-story window with offers of Atlantis.

He nudged us along a bit farther until gravity and surf began to seep in. We rose up out of the sea with our hotel in sight.

Jane and I staggered up out of the water onto Virginia Beach. It must've been late Saturday afternoon. We were soaked and exhausted, but relatively in one piece, thanks in no small part to our dolphin friend.

We walked out of the Atlantic and trudged up through the sand, fully clothed, soaking wet, huddling together for warmth. We drew some odd stares from onlookers but, thankfully, no inquiries. I pieced together a story about our boat capsizing, just in case, but the tale had so many holes in it we would have sunk long before flipping over. Most were too engrossed in their cellphones to even notice us.

Along the way, we noticed the trident was missing

from the Neptune statue. Eventually, we made it back to our room. We took an extremely long, hot shower together, embracing under the stream until we began to feel warm again. Until we began to feel normal.

It took a long time.

At last, we crawled into bed, the same bed, reluctant to leave each other. We slept for the rest of the day.

I woke around midnight, surprised to find Jane awake as well. We made love. Slowly, softly, for quite some time, then fell asleep again wrapped in each other's arms.

***

The next morning, we awoke early. We made love again, then showered...again.

"What do you think?" I asked, as Jane and I got dressed. I'm not sure why I asked, but then, it hadn't been the first time I opened my mouth when it should have stayed shut.

Jane burst out laughing, and I joined her for a bit. I realized it was a pretty open-ended question to ask after flying to Atlantis via magic dolphin, almost drowning under the Atlantic at least twice, and meeting a living goddess. When her response finally came, I was happy to note we were on the same page.

"I think last night was a good start," Jane said as she buttoned up her blouse.

"Yeah, but—"

"I liked it," laughed Jane. "Let's just leave it at that for now."

We took a quick inventory. The Magic Dollars I had wrapped in foil were gone, but Jane still had two.

We had the Crystal Gun, the Eldritch Dowser, the migraine-inducing ID, and of course, the Answering Hand in the Lincoln's glove compartment. Also, for what it was worth, Jane had a souvenir technician jumpsuit from a secret underwater base. She was only mildly upset to have lost one of her favorite nightgowns.

I was surprised the dollars and ID survived the great MIB migration, but then, that's magic for you. The stuff you think should go, stays, the stuff you think should stay, goes, and the stuff you think is lost forever, eventually winds up being found again.

Maybe.

***

We ate breakfast at the hotel, pausing for a moment to toast absent friends, our coffee mugs held high.

At the front desk, while checking out, I made a casual inquiry about the Neptune statue. It seems the unveiling that was originally scheduled for Saturday morning had been canceled indefinitely.

"Indefinitely," I echoed as I signed off on the receipt. "I'd say...definitely." We loaded our bags into the trunk, then climbed into the Lincoln.

"Where to?" I asked.

"Well," Jane reasoned, "there are still things out there, right? I mean, it didn't all go away when the MIBs left."

"I guess not. Wendigo did say there were worse things out there than MIBs."

"And probably magic that shouldn't fall into their hands, right? There's still thwarting opportunities for us," she said with a grin.

We discussed the possibility of contacting the FBI, maybe doing some freelance work for them—after all, as far as we knew their whole Special Magic Division was currently sunk at the bottom of the Atlantic, or piloting their escape subs off to the Bahamas.

"Maybe we could just try this ourselves for a while?" Jane offered.

I told her about my Plan B, from days ago in Baltimore, when I was thinking about what I'd do if Wendigo failed to pick me up at the car rental place. About going off and just doing it myself. Walking the Earth.

"You still want to do this?" I asked. "Hunt magic and deal with things worse than MIBs? Walk the Earth like Caine in Kung Fu?"

"How about we *drive* the Earth? And how about we stop off in Pennsylvania to pick up one of our cars? Either one's fine, as long as your back windshield's intact as well."

"Yeah? You want to do this?" I reached over to the glove compartment.

"As long as it's with you. And we keep making two plus two not equal four. I can't go back to normal. Not after this."

"One plus one equals us. Let's see if *worse than MIBs* are ready for that!" I pulled the Answering Hand out of the glove compartment and started tearing off its foil cover.

"You think Wendigo's okay?" Jane asked. "Back wherever he is?"

"Wendigo's fine," I laughed. "Those coin tricks never should've worked like that. He was operating on a whole other level out there." Jane stared at me with a blank look. "Submarines have decks," I explained. Jane still stared.

I brought the hand up to my mouth and whispered, "Find us the closest Boston cream pie." I moved to place the hand upon the dash, then thought for a moment. Bringing it back up, I whispered, "On second thought, find Wendigo."

I set it down, and it skittered back and forth across the dash a few times, then paused. For a moment I thought it was going to flip over on its back, give up, but then it slowly pointed a finger north.

The bastard did it, I thought while starting up the Lincoln. The greatest card trick of all.

He pulled himself out of the deck.

About the Author

Matthew Kline has written and designed over one hundred pen & paper RPG titles for Creation's Edge Games.

Recently he was referred to by one reviewer as being a "prolific writer." He considers this to be one of the greatest compliments he's ever received.

He's currently working on several comic book projects, one of which he's told will soon see the light of day.

Matthew currently lives in Eastern Pennsylvania with his girlfriend, her three kids, her three grandkids, and a very good dog named Peanut Brindle.

He wishes his house were bigger.